Copper Hill

Stephen and Janet Bly

Thorndike Press • Thorndike, Maine

Published in 1999 by arrangement with Servant Publications.

Thorndike Large Print ® Christian Fiction Series.

The tree indicium is a trademark of Thorndike Press.

The text of this Large Print edition is unabridged. Other aspects of the book may vary from the original edition.

Set in 16 pt. Plantin.

Printed in the United States on permanent paper.

Library of Congress Cataloging in Publication Data

Bly, Stephen A., 1944–
    Copper Hill / by Stephen and Janet Bly.
      p. cm.
    ISBN 0-7862-1805-3 (lg. print : hc : alk. paper)
    1. Large type books. I. Bly, Janet. II. Title.
[PS3552.L93C66   1999]
813'.54—dc21   98-53620

For
Chuck and Betty

Copper Hill

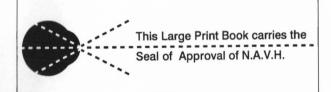

This Large Print Book carries the
Seal of Approval of N.A.V.H.

1

From the desk of Priscilla Carey Shadowbrook:

1. Finish guest list for Melody
   (Don't forget Uncle Henry or the
   Bloomrights this time!)
2. Pack
   (Hot, hot, hot . . . shorts, shorts,
   shorts.)
3. Mend Kathy's pink blouse
   (No wearing unless top button
   is buttoned.)
4. Pick up the house key from Dick
   & Natalie Winslow
   (Get street address of Jerome house
   for Fed. Ex.)
5. Talk to Kit
   (About ???)
6. Remind Tony to call Terry Davidian
   (Can they guarantee the movie
   won't be R-rated?)

7. Call Becky at ASU
   (Leave phone and fax numbers.)
8. Call Mom & Dad
   (Remind them about meeting
   at Mark's on the 4th.)
9. Take the Women's Association
   minutes to Audrey
   (32614 Stallion Way)
10. Have Tony talk to Kit
    (About ???)

All the items on Price's list were crossed off.

Except numbers five and ten.

The once-neatly folded "things to do" list lay crumpled somewhere in the bottom of her cavernous purse, as did the keys to the Winslows' home in Jerome, Arizona.

Still on Highway 89A, Tony and Price Shadowbrook left the Verde Valley and ascended steeply to the west into Arizona's Black Hills. Perched halfway up Mingus Mountain, two thousand feet above the valley floor they could see the billion-dollar copper camp of Jerome where every road, every building, every creature . . . four-legged or two-legged . . . lives and moves on a steep slope.

Flat land is not at a premium in Jerome.

It just doesn't exist.

Price, dark glasses balanced on top of her shoulder-length brunette hair, rummaged down one side, then down the other of the dark leather bag. Tony's narrow, blue-grey eyes flitted between the winding, uphill mountain road and the 1957 Chevy pickup crowding his metallic blue Jeep Grand Cherokee on a curve.

"I can't believe it!" Price fumed, still raking through her purse.

"It's absurd!" Tony roared, banging the palm of his hand on the oak steering wheel.

"It is?"

"He's a complete and utter jerk!"

"Who?"

"Mr. I'm-going-to-pass-even-if-it-kills-me in the old grey pickup." Tony eased on the brakes. The old Chevy roared across a double yellow line, passed them and sailed into the hairpin curve.

"Tony, he's fishtailing!"

"He's losing it! Hang on, darlin'!" Tony slammed the brakes and peeled off into the steep culvert on the right side of the two-lane highway. Their rig took a hard bounce over a football-sized boulder, teetered, then the rear end slid down the bottom of the drainage ditch. They faced the road, but were well off the pavement.

A loud crash and a plume of dust from the

now-obscured other side of the roadway spurred them out of the Jeep.

"Are you all right, darlin'?" Tony yelled as he hurried around to Price.

"Just a little shook up. He crashed, didn't he?"

"Sounded like it . . . take my hand . . . we'd better hike up there."

The rust tones of Cleopatra Hill dirt quickly dusted their shoes. The pungent smell of sage and the dry summer air reminded Price of a hundred other Arizona locations, but there was a faint scent of something else, too. Something familiar. Something too close. It had the feel of hazard . . . or adventure. She couldn't tell which.

From the crown of the paved highway, Tony and Price spied the grey pickup that miraculously had not rolled over when it left the roadway. With busted axle, blown tires and a popped-out front windshield, it crouched at the bottom of an arroyo aptly called Deception Gulch.

Tony glanced up and down the vacant highway. In the distant east, he could see Clarkdale and the Verde Valley far beneath them. "You wait here, I'll go check . . ."

"I'm coming with you." Although the June day was already at an Arizona swelter, Price rubbed her suntanned, bare arms as if they were cold.

They inched their way down the embankment of rocks, sage, and dirt. Mainly rocks.

"It could be gruesome," Tony warned.

Price clutched Tony's shoulder as he descended ahead of her. "Do you see anyone?"

Tony dug his boot heels into the rock with each step. Price carefully stuck her tennies in his size twelve prints. A dead tumbleweed rubbed against her bare legs. Tony pushed his cowboy hat back and rolled up the sleeves of his print-on-white western shirt.

"I should have worn pants!" Price puffed.

"You might wish you'd waited at the road."

A thin man of medium height, wearing sandals, cut-off jeans, a black T-shirt and dark glasses, staggered out of the brush next to the dry creek bed. He was about thirty yards below Price and Tony when he reached the driver's door. His full mustache drooped slightly on the ends, giving his expression a permanent frown.

"You all right?" Tony yelled.

The man spun around and shaded his eyes.

"Was anyone with you?" Price called out as they continued their descent. "Is anyone hurt?"

Both hands flung to the top of his shaggy

dark brown hair, the man danced around, shouting, "I'm invincible!"

When Tony arrived at the bottom of the dry, sandy gulch, he reached back and took Price's hand, assisting her off the rocks. They hiked over to the man, who excitedly inspected something in the back of the pickup.

"Are you sure you're doing all right?" Tony asked again.

The man leaped wildly out of the bed of the pickup. Price bolted backwards. The man let out a whoop, "It wasn't my time! I came out over the steering wheel . . . hit the windshield, popped it out and landed in the brush. Look at me! Not a scratch!"

"You're a very fortunate man. You were taking that corner too fast," Price lectured.

His wide, unblinking eyes stared at her. "I'm invincible!" he shouted.

"Well, Mr. Invincible, if you're all right, we're going to hike back up and try to drive our rig out of the ditch." Tony glanced up the steep incline to see several people standing by the roadway gawking down at them.

He was about to wave them off when the man grabbed his arm and spun him around. "Hey, buddy! Help me carry this to the top!"

Tony pulled back from the man's grip. "What?"

The man waved toward the back of the

truck. "This marker."

Tony and Price stepped over and peered in. A black granite gravestone lay lengthwise, three-feet wide, four-feet long, and over a foot thick. The top side was polished and had been chiseled out.

"How much does that thing weigh?" Tony asked.

The man stuck both of his little fingers into his ears and puffed his cheeks out as if blowing up a balloon. "Three hundred and fifty to four hundred pounds."

Price rolled her eyes at Tony.

Tony whistled. "Whew! It'll take a lot more than two of us. You'll need a crane or something." Tony eased toward the incline out of the gulch.

"You aren't going to help me, then?" the man howled.

"We'll go into Jerome and send someone back. Were you headed to a cemetery? I thought the old cemetery was closed."

"I'm not ready for the graveyard yet," the man hollered. "Didn't you read the stone?"

Tony glanced at Price, then stepped up on the tailgate of the truck and read the chiseled words aloud. "Clayton V. Gilette: born May 4, 1962, Lodi, California; died August 15, 1997, Jerome, Arizona."

"August 1997? That's two whole months

away!" Price blustered.

"Two months is a very short time, if your name happens to be Clayton V. Gilette."

Tony stared back at the stone. "This guy knows exactly when he's going to die?"

"Precisely. And he knows he's going to be murdered by a gunshot in the back of the head."

Price winced and clutched Tony's arm as they pulled away from the man.

"Who is this guy, Clayton V. Gilette?"

"That's me!" the man yelled. "Ah, hah! I'm invincible!" Then his shoulders slumped. "At least until August fifteenth!"

Tony glared over the top of his wire frame, BluBlocker sunglasses. "Come on, Mamma . . . we've got a book to write."

By the time they reached the roadway, both were bent at the waist, gasping for air. Two Arizona state patrolmen pulled over in a wide spot of the road and hiked toward them. A half hour later Tony and Price had given their statements, driven out of the ditch and gone on their way back up the mountain.

Price groaned at the sight of her stained white tennies and white shorts. *I should have brought some bleach. We shouldn't even be here. We should be in a nice, quiet, little clean town like Columbia Falls . . . instead of a wild and reckless place like this.*

"Is this the road leading to the Winslows'?" Tony slowed the rig and pointed to the north.

"Yes, it's really a beautiful summer house . . . but what would you expect from Richard and Natalie, Scottsdale's leading architects?"

"I thought you said the road was gravel."

Price searched her purse and plucked out a small tan brochure. "It turns to gravel right past the museum. Let me read you the Chamber of Commerce blurb."

The United Verde Extension Mining Company (UVX), one of two big mines at the billion dollar copper camp of Jerome, was purchased in 1912 by James S. Douglas and Associates. In 1915, Rawhide Jimmy struck rich ore which would become the fabulous Little Daisy Mine. By 1916 Douglas built himself an 8,000-square-foot mansion overlooking the mine. It's now a state historic park and museum. Looking north, across the canyon from the museum sits the Honeymoon Cottage which Rawhide Jimmy built for his son, Lewis Douglas, and bride.

Only a few hundred feet away from the cottage is a contemporary two-story home

15

with a huge deck shaded by tall elm trees planted by Lewis and his wife in the 1920s. From that deck one can look up the mountain at decaying facades of old Jerome, or down the hill at Clarkdale and the ever-growing population of the Verde Valley. Straight to the east is the expansive Mogollon Rim, and in front of it the inspiring red rock cliffs behind Sedona. To the northeast, towering over northern Arizona, loom the San Francisco peaks.

"Well, there you have it," Tony teased. "What is there left to say? Perhaps we don't need to write a book about Jerome, after all."

"Oh, no, you don't, Shadowbrook. We've got the next installment in The Hidden West Series. You're just looking for an excuse to get back to your westerns."

"You have to admit . . . perched up on the mountain . . . this is not exactly a hidden location."

"At least it's biblical."

"You mean, how a city set on a hill can't be hidden?"

"Yes." Price waved her hand toward the windshield. "There it is . . . up there in the trees."

Tony pulled into the empty, wide carport and glanced up at the sprawling house above

16

them. "This is some place! It should make for a relaxed, quiet summer."

"Somehow . . . there isn't much confidence in your voice, Mr. Shadowbrook." Price searched through her purse. "Did I give you the keys?"

"No, they're in your purse."

"Well, I can't find them."

"It's a wonder you find anything in there! I'll start unloading. You find the keys."

With three suitcases, two briefcases and a box of books resting on the deck near the kitchen door, Tony stood impatiently waiting as Price again searched her deep, leather purse.

"They have to be in here, somewhere."

"They are *not* in the purse," Tony asserted. "You and I have searched every square inch of it."

"I put them in my purse. Look," Price held up a yellow slip of paper, "here's the security code for the alarm system. Natalie gave me that and the keys."

"We'll have to drive up to town and find a phone . . . call the girls . . . maybe they can meet us halfway," Tony babbled. "What's midway between here and Scottsdale? Maybe that new drive-in at Black Canyon . . . but Kathy's got a date tonight, doesn't she? Well, Kit can . . ."

17

"Tony, I didn't leave the keys at home. They are here, someplace!" Price fumed. "Let me look again."

"You know they aren't there. We've looked and looked. At least we aren't in Columbia Falls, Montana. We could always hike home and get the keys . . . shouldn't take more than three days." Tony walked to the east edge of the deck to stare out across the Verde Valley.

Price scooped the contents off the deck and shoved them back into her purse. "They aren't in here," she sighed.

"Incredible!" Tony muttered.

"Not finding the keys?"

"No. I was just thinking . . . so far absolutely nothing about this summer is going according to design. We're not even supposed to be here. For months we made plans to write *Columbia Falls* next in the series . . . and then, surprise . . . Josh and Melody decide to get married in August. Mamma's got to stay close to home to make plans for an Arizona garden wedding. . . . I thought parents of the groom didn't have to do much wedding preparation. When Mark and Amanda got married, all we did was show up in Tucson and pay for the rehearsal dinner."

Price slipped her sunglasses down off her hair and set them on the bridge of her nose.

"Well, when the wedding's going to be in the groom's parents' backyard, I'd say they have a few things to take care of. Actually, we're doing quite well, for such little advance notice."

"It's been a harried two weeks. We shifted plans, put Montana on the back burner until next year and decided upon Jerome."

"Yes, but now we're only three-and-a-half hours from home. It's handy." Price slipped her arm in Tony's.

"It's hot."

"The house has air conditioning."

"Well, that would be delightful," he stewed, "if we were in the house."

"Tony, you saw me put those keys in my purse. Remember, you left your set of keys with the girls? You took mine out of the purse and said, 'Are these the keys to the Winslows' house?' And I said, 'Yes, there's a little black "W" key-chain.' "

"Little 'W'! Oh, man . . ." Tony jammed his right hand into the pocket of his Wranglers, past the buckhorn knife to the spot normally reserved for denim lint. "Eh," he blushed as he pulled out the keys. "*This* little 'W' key ring?"

Price stood at the kitchen sink, tearing iceberg lettuce that had been left along with other garden vegetables in a brown paper sack by their front step. Out the window, a black cat with three white paws balanced on the railing of the deck. The telephone jarred her out of a mental debate over what kind of dress the mother of the groom should wear to an Arizona summer backyard wedding.

Tony burst into the room just as she put the teal green telephone to her ear. "Hey, would you believe that we . . ."

She silenced him with her upheld hand.

"Hi, Dr. S. It's me," said the familiar female voice.

"Melody! How's everything up on Fox Island?"

"Oh, you know . . . it never changes. Except my best friend, Kim, ran off to Lake Tahoe with Amigo . . . to get married."

"Really? When?"

"Last Saturday."

"What color was his body paint *this* time?" Price questioned.

"Black and white, I suppose. That's Amigo's more formal body paint."

"So they eloped?"

"Yeah, is that totally dumb or what?"

Price shifted the phone to her other ear. "I finished the guest list. I'll mail it up to you . . . or do you want me to fax it?"

"Well . . . eh," Melody hemmed and

hawed, "Here's the thing. Why don't you just keep it there, and I'll pick it up?"

"What do you mean 'pick it up'?"

"It was just a spur-of-the-moment deal. Josh said, 'I really, really wish you'd fly down and spend a few days,' and Kathy invited me to stay with her and Kit, so . . . Dr. S., you know I can't resist Josh's awesome smile!"

She sees the smile through the telephone? "Where are you now?"

"About thirty-seven thousand feet over Reno, I think."

"You're calling from the plane?"

"Isn't that cool? Anyway, I know you said I was always welcome at your house . . . but, I just wanted to double check. Is it all right to stay there for a few days?"

She decides to ask me when she's seven miles above Nevada?

Price lifted her brown, shoulder-length hair off the back of her neck and held it above her head. The cool draft of the air conditioner blew the back of her neck. "Of course . . . you're always welcome at our house. You know that."

"Thanks, Dr. S. This is all so incredible. So absolutely incredible, isn't it? Hey, how's the new book?"

"We just walked in the door," Price admitted.

"What did you decide for a title?"

"It should be called *Jerome*, of course."

"Deception Gulch!" Tony shouted out from across the room. "We're going to call it *Deception Gulch*!"

"Tony, we are not calling it . . ."

"Oh, hey . . . creative differences! I've got to go. I'll call you from Scottsdale. I love you two."

"We love you, too, Melody."

Price folded her arms across her chest. "Tony, we are not going to call this book *Deception Gulch*! That sounds like one of your westerns!"

"What's wrong with that? They've been selling pretty well, haven't they?"

"But the town's name is Jerome. We'll call the book *Jerome*."

"*Jerome*? That sounds like the male protagonist in a romance novel!"

"I hear romance novels have been selling pretty well, too," Price retorted. She thought she heard a car backfire or a gunshot filter down the hillside. The air felt stifling.

They glared at each other.

"All right!" Tony broke the silence. "Our first argument over the book . . . It looks like we're on our way! The Hidden West Series continues."

Price tugged off her light blue, star-shaped

earrings. "You love it, don't you?"

"Love what?"

"The arguments." She rubbed her earlobes. "You get pumped up to write as soon as we get a good heated discussion going."

"That's not true."

"Sure it is." Price turned back to the sink and the salad fixings.

"I'll go hook up the laptop and get started," Tony said. "I think we ought to open the book with the scene of the guy in the truck carrying around his own tombstone."

"This time, Mr. Shadowbrook, I agree with you. I hope the sudden glimmer of harmony doesn't spoil your creative juices!"

"Hey, I can write without arguing. Call me when you have lunch ready."

She pointed to a long roll of paper in his hand. "What are those?"

"Oh, yeah. That's why I came in here in the first place. We had all these faxes waiting for us."

"Who from?"

Tony scrolled through the pages. "Well, there's a six-pager from Terrance Davidian."

"What does he want?"

"There's a long diatribe about why we can't put in the contract that we don't want

Shotgun Creek to be made into an R-rated movie."

"That doesn't sound fair."

Tony scanned the pages. "But that's what he seems to be saying."

"What else is there?"

"Liz sent a summer PR schedule. Guess when she booked me on the 'Good Morning, America' show?"

"August sixteenth? No, that's a Saturday. . . ."

"August fifteenth."

"You can't fly to New York on that day. There's the wedding rehearsal, and the dinner and everything."

"Yeah, I know. I'll call Liz. Didn't we tell her when the wedding was?"

"She knows," Price insisted. "I don't know why she did that. Was that all the faxes?"

"This other one is from someone called Dr. Icing. . . . Do you know a Dr. Icing?"

"That's the caterer who's making the wedding cake. He was going to send me an estimate."

"I hope he makes enough this summer to buy a new fax. . . . His transmission came across garbled."

"What's it say?"

Tony held out the fax. "Look at this. If you

24

hold it just right it looks like the price of the wedding cake is $1,269."

"Oh, really?" Price took the fax from his hand. "That's a couple hundred less than I thought."

"What?" Tony boomed. "Twelve hundred dollars for a wedding cake that will be consumed in thirty minutes! That can't be!"

"But it includes a waterfall."

"The cake has a waterfall in it?"

"Yes, it's the one Josh and Melody picked out."

Tony shook his head. "I'll have to sign that movie contract just to pay for this wedding."

"Go write, Mr. Shadowbrook. You're so emotionally charged you'll probably write an award-winning paragraph."

"Paragraph? I'm buzzed enough to write a whole chapter!"

The morning sun had just crested on the Mogollon Rim. Tony stopped at the upper park on Clark Street to catch his breath.

This is not working. How can I go running every morning? There isn't a level stretch in this whole town. There isn't even a gradual slope in this town. I'll bust a lung going uphill and blow out a knee going down. The country around Columbia Falls is beautiful! I was looking forward to the glacier view. It's going to be a long sum-

25

mer, Shadowbrook . . . a very long, hot summer.

Tony leaned against a black iron fence and watched an old man ascend the steep, concrete steps between Main Street and Clark Street. His tanned and twisted right hand gripped the railing; his left hand made repeated journeys to his mouth as he dragged on a poorly rolled cigarette. The long-sleeved khaki shirt was frayed and tattered at the cuffs. The top button was missing, revealing a less-than-clean white knit undershirt.

The old man stopped, coughed, puffed on the cigarette and stared up at Tony. His beltless khaki trousers were worn slick in the knees. The work boots were held together by aged duct tape. A gray and white mustache rested on his upper lip, a week's stubble bearded his chin. His bronze face looked so leathery and wrinkled that his eyes were merely window slits, like the cracks between Venetian blinds. The narrow-brimmed, brown canvas hat looked sat on . . . or slept in.

As the man puffed his way closer to the top, Tony could see caked dirt on the back of his hands and black grease under his squared-off fingernails. Even though the sun was to his back, he stopped near the top and squinted at Tony.

"I don't believe I caught your name." The old man had a tight, gravelly voice.

"You can call me Tony. Come on, old timer, and sit a spell. You look plum tuckered."

Deep in the recesses of those brown eyes, Tony noticed a sparkle. "Yes, sir . . . I believe I will."

Dressed in jogging shorts, sweaty T-shirt and tennis shoes, Tony remained standing at the fence. The old man plopped down on the top step beside him. They faced the rising sun.

"That's quite a hike," Tony motioned to the stairs.

"Yep. Tough on the lungs. Doctor down at the hospital in Cottonwood told me if I quit smokin' I'd live longer."

"How old are you?"

"Eighty-six. How much longer does he think I want to live?"

Tony grinned. "At eighty-six, a man can do about anything he wants . . . as long as it isn't sinful."

"At eighty-six, you can't *do* the sinful things!" The man laughed, then coughed. "I've been hikin' up them stairs for seventy-two years. I ain't goin' to stop now."

"You've lived in Jerome for seventy-two years?"

27

"Except during the war. I worked in Alameda at the shipyards then. But I moved right back here in '46."

"Did you ever work the mines?"

"They don't call me Dynamite Vic Lucero for nothin'. I worked for the company twenty-two years and never missed a day. Not one day. No one else could say that. Look it up in the company records. 'Course, they're all gone now. Just me and old man Morvant."

Tony sat down on the step next to the man. "Old man Morvant? Is he older than you, Vic?"

The ashes of his cigarette almost reached his yellowed fingers. A wide smile sprung up on his face. "Shoot, no, he ain't older than me. But he was my shop foreman, and we always called 'im the Old Man. I reckon he ain't much over eighty. Don't see him much, though. Lives in one of the fancy houses down at Clarkdale."

Lucero's aroma caused Tony to scoot over on the step toward the closed cafe. "Tell me about the old days, Vic. What kind of place was Jerome?"

"One swell fine town, she was. Runnin' three shifts a day, the town never closed. Ol' Glen Bayliss ran that cafe right there twenty-four hours a day. He only closed on

Christmas Day and Easter. Sort of a religious feller, I surmise."

"I suppose it was a little rough at the edges, being a mining town and all," Tony pressed.

"Don't you believe everthing you read in them books. Sure there was two saloons on ever' corner, and the girls over on Hull Avenue. There was fights, knifings and shootin's. But what do you expect? This is Arizona. Back then we had a tradition to uphold. But there was good folks, too. Lots of 'em." He leaned close enough for Tony to smell his tobacco breath. "What did you say your name was?"

"Tony. Tony Shadowbrook."

"No foolin'? You live in Jerome?"

"We're staying here for the summer."

"Ain't that somethin'? You wouldn't think there was two of them in the state."

"Two what?"

"Two Tony Shadowbrooks."

"You know someone else named Tony Shadowbrook?"

"Well, I don't know him personal," Vic dropped the remains of his cigarette and stomped it out on the steps. "There's that Shadowbrook fellow who writes westerns. I heard he built himself a large mansion down in Carefree."

"Actually, he has a house on Hearthstone Drive in Scottsdale. In fact, he's still making sizable payments on it."

"You don't say? You know him?"

"I am him."

"You're the writer?"

"That's me, partner."

The old man slapped his knee and showed a yellow-toothed grin. "I've been meanin' to write to you! I like your books. Check 'em out of the library as soon as they come out, I do. Just ask Sheila, the librarian, she'll tell you. Dynamite Vic reads Shadowbrook and Hillerman. . . . But, you've got a mistake on page 186 in *Blowout in the Black Hills*."

"What's that?"

"If you remember, you describe how they shored up that horizontal shaft with timbers? Bob Underwood invented that pattern you described on the Iron King Mine in 1896. *Blowout* takes place fifteen years earlier."

"You got me there, partner," Tony admitted.

"Well, I figured you might like to know."

"You find any other errors?"

"None that amount to much." The old man looked up the sidewalk. "Here comes that hippie that runs the Flour Power Cafe."

A woman in her fifties approached, her long grey and black hair pulled back in a ponytail. She wore an ankle-length, multicolored prairie skirt and a turquoise peasant blouse. "A hippie?" Tony questioned in a low voice.

"They moved in here in the late '60s."

"That's almost thirty years ago."

"Some of 'em never left. We was down to less than a hundred people when they moved in. It was nice to have some company," Vic reported.

"Can she cook?"

"The best in town."

Tony dug into the tiny pocket inside the waistband of his jogging shorts and pulled out a tightly folded twenty dollar bill. "Tell you what, Vic. When she gets the grill hot, I'll buy you breakfast. Providin' you don't have other plans."

The old man's eyes glistened as he rubbed his soiled hands across his stubbled beard. "Sounds good to me. When a man's self-employed, he can set his own hours."

"What kind of work do you do nowadays, Vic?"

"Same as always. I work the mines. 'Course, now I'm on my own. There ain't no steady paycheck, except for Social Security."

"You doing some gold panning?"

31

"Pannin', nothin'! I leased me part of the shaft."

"There's still good ore down there?"

"You bet there is! It could be sweet . . . mighty sweet. But those college graduate scientists cain't figure out how to process the ore to remove the gold, silver and copper. You'd think they would have gained a little knowledge over the past hundred years. Shoot, no . . . they're still actin' like we're livin' in the nineteenth century."

Tony watched as the "closed" sign on the cafe was turned to "open." "Let's go grab some breakfast," he motioned.

"She'll make us sit on the patio."

"Why's that?"

"Says I pollute her environment. Listen, I tell her, I've spent more time in this building over the past seventy-six years than you have!"

"What does she say to that?"

"Says I still have to sit on the patio. You know, I think I liked 'em better when they didn't bathe so much, either."

"I'd rather eat outside myself," Tony offered.

"You're right about that."

The shadows had crept down to street level by the time Vic finished breakfast and

Tony sipped his second cup of coffee. They sat at a round, green metal table with a yellow and green canvas umbrella. Dynamite Vic Lucero rolled himself a cigarette and then dug out a tattered gold foil book of matches that read *The Mirage* and lit the smoke.

"You don't eat breakfast?" Lucero prodded.

"Not until I finish running."

"Where you staying?"

"At a friend's house across the way." He pointed down the hill towards the museum.

"You in the Honeymoon House?"

"Next to it."

He leaned close to Tony. "I like you, Shadowbrook. You ain't stuffy like them other writers."

"You know other writers?"

"Oh, shoot, yeah. This town is jammed with artists and writers and poets and musicians and historians. 'Course, most of 'em ain't sold nothin' more than used furniture at a garage sale. But they act as if they was Ernest Hemingway himself. Now, there's a writer! Say, whatever happened to him?"

"He killed himself."

"You don't say?" Lucero scratched his temple. "Listen, Shadowbrook. . . ."

"Why don't you call me Tony?"

33

"I don't want you to think I'm just panhandlin'. No sir, I ain't askin' for no gift. But, bein's you seem to be a square fella, with some sand . . . I was wonderin' if I could borrow sixty off you?"

Tony tipped the blue enamel mug and swigged down the last of his coffee. He looked over at the expectant eyes of the old man. "I don't know, Dynamite Vic. What would you do with sixty dollars?"

"Sixty dollars? Shoot, that ain't enough to go to Prescott and buy some pretty lady supper." He leaned over until his face was only inches from Tony's. "I meant sixty thousand dollars."

Tony's eyebrows raised. "You want to borrow sixty thousand dollars?"

"Shhh. Not so loud. Keep it on the quiet," Lucero insisted. "It will take that much to file a patent on the extraction process I developed. I don't even have money to make a full-sized prototype, but it will revolutionize prospectin'. Phelps-Dodge would pay millions for this. But if I don't make the prototype and get the patent . . . they'll steal it from me."

"You really think a mining corporation as big as Phelps-Dodge would pirate your invention?"

"Yep."

"Vic, I don't have that kind of money to loan."

"You mean, your books ain't sellin'?"

"Oh, they're doing fine. But I have a family to raise . . . a couple girls in college. I'm afraid I just don't have extra funds for speculative investments."

"Ain't no speculation about this. It's a sure thing."

Tony fiddled with his empty coffee cup. "Can't you get a bank to back you?"

"I ain't goin' to show my idea to no bank! They'd steal it as quick as you could say Hoover Dam. Besides, I haven't been inside a bank in thirty-seven years."

A slightly cool breeze drifted down the mountain. "Sorry, Vic . . . I just don't have that kind of money."

The old man shook his head. "Well, sir, that's too bad. Maybe them book sales will pick up and you'll be able to send them girls of yours to college after all."

"Well, it's not that . . ." Tony began, then just let it drop.

The two men walked to the top of the stairs. "It's about time for me to jog back to the house before the wife dials 911."

"Wish you'd reconsider makin' that loan," the old man pressed.

"Vic, I just don't have the funds. But I'd

enjoy visitin' some more. My wife and I are writing a book about Jerome."

"You are?" The old man shoved his canvas hat back. "You think it will get published?"

"Next June. We already have a contract for it. How about you and me meeting for breakfast again? Where do you live? I could pick you up some morning."

"Don't need to do that. I've walked this town for more than seventy years . . . ain't goin' to start shirkin' now."

"You'll have to tell me all about minin' in the old days. In fact, I'd love to go down and see firsthand exactly what you're doin' now."

Lucero recoiled. "Listen, Shadowbrook, knowin' you like I do, I wasn't offended by that. But let me explain to you how it is. You don't ever ask to see a man's diggin's. That location is between him and the Good Lord. And nobody . . . I mean nobody . . . better try to find out where it is. That's why I always carry a Colt .45 when I go to work."

"I apologize for my obvious lack of etiquette."

"Ever' man is entitled to one mistake."

Tony lifted his right leg to the top of the fence railing and tried to stretch out. "Have you made your one mistake?" he asked the old man.

"Yep."

"What was that?"

"I should've married Verna Radford."

"Good lookin', was she?" Tony jibed.

"Had a face like a bulldog."

"And you thought about marrying her?"

"Oh, lordy, how she was rich."

"If you had married her, you wouldn't have been motivated to develop this great new extraction process."

"Say, you might be right about that. Besides, I'd had to live in one of them big old Sedona houses and gulp them watered-down drinks with little umbrellas."

By the time Tony reached the house his knees burned from the constant downhill jarring. Price was sitting on the deck reading a book. "You get lost, Mr. Shadowbrook?"

"Sorry, I ran into an old timer who volunteered some oral history of the town. He's quite a character. He talked my leg off. You're up and reading awfully early. Must be a good book."

"It's a fascinating biography," Price reported. "It's all about Frances Willard."

"The one who headed the Temperance Union?"

"No, it's a different lady . . . with the same name and the same priorities."

"Really?"

37

"She taught school here, was a state senator and temperance leader. Her brother started the town of Cottonwood, her father-in-law was Jerome's first mayor, and her husband, Johnny Munds, was a Yavapai County sheriff of some notoriety."

"I've heard of Sheriff Munds! Some kind of big gunfight. Hey, this is good stuff you're finding. But that still doesn't tell me what in the world you're doing up. It's still quite early for a non-morning person like Professor Shadowbrook."

"I've been on the phone," she admitted. "I've had three phone calls already."

"Who called?"

"One was from Kit, another from Kathy and the third from Melody."

"All three of them called separately?"

"Yes." Price rubbed her clearly defined eyebrows. "It seems they aren't speaking to each other."

2

From the desk of Priscilla Carey Shadowbrook:

1. Speak at Bed & Breakfast conclave (Wednesday noon, at Flowers & Frills.)
2. Mail present to Cooper Jarrett Shadowbrook
(Two months old on Friday!)
3. Lunch with Danae Pettybone at Emile's in Sedona
(Don't wear anything that clashes with hot pink.)
4. Call Dr. Icing
(Abolutely no goldfish swimming in the waterfall!)
5. Find out who's leaving vegetables by the front step
(More zucchini recipes?)
6. Remind Tony of radio interviews

(WSAB, Miami, Tuesday. KJRC, Austin, Friday.)
7. Ask Kit about the pills!
   (Who is this Dr. Neustatt?)
8. Finish Isaiah study
   (26:12 . . . yes! yes! yes!)
9. Edit Chapter One
   (Find a more creative way to open each chapter.)
10. Get Another bid on backyard landscaping.
    (More rock and succulents.)

Price could see the supermarket from the big deck.

At least she could see the generally green area that represented the trees that surrounded the shopping center that housed the supermarket. Unfortunately, it was over ten miles from the house, down the mountain and over the twisting highway. She drove the few blocks to the little market in Jerome instead.

Price was surprised to see the old grey Chevy pickup that had spun off the highway the previous week parked across the street. The vehicle looked mostly repaired. The gravestone now stood upright in the bed of the truck and a shorts-clad Clayton Gilette sprawled sound asleep on the hood.

When she exited the store carrying a sack of groceries in her left arm and a gallon of nonfat milk in her right, Gilette was standing on the front bumper of his pickup, yelling down at the lower level of the city parking lot.

"The time is coming when you will no longer see Clayton V. Gilette. I will be murdered, and you will be surprised at the killer!" he shouted.

Staying at a distance from Gilette, Price hiked to the front of the Cherokee and gazed down into the open parking lot, twenty feet below.

There's no one down there! Who's he talking to?

"I know you're listening!" he screamed. "You will be my witnesses. I told you ahead of time this would happen. I am a prophet of doom! And I will die in this doomed town!"

This guy is crazy! He needs to be committed.

"My death will be a sign. Run to the valley . . . move to the plains . . . flee this wicked and perverse place!" Gilette spun toward Price. "Lady, can you buy a condemned man breakfast?"

Price ignored him and stuffed groceries into the Jeep Cherokee.

Scooting toward the front of her rig he hollered. "I said, Lady, can you buy a doomed man breakfast?"

"Get a life!" Price mumbled.

He spun back to face the east and the empty lower parking lot. "I'm going to be murdered in less than eight weeks and all she can say is 'get a life'?"

He was still screaming when Price backed up into Main Street and drove south.

Jerome was once called "The Most Unique City in America" for its incredible ability to cling to the implausibly steep, sunny side of Cleopatra Hill. Some of the streets drop at a thirty-three degree angle. Since 1953, Jerome had clawed out a new life for itself with as much tenacity as Angus McKinnon and M.A. Ruffner, who filed claims on the copper outcroppings in 1876.

In the 1920s over fifteen thousand people perched in this hawk's nest of a town. At that time it was the fourth largest city in the state. By 1955 the population had plummeted to barely over one hundred. Today, the year-round residents number closer to four hundred.

Boom or bust, miners or tourists, Jerome attracts the eccentric, the gifted, the bizarre and the talented. They are the new adventurers on the pockmarked, scarred, and disemboweled mountain.

A woman wearing an olive, orange and brown broomstick skirt, triple-buckle olive leather sandals and an olive drab tank top sat on the concrete retaining wall near the carport as Price pulled into the Winslows' house. Grabbing her groceries and milk, Price shoved the door closed with her bare knee.

She stopped about ten feet away. "Are you the one who's been leaving the vegetables?"

"Vegetables?"

"Oh," Price mumbled, "I thought . . . May I help you?"

The woman looked somewhere between a hard twenty-five or a soft forty-five. "Are you the one writing the travelogue about Jerome?"

Price shifted the sack of groceries on her hip and let her right hand down with the plastic jug. "My husband and I are writing a book about the area, but it's not exactly a travelogue. There'll be lots of history, plenty of character sketches . . . things like that."

"That's what I meant."

"What can I do for you?"

"It's what I can do for you that's important." The woman stood up, walked toward Price, and examined her from head to toe.

Feeling like the last applicant in a beauty queen contest, Price repeated, "Do for me?"

"My name's Isabelle Broussard. I can give you a private ghost city tour."

Price set the milk down on the stairs and changed the groceries to her right arm. "I suppose you could call Jerome sort of a ghost town, but since it's still populated it doesn't quite fit the image, does it?"

The woman threw her head back. Her long dangling gold earrings jingled. "Ha! Not a tour of a ghost city . . . but a tour of the city's ghosts. Jerome is haunted, you know."

"Haunted, you say?"

"That's right. The tour begins at midnight and ends at dawn. The private tour is five hundred dollars. I can guarantee you'll get your money's worth!" The woman accented the point by raising her dark eyebrows to a sharp crease.

Price stared the woman down in her deep-set brown eyes. "Mrs. Broussard, I . . ."

"Ms. Broussard."

Price took a deep breath and let it out slowly. "Thanks for the offer. But, frankly, I'm not interested. Sorry you wasted your time coming out here."

The woman leaned only inches away from Price's face. Her voice was husky, much deeper than previously. "Oh, I have plenty of time for you."

Lord, this is getting creepy.

"Well, I don't. So, perhaps you're wasting *my* time."

"You don't want to talk to the ghosts?"

"Ms. Broussard, I do not want to talk to them, see them, or receive a fax from them! Besides, no tour of Jerome, even if 'Rawhide Jimmy' Douglas was here in person, would be worth five hundred dollars a night."

"Douglas' ghost is at the ruins of the Little Daisy Hotel. He refuses to go home as long as it's a museum," Broussard reported in the same deep voice.

Tony Shadowbrook, this would be a real good time for you to step out here and handle this!

"Actually, I wouldn't go on a ghost tour if you paid *me* five hundred dollars."

"You afraid of ghosts?"

"Ms. Broussard, there are no such things as ghosts. But there certainly is a demonic world that is able to convince some they are the spirits of departed souls."

"Ha!"

I said all that . . . and she just answers, "ha"?
"That's a destructive game you're playing. The Evil One's only purpose is to steal, kill, and destroy."

The lady's face flushed red and her voice, still distorted, flashed hatred. "And we hate

45

you, too, Priscilla Shadowbrook!"

Price looked back toward the house, searching for an opening door. *Shadowbrook, get out here!*

She tried to look straight into the distorted face of Isabelle Broussard. Suddenly an idea flooded her mind. She spoke forcefully, yet quietly. "In the name of Jesus, be gone!"

The lady's face turned sheet-white. She staggered back a step. The hateful expression melted into one of fear and bewilderment.

"Ms. Broussard, I believe you're experimenting with something far beyond your understanding. It's a deadly power you're plugged into. I urge you to pull away while you have the ability to do so."

"I'll see you again," Broussard vowed.

The woman turned toward the road and scurried out of sight.

Price wanted to run into the house. She thought about screaming for Tony. She hoped she would wake up from an onion-and-garlic-pizza dream. Instead, the same words kept recycling themselves in her mind: *In the name, power and blood of Jesus, hedge this property from the dominion of the Evil One.*

Price had just put the groceries away when Tony bounded in from the back room, tucking in his purple-and-white, long-sleeved western shirt.

"Were you talking to someone out there?"

Price bit her lip and nodded.

"Who was it?"

"The devil."

"No, really, . . ." he urged, "who was out there?"

"I told you. It was Satan himself."

Tony was lost in the screen of his laptop computer when Price barefooted her way to the deck. The almost-orange Arizona sun was three-quarters of the way across the sky.

"Are you all right, darlin'?"

"I took a nap." Price stretched her arms straight out and stared up at the blue clear sky.

"I didn't know you were that tired."

"Neither did I. That deal with Broussard sort of zapped my energy, or something. I feel better, but I sure didn't get any work done today. How about you?"

"Listen to this. . . ." Tony shaded the screen of his laptop and leaned close as he began to read.

Mr. Eugene Murray Jerome never set foot in the town named after him. He was content to finance the mining operation, while his name lived on with the notorious reputation of the rip-roaring copper camp. Perhaps he was too busy in New York City shuffling stocks and making money to bother with a journey west. Or perhaps the social calendar kept him hopping.

He traveled in the right circles. After all, his cousin, Jennie, had married that English chap, Churchill, and moved to Great Britain. Her infant son, Winston, would one day make a fair name for himself.

Price stepped over behind him and stared at the screen. "Think I'll do a little more research on the Jerome family. Go ahead, read the rest."

The United Verde Copper Company was formed in 1882 and was purchased in 1888 by William A. Clark, who would go on to be a U.S. Senator from Montana. But the camp was named and the best he could do was call the neighboring smelter town Clarkdale.

When Dr. James Stuart Douglas struck valuable ore on the lower side of town in 1915 he already was a well-known mining man. Years before, following that glorious tradition of the times, the smelter town of Douglas, Arizona, had been named in his honor.

Price turned east and stared down at the treetops of Clarkdale, two thousand feet below them. "Everyone wanted a town named after them, I suppose."

Tony pushed his silver-frame glasses up on the bridge of his nose and squinted.

From the United Verde Copper Company (1888-1935) to the United Verde Extension (1915-1938) to the giant Phelps-Dodge Corporation (1935-1953), Jerome was seen by many as merely a company town dominated by strong personalities.

Although Phelps-Dodge Corporation is still a principal landholder around the copper hill, Jerome is no longer a company town. It is, however, still home to a robust citizenry of rugged individuals, some of whom are only temporary residents.

"Davidian is flying in to negotiate? What is there to negotiate?" Tony sputtered.

Price glanced up from the laptop computer that rested on the glass table in the sun room. The oak and leather director's chair squeaked as she leaned back and stretched her arms. "All I know is that Davidian called and said he was coming today to talk to you

49

about the movie deal on *Shotgun Creek*. He said if you agree to this deal, they'll pick up an option on *Standoff at Rifle Ridge*."

"They've seen *Standoff*? I haven't even seen the author's proofs on it yet!"

"Well, he's on his way. He wants you to pick him up at the airport."

"Which airport?"

"Sky Harbor."

Tony paced the room, slamming his right fist into the palm of his left hand. "He thinks that I'm going to drive three hours to Phoenix just to pick him up at the airport? That's the most absurd, presumptuous thing I ever heard of in my life! There's no way on earth that I'm going to drive clear down there."

"I know."

"So what did you tell him?"

"I screamed into the phone, 'That's the most absurd, presumptuous thing I ever heard of in my life! There's no way on earth that Tony's going to drive clear down there!' "

Tony stopped dead still. "You did?"

"Of course not. But I did tell him we were too far from Phoenix to offer a ride. He'd have to make other plans."

"I hear John Grisham gets final approval of which actors play in movies based on his books . . . and I can't even get my opinion heard on them twisting my book with sex, gore and blasphemy."

"Maybe you ought to just forget the movies and stick with books," she suggested.

Tony wandered into the kitchen, grabbed the coffee pot and meandered back to the desk in the corner of the sun room.

Price held up her cup. "Man at the pot!" she called.

Tony spun around. "Where did you learn that old chuckwagon line?" He came over and poured her cup full.

"From that famous writer, Anthony Shadowbrook!" She tilted her head sideways and batted her eyes.

"You two good friends, are you?"

"He's such a dear," she cooed. "And he reminds me of my . . . father!"

"Listen, Grandma Price . . . don't pretend you're some young thing."

"I'm not quite ready for this grandma bit," she admitted.

"Cooper Jarrett Shadowbrook, aged two months, thinks you are."

Price sipped on her coffee. They stared out across the now hazy Verde Valley towards the timeless Mogollon Rim. "He is a darling. Seems to have his daddy's looks and his mamma's sweet disposition. Amanda said he has the awesome Shadowbrook smile. I love him dearly, but I'm really having a tough time with being called grandma." She gazed at Tony's rugged, squared face. "Are we really that old?"

"Yep." Sitting the coffee cup on the table, he stepped over behind her and began to rub her neck. "Where did the time go, darlin'? Mark was the cutest baby that ever existed on the face of the earth. You said so yourself. The Lord's right. A person's life goes by awful quick. Grandparents? Some days I don't feel much over thirty."

"And others . . . ?"

"And other days I feel seventy." Tony released her shoulders and walked to his computer. "How's Chapter One look?"

Price glanced at her computer screen. "Great!"

"You mean, we agree on it?"

"No major problems at all. Except, you still need me to clean things up a bit," she chided.

"Clean it up? Where?"

"Well, like this line: 'Douglas stood to his feet.' That's redundant. If he stood . . . he stood on his feet. . . . What other way to stand is there?"

"I just leave those in, you know . . . to make you feel useful."

"Oh, thank you, Mr. Famous Writer. It must be working, because I do feel useful." She saved what was on her screen, then scooted to the floor-to-ceiling window. "What did you decide about the Broussard woman? You going to include something about her in Chapter Two?"

"I'm convinced that we can use Vic Lucero's story in the book. It's kind of a human interest feature that ties along the narrative. I think the verdict is still out on Gilette. He's a newcomer, but he typifies the craziness of a mining town. But Broussard is too far out to mention by name. I thought about just alluding to a tour available to Jerome's haunted places. What do you think?"

"You know what I think. She's playing around with the demonic. I don't want to mention anything in our book that could be misused, that would be spiritually harmful to a reader."

"You're right."

"I am?"

"Yep. No mention of haunted places . . . or ghosts."

"Thanks, Tony. I appreciate it. That bout with Broussard kind of pushed me to the wall the other day. That's about as much confrontation as I want. But I suppose we'll have to mention the Halloween Reunion at Spook Hall."

"Yeah, this must be the only town in America with a community center called Spook Hall. Hey, I forgot to ask you when you came home. . . . How was your talk at the Bed & Breakfast conclave?"

Price's face brightened. "They seemed to like it. Everyone there had a wealth of information about the history of their particular buildings . . . who lived there . . . what happened . . . the famous and the infamous. I set up eight interviews."

Tony stepped to the bootjack and began to tug on his lizard-skinned Justins. "Anything new? Anything that hasn't already been included in a dozen other books?"

"A few interesting stories. I'm not sure how we use some of them. For instance, there was a character named Box Car Riley who recited long passages of Scripture or Shakespeare only when he was drunk. But I couldn't find anyone who could set the context of a particular diatribe."

"Maybe we should have a chapter titled 'Unsubstantiated Wild Stories of Deception Gulch.' "

"Jerome."

"Whatever."

Price doodled on a piece of paper. "Maybe

54

. . . you're right."

"About using the title *Deception Gulch*?"

"No. About the Wild Rumor Chapter. You can learn a lot from considering the type of rumors that get started in a place, even if they turn out to be false." Price glanced at the pink note pad by the phone. "Any calls while I was gone?"

"Your daughter called."

"Which one?"

"The one that's a twin."

"Who called, Shadowbrook!"

"Kit."

"How are things going? Did the daddy-brokered truce hold?"

"So far. I still can't believe who the bridesmaid walks down the aisle with is all that big a deal."

Price slipped off her heels and padded her way to the kitchen. Tony trailed behind. She rummaged in the fridge and pulled out a large fresh carrot. She then washed and peeled it. "When one groomsman is your oldest brother . . . and the other just happens to be one of Hollywood's ten most eligible bachelors for the past three years . . . it makes a difference."

"Well, at the rehearsal they'll draw names out of a hat to see who walks with whom. They agreed to that," Tony concluded.

"Can you imagine the tears we'll have to put up with on Friday night?"

Tony rummaged through the refrigerator. "Oh, Kit will pout, but she won't cry."

"Speaking of the only female mechanic at the Valley of the Sun Auto Village Service Center. . . . Did you talk to Kit about the pills we found?"

"Yep."

Price spun around. "You did?"

"Sure, I said I'd talk to her."

"You said you'd talk to her two weeks ago . . . and last weekend . . . and on Monday. Anyway, what did she say?"

"She said Dr. Neustatt, a dermatologist, recommended them to help her with her acne."

Price cocked her head sideways. "Acne?"

"Pimples . . . zits . . . something about birth control pills that help the skin. Must be the hormones."

"Then exactly why has she been so secretive so neither we nor her sister knew anything about them?"

"She said she was afraid we'd think she wanted them for other reasons. I guess she was a little embarrassed to talk about it."

Price dug out a half-empty bottle of low-fat ranch salad dressing and squirted it across the carrots. "How long has she been taking them?"

"About six months."

"She's been taking birth-control pills for acne for six months and didn't bother to tell us?" Price fumed. "Did you tell her that we've known about this for weeks?"

"Yep."

"What did she say?"

"She said she couldn't believe we've known about it for weeks and never asked her anything."

Price and Tony focused their eyes out the front window up the mountain at the crumbling, braced buildings of downtown Jerome.

Their hearts were focused elsewhere.

Price slipped her hand into Tony's. "They're almost twenty, Daddy."

"I suppose they do a lot of things we don't know about?" he mused.

"Did you tell your parents all that you did when you were twenty?"

"Not hardly."

"Me either."

"It doesn't get any easier, does it?" Tony slipped his arm around Price's shoulder and gave her a gentle squeeze.

"You mean, letting them go?"

"Yeah." He dropped his hand to his side and turned to face Price. "Now, tell me the truth, do young ladies actually take birth-control pills to help their complexion?"

Price laid her reading glasses on the counter and rubbed the bridge of her nose. "That's what I've heard. Didn't you believe Kit?"

Tony ran his hand through his grey-flecked, dark brown hair. "Yep, I believed her. Of course, I don't think she's had a date since last summer. But I must admit if Kathy gave me that same reason, I'd have serious doubts."

"Kath doesn't have any skin problems," Price commented.

"Exactly. And she hasn't gone five days without a date in years."

"Oh, you'd believe Kath, too, Tony. Both girls have Daddy wrapped around their little fingers."

"What do you mean both girls? All three girls."

"Melody, too?"

"No, I mean Priscilla."

Price's smile revealed deep, suntanned dimples. "Come to think of it, you are an easy target. Papa told me that before we married."

"He told you I was an easy mark?"

"No," she sipped from her tea cup. "Back in those days we didn't have any idea you'd turn out to be a writer. But my papa said, 'Price, honey, you marry that cowboy and you'll have to live on a pedestal all your life. You'll be pampered, spoiled and zealously overprotected . . . but there's worse things that can happen to a woman.' "

"Your father told you that?"

"Yes, he did."

"What did your mother tell you?" Tony quizzed.

"She said I was probably in for a wild ride, but at least my life would never be boring."

"Which one was right? Mom? Or Dad?"

"Both." Price thought Tony suddenly looked twenty years younger. "Now, what did your parents say about marrying me?" she quizzed.

"My daddy said if I didn't marry you it would be the stupidest thing I ever did in my life and he'd seriously think about writing me out of his will."

"He did?"

"Something to that effect. I believe his exact language was a little more blunt."

"And what did your mother say?"

Tony glanced back out the window. "She said I shouldn't worry if you couldn't cook and clean house too well . . . she was sure you'd make up for it in other areas."

"Other areas? Just what did she mean by that?" Price demanded.

"Eh . . . well . . . ," Tony stammered. "There was one other thing she told me."

"What's that?"

"She said, 'The day after your wedding I'm turning your bedroom into a sewing room. So don't plan on coming back.' "

"And she did, didn't she?"

"Yep."

Tony was sipping boiling hot coffee from a chipped porcelain cup at the counter of the Ireland Cafe, glancing through the *Wall Street Journal* when Dynamite Vic Lucero ambled in. The old man plucked off his dirty brown hat, slid up on a stool next to him and signaled the waitress.

"Two sugar doughnuts and the hottest, blackest coffee you can find. Afternoon, Tony."

"How was the diggin' this morning?"

"Sorry as could be," he reported in a loud voice, then winked at Tony. Lucero scooped spoon after spoon of sugar into his cup of coffee. "I know . . . I know," he protested, "you're goin' to tell me sugar is bad for me and it will shorten my life span. . . ."

"Nope," Tony grinned. "Have all the sugar you want. You did put me in your will, didn't you?"

Vic's smile revealed yellowed but straight teeth. "Now that's what I like about you, Shadowbrook. You just come right out and say it." Then he leaned over closer to Tony. "You ain't too far off in your thinkin'."

Tony laid the newspaper down and swiveled toward Lucero. "What do you mean?"

"Well, you ain't gettin' in my will. But I was thinkin' someone ought to know where my diggin's are . . . just in case, you know, there's some foul play, or some claim jumpers start actin' up. Who knows when I might need a witness in a court of law to say, 'Yep, that's Dynamite Vic's claim, all right'?"

"You're expecting trouble and you want me to witness your claim?"

"I ain't expectin' nothin'. But a man's got to keep all the pillows warm. I'm jist thinkin' about it, mind ya. Ain't made up my mind quite yet. You pack a gun, Shadowbrook?"

"Not unless I need to. Why?"

"Probably nothing." Vic Lucero bit into a doughnut, spraying powdered sugar across his beard, then washed it down with steaming coffee. "Say, did your book sales perk up any this week?"

"I don't really check on them week by week," Tony admitted.

"My offer still holds. You want to invest that sixty thousand dollars . . . we'll be partners."

"Partners? I don't remember you offering that before."

"Did I forget to mention that part?"

"I'm afraid so."

"Does it make any difference?"

Tony slapped him on the back. "I'm afraid not, Dynamite Vic. I still don't have the fund."

"Well . . . it's all right. I like you, Shadowbrook. And to tell you the truth, I think I've got me another backer anyway."

"That's great, Vic. Who's the rich hombre that's giving you a stake?"

"Cain't say . . . just yet. Don't want to jinx the deal. But it might be just the ticket, yes sir. Say, do you know a good patent attorney?"

"You're serious about this, aren't you?"

"Yep."

"I do know a copyright attorney that does a good job for me. But I don't think he knows squat about mining. Maybe you'd be better off with someone more expert in the field."

"I don't want one that knows a whole lot about mining. When he sees what I've come up with, he's liable to steal it. Suppose he tears up the papers I sign and files it under his own name? By the time I discovered the deception, he'd sell out to Phelps-Dodge for millions and be livin' on some South Pacific island with a harem of sweaty, half-dressed women."

Tony spun back and forth on the cafe stool, trying to keep a straight face. "I can see the dilemma that puts you in. Why don't I check around with some friends of mine next time I'm in Phoenix? If I run across a reputable mining attorney, I'll bring you his name and number. Then you can check him out if you want to."

"I'd be obliged." Lucero took another swig of coffee, grimaced, then held his jaw.

"You got a toothache, Vic?"

"Ain't bad. Just if the coffee hits it right. These ain't store-boughts, you know. I got all my own teeth, and I ain't been to a dentist since Doc Hawkins died."

"When was that?"

"In 1932. Did you ever hear about Doc Hawkins?"

Tony finished his coffee and folded up the newspaper. "I hear he was quite innovative."

"Innovative . . . he was a loony! On little cavities, he'd numb you up and then drive in a cactus thorn. On the big one's he'd use asphalt. Same stuff that's on the highway!"

"Did it work?"

"Ain't none of 'em still livin' but me. Old Doc was nice enough, though. He bought us a baseball one time. The grade school had a team right after the war. That's World War I. And we was playing Prescott. They had come over on the train. The UV and Pacific was still runnin' that little narrow gauge railroad from Jerome Junction back then."

"Where did you have a level enough field to play on?"

"We was out there on the point. That was before the high school was built out there. It weren't much of a ball field, but it's all we had. Anyways, we was playin' Prescott, and Nate Mack Cunningham came up to bat in the bottom of the second. His daddy was the postmaster, you know. And his mamma, too. Well, Nate Mack was a big kid, and he plows into one, sending it over the right fielder and down off Cleopatra Hill.

"They say it took two bounces and landed in the back of a Model T that was snakin' its way down to the valley. Well, we started searching around and discovered that we didn't have another ball. The boys from Prescott didn't have a ball either. So they got on the train and went home. We always claimed to have won the game one to nothing, but them Prescott fellas insist the game didn't count. People from over there always was stuck-up like that, you know what I mean?"

"Thanks for the story, Vic. I've got to head out to the house. We've got company coming for supper and I promised Price I'd be there when they arrived."

Vic shook his head. "You're a busy man, Shadowbrook. It beats me how you find time for research, let alone write."

"Well, Vic, you'd be surprised how much a man can cram into an afternoon at the Ireland Cafe."

"What time did Davidian say he would be here?" Tony asked as he sat on the couch in the living room, tugging on his full quill ostrich boots.

"His plane was arriving in Phoenix at 2:10. By the time he rents a car and all, I suppose it will be at least six before he drives up." Price pulled a long turquoise apron over her short-sleeved, white cotton dress with teal-green and peach southwest designs. She began to scrub fresh potatoes and slice zucchinis that lay on the white tile counter next to the sink.

Tony wandered into the kitchen. "Is it just me, or does Davidian always show up at meal time?"

"I'm wondering if he's going to want to stay the night?" Price placed the potatoes on the microwave tray.

"There are plenty of motels in Cotton-wood and Sedona. We are not inviting him to stay with us," Tony insisted. "We had all the houseguests we could handle last year. This time, it's just you and me."

Price glanced at her watch. "Think I'll bake these half through now, and just wait until Davidian arrives to finish them." She punched several buttons on the microwave, then wiped her hands on the apron. "You know, I love Melody dearly . . . but having her in the garage room last year slowed down our writing. Have you noticed how much faster things are going this summer?"

"We do seem to be buzzing along. What can I do to help you?"

"You could set the table."

Tony rattled his way into the silverware drawer.

"How about you and Davidian discussing your contract stuff at the table. Then after supper, he can go his way, and we'll still get a couple hours of work in?"

"I really don't have much to say. He knows what I want. I don't know why he's coming over to see us." Tony stared out the living room window past the trees planted by Lewis Douglas in 1932. "There's a car tooling up the road. Maybe it's Davidian."

66

"What kind of car? Does it look like a rental?"

Tony squinted as the sun hovered above the ridge of Mingus Mountain. "I can't tell . . . there's too much dust. But the neighbors are in Europe, so I doubt if anyone's headed to their place."

"This is earlier than I expected," Price called out from the kitchen. "Oh, well . . . get all your discussion done before supper and we'll still have plenty of time for writing."

"It looks like he's driving a Mustang."

"That's a nice rental."

"A Mustang convertible."

"Like mine?" she asked.

The rig pulled into the carport next to their Jeep Cherokee. Tony pulled the blinds open wider. "It is yours!"

"What?" Price scurried out into the living room next to Tony. "He drove *my* Mustang?"

"Not exactly." A young woman got out of the driver's side of the car.

"Melody! She drove him up here? In my car?"

Tony shrugged. They stepped out on the porch as Terrance Davidian and Melody Mason hiked up the steps.

"Hi, guys!" Melody called out. "Is this cool, or what?" She gave Price a hug, then

Tony. "Hi, Pop!"

"Hi, kiddo . . . you gave Davidian a lift, eh?"

"Tony, my man . . . I thought to myself, why bother the Shadowbrooks and make them phone their research assistant? So I just called Ms. Mason myself."

"He said you wanted me to drive him up here," Melody added. "Kit and Kathy have their rigs at work, so I presumed you wanted me to drive the Mustang . . . right?"

"Eh . . . well . . ." Price stammered. "Sure."

"Mel," Davidian motioned, "be a star and bring in our suitcases, would you?"

"Suitcases?" Tony quizzed.

"Oh, I couldn't get a return until noon tomorrow. Hope you don't mind."

"Actually, as large as this house is, it only has one guest room. Naturally, Melody should. . . ." Price began.

"Oh, no problemo! I can bunk on the sofa. Say, did I ever tell you about the time that Keanu Reeves had to spend the night on my couch? Talk about the phone ringing off the hook!"

"Keanu Reeves was at your house?" Melody choked out each word.

"Oh, sure . . . didn't I tell you about that? Grab the suitcases, would you, sweetheart?"

Tony gave the guests a panoramic tour of the Verde Valley and Cleopatra Hill from the expansive front deck. Price puttered in the kitchen. When they finally sat down at the glass-and-chrome table, Davidian sat next to Price, so Melody plopped down by Tony. Their plates were soon heaped with pepper steak, waldorf salad, homemade zucchini bread, and baked potatoes.

"Terry," Tony began, "I think you know exactly how I feel about the contract."

"Dr. S.," Melody inserted. "Did Kit and Kathy tell you that I changed my colors?"

"Tony, I hear you, pal. Believe me, I'm with you on this."

Price stared into Melody's big round eyes. "You did what?"

"Good," Tony nodded, "then we see eye to eye. You know what kind of contract I need."

Melody looked down at the table and fiddled with her water glass. "I only changed them a little, Dr. S. Instead of Dream Blue and tangerine, I'm using Dream Blue and watermelon."

"But here's the thing, Tony," Davidian sputtered, "the contract you want is not available. We have to work within the parameters of the system."

"Watermelon? You mean, red? You're changing from orange to red?" Price studied the girl's bowed head.

Tony glared at Davidian, who was about to spear another piece of steak. "Why?"

Melody peered up, her eyes silently pleading. "Well, see . . . yesterday I went to the florist to finalize the flowers and they had a picture of the bouquets . . . in dream blue and watermelon . . . and I said, that's exactly what I always wanted for my bridesmaids, and they said we can't do them in tangerine, so I said . . . hey, the bridesmaids dresses are all dream blue anyway, what would it hurt to change . . . right? You and Mr. S. told me I ought to make sure the wedding was just the way I wanted it."

"Why, what?" Davidian asked.

Price wiped her mouth, harder than she intended. "But, Melody, what about all the other things?"

Tony waved his hands. "Why do we have to work within the parameters set by others? Why not just say, this is the way it is with Shadowbrook novels?"

Melody furrowed her brow. "What other things, Dr. S.?"

Davidian waved his fork, his mouth full of steak. "Tony . . . my man . . . listen to me. I'd like to get you everything you asked for. It's all reasonable. But no one, and I do mean no one, gets everything! You have to give and take. Now it's time to give. Look, I'm a practical man. I get paid only if they buy the movie rights . . . I'm going to bust my, eh, backside to get you the best deal I can, but neither of us earns a dime if we don't give in a little. Comprende?"

Price pushed her sun-streaked brown hair behind her shoulder. "Melody, how about the napkins, the candles, the ribbons and bows . . . even the cake! The cake has tangerine on it."

Tony carefully swallowed. "Terry, I do appreciate your enthusiasm over this deal. I surely don't fault you for that. But this is what I don't understand. Why did you think flying all the way to Arizona was going to change my mind? I will never agree to a movie from one of my books that . . . for instance, blasphemes the Lord."

"But they haven't made the cake yet," Melody protested. "We can get it changed!"

Davidian's face flushed a deep burgundy. "Tony, I was hoping for a little more negotiating room here. No blasphemy, but a little more graphic detail between Jake and the dance hall girl. You know what I mean?"

Price felt her jaw set. "But the invitations

are all printed and they have dream blue and tangerine."

"Terry, are we going to have a movie you'd take your twelve-year-old daughter to see?" Tony felt his left eye begin to twitch.

"Maybe they could be reprinted. Or maybe we could send out a little disclaimer . . . 'These are not the wedding colors.' " Melody suggested.

Davidian shrugged. "I'm not even married, let alone have kids."

Price's whole face tightened. "There's no way, Melody. I'm sorry, but you just can't change the colors now."

"Maybe that's my problem, Davidian," Tony lectured. "Don't take this wrong, but perhaps I need an agent who's a family man. It might make it easier for him to understand where I'm coming from."

Melody sported the scolded puppy look on her face. "Are you sure?"

Terrance Davidian scooped up the last bite of meat on his fork and pointed it at Tony. "Couldn't you see your way to flex just a little bit on this?"

"Positive. There's absolutely no way," Price insisted. "Right, Tony?"

Tony drew an imaginary fixed line on the glass table top and glanced around at the other three. "No way."

3

From the desk of Priscilla Carey Shadowbrook:

1. Get party stuff on the way home Thursday —
   steaks (chicken for Kath), potatoes (rice for Amanda), fruit (plain Jell-O for Mark), zucchini (corn for Kit), green salad (low-fat raspberry vinaigrette for Melody), and mint chip ice cream (nonfat yogurt for Josh.)
2. Call Pastor Jacobson (Book on spiritual warfare?)
3. Synopsis on Jerome . . . (D.G.?) to Liz by Friday
   (Decide on the title BEFORE we send synopsis.)
4. Call Dr. Icing
   (The bride and groom figurines are hang-gliding.)

73

5. More research on fire of 1899 and the prophetic, colorful Mrs. Thomas from the Salvation Army ("God isn't going to give up the fight with Jerome. He'll burn it down a dozen times if need be. His hand holds the torch.")
6. Check with Mom on Wednesday (Results of Dad's CAT scan?)
7. Shop Dillard's in Sedona for dress (Take Kathy, leave Tony at home!)

The morning opened Arizona-hot. Price knew it would only get worse.

Wearing teal shorts and a white cotton scoop-neck T-shirt, she planned to sit out on the deck and edit right after her morning walk, but the blazing Yavapai County sun drove her inside the air-conditioned home. Perched in a leather and oak director's chair, she balanced the laptop computer and stared at the grey words on the blue screen.

Tony dug through a collection of old maps that blanketed the glass and chrome table.

"It's just plain hot!" Price declared. "Even in here with the air conditioner running, it's warm . . . and stale-feeling."

"It's ten to twenty degrees cooler than home."

"The nights aren't bad . . . if you're out on the deck," she admitted.

Tony continued to shuffle through the papers.

Price stared over the top of her computer glasses. "What's another word for steep? I've already used abrupt, craggy, sheer, vertical, angular and precipitous."

"How about . . . rawboned?"

"A rawboned mountain?"

"Why not?" Tony muttered. "Have you seen that old United Verde Extension tunnel map?"

"You're asking me? You're the map expert." Price typed in 'rawboned,' stared at it, then deleted it. "I'm sure it must be on the table there somewhere with the hundred others."

"Forty-two. I've only got forty-two maps and I can't find the one I want! Why does this happen to me?"

"Relax, Shadowbrook."

"Do you think Tom Clancy goes through this?" Tony stalked around the table. "No way! Some research assistant runs down stuff like this. All he has to do is write!"

"I'm sure even Clancy has a few frustrations."

Tony flailed his way through the stack one more time. "Do you know how much time I spend looking for something that's supposed to be right in front of me?"

Price saved the screen, set the laptop in the chair, and strolled to his side. *Do you have any idea how many times in the past thirty years I've heard you say that?* "Let's review. If it's not on the table, what other conceivable place could it be? How about your briefcase?"

"My briefcase is empty. Besides, I had it right here just five minutes ago!"

"Then keep looking." She picked up a railroad map dated 1888. "It's got to be here."

Tony dropped the maps and slammed the table. "That's the whole point! It's not here! It's disappeared!"

"This one says 1916 . . . can't you use it, instead?"

"No . . . only the 1920 tunnel map will work," Tony circled the table. "I think I'm onto old Vic's diggings. At least, it's a good possibility. All that blasting in the 1920s caused some tunnels to collapse. The buildings started sliding down the hill. So they stopped digging in those areas."

"What's your point?"

"I think there's still good ore down there."

"Are you getting prospector's fever?" She stared out the floor-to-ceiling windows at the clear blue Arizona skies over Verde Valley.

That's the color! I need to find a dress just that color!

"Of course not!" Tony protested. "But this whole side of the mountain was copper, gold, silver and zinc. Mainly copper. This was almost a pure copper hill. Every shovelful under this town is bound to have traces. But I need that map!"

Price flipped her hair back and rubbed the lobes that sported light teal and silver star earrings. *I won't get a thing done until he finds this map.* "What's so special about the missing one?"

"It should reveal how extensive the United Verde Extension diggings were on the east side of town. I think there's an underlap."

"An underlap?" she laughed. "Is that the opposite of an overlap?"

Tony waved impatiently. "There's some good ground down there that hasn't been dug."

"Why has it been ignored?"

Tony locked his thumbs into the front pockets of his Wranglers. "Because it would collapse the town on top of it. I'm looking for a yellowed map . . . like this big United Verde Copper Company one."

"I know you're a brilliant writer, Mr. Shadowbrook, but . . . surely others have thought of this, too?" She reached up to rub his shoulders and neck.

"Oh, sure. They thought of it. In the early seventies a Canadian outfit wanted to buy the whole town, raze it and put in a huge open pit operation."

She continued the massage. "Why didn't they?"

"The state pitched a fit, Phelps-Dodge held out for an exorbitant price, and the price of copper fell." Tony slumped his shoulders, leaned his head forward and stretched his neck. "But here's the thing. Dynamite Vic claims to have a revolutionary new mining process or gizmo."

"You think he does?"

"Just could be. That's why this has been overlooked. There's a lot of good paying ore in this country just waiting for someone to figure how to get it out without collapsing the town on top of it."

Price kicked off her sandals and enjoyed the feel of the cool tile floor on the soles of her feet. "You're not thinking about investing in his idea, are you?"

"Nope." He rolled up the sleeves of his longsleeve turquoise shirt. "But I'd sure like *Deception Gulch* to be the first book to put it in print. It's just the kind of freshness that makes a book unique."

"Tony, we are not going to call this book

Deception Gulch!"

"I don't know why you keep saying that. Can't you see? Our whole book is about deceptions." Tony paced toward Price as she backed her way around the table. "This guy Gilette is not going to be murdered on August fifteenth. It's some sort of deception. Ol' Vic has kept his claim hidden while he perfects his mining technique and digs away in secret. The Broussard woman with her tour of all the ghosts, that's a deception. How about the guy with his fake mine and gift shop for tourists? This whole area breeds deception. It's got to be called *Deception Gulch.*"

"The town's name is Jerome." Price stopped to shuffle the maps on the table. "Look . . . here's an 1895 Map of Arizona . . . there it is . . . Jerome! Deception Gulch is not on the map. And look at this yellowed one from . . . eh, from 1920 . . . look, it says, 'The Jerome Holdings of the UVX.' They all say . . ."

"That's it!" Tony shouted. "You're wonderful!" He grabbed her by both shoulders and gave her a quick platonic peck on the cheek.

"I don't suppose that's a sign that we're going to call the book by its rightful name, *Jerome?*"

"What? No, no, of course not!" He spread the map next to a bigger, yellowed one. "Now, where's that magnifying glass I bought?"

Price glanced across the table. "You bought a magnifying glass?"

"Oh, you know. . . ." Tony's voice began to softly fade. "They used such small printing on some of these old maps. When they photocopied this one, they must have reduced it."

Price stared down at the stiff, aged map. "I don't think this has been copied. Perhaps people had better vision in the old days."

"No, I think they probably used magnifying glasses, don't you?"

Price picked up a thick, four-inch magnifying glass by its black plastic handle. "Is this what you're groping for, Grandpa?"

"Grandpa? There is nothing I could do twenty years ago that I can't still do today." Tony noticed her slightly creased, teasing blue-green eyes. "I'm starting to sound a lot like my dad used to, aren't I?"

"Yes, you are, Mr. Shadowbrook. But we knew that the day would come. . . ."

"Well, it hasn't come yet!" Tony insisted. "So don't put me in a rocking chair."

She picked up the magnifying glass. "How

will we know when it's here?"

Tony turned his back. "I am officially getting old when I start telling a bunch of 'Me and Stuart Brannon' stories."

"You never knew Stuart Brannon."

"Of course not. But, neither did my dad."

"Really?"

"Grandpa moved the family from Texas to Arizona in 1916. That was two years after Brannon died."

"But all those stories he used to tell?"

"Wishful thinking. Dad felt cheated he had to live in the twentieth century. It broke his heart to read the old stories and never get to live them out."

"How about you, Anthony B. Shadowbrook? Were you born in the wrong century?"

"Nope."

"Oh?"

"Any other century, any other place, and I would have missed meeting Miss Priscilla Carey."

"You'd give up all that excitement of the late nineteenth-century west for me?"

"In a flash. There's not even a contest."

She grabbed his shoulders, pulled his head down toward hers, and planted a very non-platonic kiss on his slightly chapped, thin lips.

★ ★ ★

Tony didn't like the telephone at the Winslow house. It only had a six-foot cord. His usual procedure of roaming throughout the house and yard while on the cordless telephone was severely restricted.

"Tony? It's Marty Lawington. I finished the preliminary check on your boy, Clayton V. Gilette."

"Hey, that was quick, Marty. What did you find?"

"His last known address was Goldfield, Nevada."

"Up by Tonopah?"

"That's the place."

"He actually lived in Goldfield?" Tony pranced to the end of the phone cord, then wandered back.

"Yeah, he lived in the hotel from '93 to '95."

"The Goldfield Hotel? But I thought it'd been closed for years."

"They say he broke in and camped out, or something. Told people in Goldfield that he had inherited some mining stock and planned to reopen one of the mines."

"Reopen . . . like reoutfit the tunnels?"

"Nope. Claimed to have some backers to open a pit."

"He had that kind of money and needed to

hobo in a closed hotel?"

"Yeah, well . . . he claimed to have purchased the hotel, but no one around Goldfield believed him. They all figured he was just another bum. All except for Mr. Schrodter."

"Who?"

"Mr. Wolfgang Schrodter of Stuttgart."

"Stuttgart? As in Baden-Württemberg, Germany?"

"That's the one. It seems that he invested a considerable sum in purchasing old mining claims for a corporation, of which your boy Clayton was listed as president."

"And Gilette absconded with the funds?"

"Apparently not. All the money was invested in property and mining claims. Gilette just disappeared one day. This Schrodter fellow went back to Germany and abandoned the claims. They will be sold at auction at the county courthouse on September third."

"And he didn't try to find Gilette?"

"Rumor has it that the money wasn't clean. So he just walked away. But there are plenty of rumors around Goldfield."

"Nobody cons someone and gets nothing out of it for himself. What's the angle here, Marty?"

"I have no idea, Tony. Maybe Gilette fooled himself and really believed he was going to strike gold."

"How about before that time? Where did he live?"

"Seems to have been a perennial student at Montana College of Mining Science and Technology."

"In Butte?"

"Yeah . . . took classes for eleven years but never graduated. Worked odd jobs and lived in an old closed saloon. College records say he came down from Wildwood, Alberta. I didn't fly up there and check it out. But if you want to pay the bucks, I will."

"No . . . no, that's fine. You said he was in Goldfield from '93 to '95? What about the past couple years?"

"Nothing, Tony. I can't find him. Folks around Goldfield thought he fell down an abandoned shaft or something. Some were surprised to hear he showed up in Arizona. The guy at the mini-mart says Gilette owes him $16.24. That's all I've got. I can't legally check driver's licenses, police records or any of that. So who knows? Maybe he was in jail. Or, maybe he moved to Reno . . . or Fresno."

Tony switched the phone from one ear to the other and paced in place. "But it sounds like he does have some mining background?"

"At least he can talk a good claim.

Jerome's a mining town, right?"

"Yeah."

"Why are you so interested in this guy? What's the deal? Is he trying to swindle someone into investing in a claim?"

"Nope. It's just that tombstone thing I told you about. We're thinking of using him in our book and trying to see if he's typical of the crazy characters who come and go or if he's a different breed, with an ulterior agenda."

"Well, that's all I've got for now. The boy sounds like he's been out in the desert sun too long, but fairly harmless. Anyway, a buddy of mine in Carson City is on vacation. I'll check with him, and with another friend in Sacramento. Maybe we can spot where this guy Gilette has spent the past couple of years. I'll call you in two weeks."

"Thanks, Martin."

"Hey, don't thank me too much. . . . You haven't seen my bill, yet. I want two auto-graphed sets of *River Breaks* books for my dad and brother."

"You got it."

"Listen, partner, when's the next one coming out?"

"Have you read *Standoff at Rifle Ridge*?"

"Finished it two weeks ago."

"Well, I haven't written *Bushwhacked in*

the Badlands yet. You'll have to wait until next summer."

"Next summer? Man, you've got to write faster than that. Hey, you aren't going to marry Jake off to that Spanish señorita, are you?"

"You never know what those two will do. I can't get them to listen to me at all."

"What? Yeah . . . well . . . whatever. And people say P.I.s are weird."

Tony and Price ate a late supper of tamale pie and zucchini cake on the deck. The sun had already sunk behind the crest of Mingus Mountain. Jerome was deep in a swamp of shadows. They watched the dusk creep slowly down the slope of Cleopatra Hill and on toward the Verde River. Only the highest red rock spines behind Sedona glittered with a touch of dying sunlight. Streetlights twinkled on and they watched the headlights from cars winding their way up 89A to Jerome.

One of the cars wound up in their carport.

"Kit?"

"Hi, Pop! Hi, Mom!"

"Hi, darlin' . . . what's up?"

Kit's permed brown hair bounced as she jogged up the stairs. "Didn't Kathy call?"

Price reached out her hand to Kit. "Call us about what?"

"Oh, man . . . she promised to call you. At

least, Melody said Kath was going to call you."

"What's this all about, Christina?" Price quizzed, still clutching her hand.

"Oh . . . well . . . see . . . tomorrow is my day off, and I thought maybe I should just come up and spend it with you." It was a sheepish, I-don't-really-believe-this-myself, kind of smile.

"That's nice, dear. But we're coming home Thursday night, remember?"

"Yeah . . . well. I, eh . . . thought Pop would like to see this!" She pulled a folded piece of paper from the back pocket of her faded black Wranglers.

"What is it, kiddo?"

"A fax from Liz. *Standoff at Rifle Ridge* hit number twenty-five on this week's *Times* Bestsellers List. It's the second most popular western novel! Isn't that cool?"

"That's really great, darlin' . . . but Liz called and told us about that yesterday." Tony slipped his arm around Kit's shoulder and she put hers around his waist.

"She did?"

"Yes, but I'm glad you came up." Price tugged her toward the kitchen. "Let me fix you something to eat."

"I had a big lunch."

"What?"

"Two Big Macs, fries and a Mountain Dew."

"Come on, we have some pasta salad and zuc . . . eh, vegetable casserole. You'll like it."

As Kit trailed her mother, Tony noticed both women were exactly the same height and had the same bounce in their step. "Hey, I hear you talked Mel out of changing her colors." Kit's smile was tentative.

Price dug a large green bowl out of the refrigerator. "I hope so."

Kit pulled out the carton of milk and searched the cupboard for a glass. "You know why she wanted to change, don't you?"

"You mean, the watermelon-colored bouquets at the florist? She did mention that."

"Oh, no, that wasn't it."

"It wasn't?"

"Nope. It's because Kath decided that the tangerine accessories made her look fat. She convinced Mel into trying to change the colors."

Tony sat down at the table. "Fat? Kathy couldn't look fat if she swallowed a watermelon."

"Yeah, Pop, can you believe it? You know Kath. Image is everything."

"Now don't tell me you two aren't getting along?" Tony pressed.

88

Kit bit her lip. Her dark bangs lapped over her eyebrows. Any semblance of a smile vanished.

"OK, kiddo . . . what is it this time?"

Kit continued to chew her lip.

Price stepped behind Kit and began to rub her shoulders and neck. "You did come clear up here to talk to us, didn't you?"

"Yeah, Mom."

"Well?"

"Well . . . I think I'd like some pasta salad."

"Just when are we going to get around to the important part?" Price insisted.

"Later."

"Who's got the problem?" Tony asked. "You? Or Kathy?"

"Me."

Price sat a bowl of pasta salad in front of her almost twenty-year-old daughter. "Does it have anything to do with those pills you're taking?"

"Oh, no! Not really. Only, maybe . . . indirectly. Sort of."

Tony felt his heart sink. He slipped over into the chair next to Kit. Price brought her daughter a glass for the milk, then sat across from them.

"OK, darlin' . . . you've driven all the way up here to spill something. . . . Who's the guy, and what's the problem?" Tony quizzed.

Kit fidgeted with the noodles and glanced at her mother and then her father. Finally, she settled on looking only at her mother.

"I've been rehearsing all of this, and now I don't know if I can say it or not. So, let me try. Promise you won't yell or scream or get mad until I'm all through, because I don't think I'll get the nerve up again."

"You take as long as you want, honey. . . ." Price was surprised that her voice sounded so calm. She felt her heart race and a sense of dark gloom cloud her spirit.

"Well . . . see, there's this guy at work. His name is Lyle Roberts. He's the assistant service manager. He's the best mechanic I've ever seen . . . no kidding, Dad. . . . This guy knows everything about cars from lug nuts to computerized ignitions. Anyway, I've been dating him for several months and. . . ."

"Several months?" Tony gasped. "Sorry . . . I didn't mean to interrupt."

"Yeah, see . . . I didn't tell you about him because I didn't think you'd approve."

"Why did you think that?" Price blurted out. "No . . . no, go on . . . tell it your way."

"See, Lyle is into stock-car racing. Actually, his brother, Gary, is the driver. He's in the paper all the time. He's won most of the races in the state. Lyle is crew boss for the Gary Roberts Racing Team.

"Here's the thing. Lyle has been watching me around the shop, and he asked if I'd like to be a member of the pit crew. Can you imagine that, Dad? Ever since I was six and you took me out to Phoenix International Speedway you know I wanted to be on a pit crew. And now, I have an opportunity."

"Exactly what does being on the pit crew mean?" Price asked. "I don't know much about stock-car racing."

"Well, as soon as Gary and Lyle line up some national sponsors, they're going on tour."

"All over the States?" Tony asked.

"Yeah, is this an opportunity of a lifetime, or what?"

"Let me see if I've got this right," Price interjected. "One young lady traveling with a dozen men."

"But, Mom, this is like breaking ground for women. Lyle said he didn't know of a dozen women on pit crews who were real mechanics. A chance like this just doesn't come along very often."

"Is that the line that good ol' Lyle is giving you?" Tony demanded. His words brought a glare from Price. "Go on, darlin' . . . I'll do my best to be still . . . for now."

"Anyway, if they get the sponsor thing squared away by the first of August, they want to take off to the southeastern part of the country for the next six months and test their skills."

"You mean . . . the pit crew will be gone for six months?"

"Yeah. Exciting, isn't it?"

"What about the University?" Tony asked.

"I guess I'd just wait and finish that up later. Isn't that what you did, Dad?"

"Well . . . yeah, but I had a family to support. It's just not the same."

"What do you think, Mom and Dad? Is this the opportunity of a lifetime, or what?" Kit's wide smile looked as phony as a passport photo.

"Christina . . . let's save the talk about a job offer until later." Price looked her dark-haired daughter right in the eyes. "Let's get back to Lyle . . . and birth control pills . . . and why it is you really came up here."

Kit took a big, deep breath and bit her lip. "I mentioned that we've been dating."

"You also mentioned that you didn't think we'd approve," Tony added.

"Lyle is a really neat guy. He treats me really good, Mom and Dad . . . really. He always takes me to nice restaurants, and opens the door for me, and pulls out my chair and

92

all that stuff. He makes me feel like a special woman. Remember, Pop, you told me some man would come along and make me feel real special?"

"I also said the one the Lord had in mind would bring out the spiritual best in you. Does Lyle do that?"

"Oh, he believes in God. He told me so. It's just that he doesn't go to church much anymore. A lot of stock-car races are on Sunday, and besides . . . he's not comfortable . . . going to the same church as Nanci and the kids."

Price felt tears well up in the corner of her eyes. A lump caught in her throat. She couldn't speak. Her eyes spied the fire in Tony's. *Don't get angry and yell . . . Tony, please!*

"Maybe you should explain about Nanci and the kids." Tony's voice was halting, as if out of breath. But he didn't shout, a fact that surprised him and shocked Price.

"OK, here's the crux of the matter. Nanci is Lyle's wife, and they have two little children . . . Branson and Nicolle."

Price found she still could not speak.

"You mean, he's divorced?" Tony asked.

"They've been separated for over two years, but the divorce isn't final. Not for a few more months. Lyle says the lawyers are trying to work out the custody thing. I guess Nanci's being real nasty about it, and is just stalling over giving him a divorce."

"And she's a churchgoer?"

"Out in Mesa. I guess her parents sort of helped start the church twenty-five years ago. Everyone knows her. That's why Lyle doesn't feel good about going there. I know you guys would like Lyle if you just got to know him."

Price slid her elbows on the glass table, her head in her hands.

Tony reached out to touch Kit's shoulder. "Darlin' . . . I need to ask you a couple of questions. They might be difficult for you to answer. The questions are hard for me to ask."

"Pop . . . I haven't had sex with Lyle. Isn't that what you wanted to ask? Well, I haven't . . . yet. Not that I haven't thought about it some. Lyle's not pushy. When I say stop, he stops. He said he'll wait until I'm ready."

"How old is Lyle?" Tony asked.

"Twenty-eight. He'll be twenty-nine on the fifteenth of July."

"Do you love him, darlin'?"

"Yes . . . I think so. I mean . . . of course I do. Well, maybe. . . ." Kit looked into her father's eyes for the first time. Then, without warning, she began to bawl. "I don't know,

94

Daddy . . . I don't know! I want to love him."
She smeared a flood of tears across her freckled, tanned face. "I don't know, Daddy, I
don't know anything! I'm so stupid. I don't
know anything!"

Tony stood and pulled Kit to her feet. He
wrapped his long, strong arms around her
shoulders and pulled her toward him. She
laid her head on his chest as he rocked her
back and forth. Price saw the tears streaming
down Tony's cheeks as she joined the two in
the hug.

"Darlin' . . . you aren't stupid."

"I can't believe I've gotten myself in another mess. These things never happen to
Kathy!" she sobbed.

"Kit," Tony continued, "it takes a mighty
smart nineteen-year-old to come and talk to
her folks about something like this."

"What am I going to do, Pop? I really do
like Lyle. It seems so wonderful when I'm
with him. But when I try to tell you guys . . .
it all sounds really dumb, doesn't it?"

Tony released his hug. "Let's blow our
noses, wash our faces and get a glass of iced
tea. Then let's sit out on the deck with the
lights out, and just talk about it."

The moon was nowhere in sight, but the
bright stars covered the Verde Valley. The

95

breeze was cool, the air tasted fresh to Price, like virgin water from a high mountain stream. It was not nearly as tense as it had been inside.

"OK . . . time for the lecture, Pop," Kit sighed. "And please, please don't tell me to dump Lyle."

"Darlin', in a few weeks you'll be twenty. You're much too old, and I might add, too mature . . . for me to tell you what to do. You've got to make up your own mind. It will be your choice. But I'd like to remind you of a few things, to help you make a good decision."

"Yeah, I figured you would."

"First, there is right and wrong in this world. I didn't set the standard. It comes in God's Word, and every one of us has to deal with it."

"I know."

"Lyle is a married man. There's a chance his wife's a believer. Maybe he is, too. Either way, in God's eyes they are married. There are two little children who call Nanci 'Mamma' and Lyle 'Daddy.' To add to the dissolution of that family is wrong."

"But he seems so perfect for me."

"Second, sex outside of marriage is wrong. None of us, no matter how tempted, can debate that. It's the biblical injunction. Now,

96

it's my opinion that the right one for you will not ask you to do anything that is against God's Word."

"But he's not really demanding. I mean, he said he'd wait."

"How long? Will he wait ten years?"

"Ten years?" Kit gasped.

"Until he's exhausted every avenue of counseling, prayer and repentance to try and put his marriage to Nanci back together. Would he wait that long, darlin'?"

"I'm not sure he wants to wait until September."

Price cleared her throat. "Honey . . . would Lyle still be the right man if he were a shoe salesman at the Northgate Mall?"

"What?"

"Well," Price continued. "What if Lyle wasn't connected to stock-car racing? What if he didn't offer you a position on a pit crew? What if he were a twenty-nine-year-old married man with two kids selling shoes at the mall? Would he still be the one?"

"I, eh . . . but that's just hypothetical. Who knows? I mean, what if Pop wasn't a famous author? What if he didn't write books? What if . . . what if he worked at a gas station in Quartzite? Would he be the right one still?"

"Yep."

"You're kidding."

"Nope." Price glanced at Tony. "Honey, I'd follow that man to Yellowknife and live off polar bear meat if he wanted me to."

"You would, wouldn't you?"

Price nodded.

"Darlin' . . . you've got lots of time to look around and find God's best for your life. There's no need to take second, let alone third, fourth, or fifth best."

"But I won't ever get to be on a pit crew!"

"I don't know what the Lord has in mind for you, darlin'. You've heard me mention that I was pretty active in calf-roping at rodeos when I married your mamma. The summer we got married I was signed up for Prescott, Salinas, Calgary and Cheyenne. It was my chance to compete with the big boys. I was even going to travel with Dean Oliver. Now, that doesn't mean anything to you, but it was mighty important to me."

"So what happened?"

"I had a new wife to support. And not too long after that, a baby on the way. I never competed at a professional rodeo after the wedding."

"And?"

"And I never regretted it for a minute. All of a sudden there were just more important things to do. Man, were there exciting things to do!"

"So, you don't think I'll ever get to be on a pit crew?"

"Darlin' . . . if that's your dream, don't turn loose. Just make sure it's in God's timing, and in his way. Anything else, and I think you'll be disappointed."

"So, what do you think I ought to do now?"

Tony gazed up at the northern horizon and stared at the north star. "I think you ought to ponder all we've talked about. . . ."

"And pray about it, . . ." Price interjected.

"Your mother's right. Bring it all before the Lord, then make your very best decision."

"Are you saying you don't want me to date Lyle anymore?"

"Darlin' . . . that's one of the decisions you have to make alone. We're goin' to love you . . ."

"And pray for you . . ."

". . . no matter what you decide."

"I disappointed you guys, didn't I?"

"Kit . . . tonight, I am very, very proud of you."

"You mean, because I haven't had sex with Lyle?"

"Well, that . . . too," Tony sighed. "I'm also proud of you because I have an extremely attractive and highly intelligent almost twenty-year-old daughter that still cares enough about what her mom and dad think to drive clear up here and talk about it."

For a moment all they could hear were the crickets.

"Kathy's the pretty one." Kit responded in a soft, low voice.

"Darlin', I want you to understand something. I happen to be the most fortunate and blessed man in the world. I am surrounded by the three most beautiful women God ever created."

Again it was quiet.

Kit's voice broke the silence. This time there was laughter in her words. "The old man really believes that, doesn't he, Mom?"

"Yep. He's believed that from the day you were born, Christina. He made such a fuss over you two girls that I had to come home from the hospital a day early, just to get away from the total embarrassment of the glares from the other mothers in the ward."

"Really?"

"Really. He's always been pretty obnoxious about bragging on his daughters." Price could hear Kit sigh. "Are you all right, honey?"

"Yeah. I just need time to think some things through."

"And pray?"

"Yeah. Hey, can I just, maybe, you know . . . sleep out here on the deck tonight? It's so peaceful."

"You just stay out here until you get too cold. The guest room's all ready for you, if you need it. Did you bring a suitcase?"

"Eh . . . no. . . ."

"Well, you can use any of my things. You know that. I'll leave one of my gowns on the guest-room bed, in case you come inside to sleep."

"Eh . . . Mom," Kit giggled, "let's face it . . . your gowns make me feel like a ten-year-old boy . . . if you know what I mean. Can I just use one of Pop's T-shirts?"

Tony circled the empty school building and headed north on Clark Street. Vic Lucero waited for him at the top of Upper Park.

"Shadowbrook . . . you ain't never goin' to live to be ninety if you keep runnin' up these hills."

Tony collapsed by the black iron fencing. "You might be right, Vic. At this rate I'll never reach sixty. Hey, did you call that attorney in Prescott yet?"

"Ain't had time. Been busy consulting with my new backer."

"You got the money, then?"

"Well, not exactly. But he's got it. I seen his line of credit."

"That's good, Vic. I'm real happy about it. You know, Vic, I've been meaning to talk to you about something."

"What's that?" The old man pushed his grimy hat to the back of his head. A dirt line streaked across his forehead.

"I've been studying the old maps. And if I were looking for some good paying ore, which I'm not . . . well, I believe I'd rent the basement of the old Hotel Nevada. I'd sink a shaft right there through the concrete and go about twenty feet down and connect with 120E Tunnel. I bet a man could shove the dirt in the back of the basement and no one would even know it. Then I'd take the UVCC tunnel to the north, and work that area real good."

Vic Lucero's unshaven jaw dropped open. "Well, I'll be . . . !"

"But I can't figure how a person could blast and brace without everyone knowing it . . . and without the rest of the buildings on Hull Avenue sliding all the way down to Clarkdale."

Lucero pulled out a grubby blue bandanna and wiped his forehead. "Are you ready to invest?"

Tony shook his head. "No, but I surely hope this works out for you."

"You goin' to stop by the Ireland Cafe this afternoon?"

"I'll be there," Tony promised as he trotted on down the hill.

When he reached the house, Price was sipping Earl Grey tea and Kit was gulping coffee out on the deck.

"How are you this morning?" he asked.

"Better. Thanks for the talk, Pop. It sure did help to hunker down under the stars all night. All I could hear were those crickets . . . and a wild donkey braying."

"Did you come to any decision?"

"I think so."

"Are you going to tell us what you decided?"

"Not yet, Pop. I've got to talk to Lyle in person. See, I knew what I was going to tell you guys ahead of time. But when I got here . . . it all got confused. Well, I know what I want to tell Lyle when I'm up here in Jerome. But I've got to be able to look him in the eyes and say it."

"We'll be home Thursday night. Maybe

we can talk some more then," Price offered.

"Maybe . . . but the others will want to talk to you then. Did you hear about Melody's mother?"

"Barbara Mason? What about her?" Price asked.

"She refuses to wear the tangerine dress Mel picked out for her. She says it makes her look like a giant Sunkist orange."

"Well . . ." Price grinned, "she may have a point there."

After breakfast, Tony walked to the car with Kit.

"You mad at me for not making up my mind yet?"

"Nope. Just keep thinking. It's when we base our decisions on feelings that we get in the most trouble. You're one smart girl, darlin' . . . you'll figure it out."

"If I break up, I'm going to miss him, Pop. There aren't many guys around who treat me like a lady."

"Listen, kiddo, there aren't many guys around who know you want to be treated like a lady. You've got to give them a hint now and then."

"You mean, like wear dresses?"

"Well . . . at least to church," he laughed. "Look, darlin', don't worry about it. Just be yourself. There's only one Kit Shadow-brook."

A grin broke across her freckled face. "Kit Shadowbrook . . . man, I have a great name! Did I ever tell you I think I have a great name?"

"I think you mentioned it once or twice."

"Kit Shadowbrook, stock-car driver. Is that cool, or what?"

"I don't want you racin' this pickup all the way back to Phoenix."

"Yes, Daddy, dear . . ." Kit intoned in her best Kathy impression.

4

From the desk of Priscilla Carey Shadowbrook:

1. Research Jennie Banters
   (The richest woman in northern
   Arizona in 1900?)
2. Answer Isabelle Broussard's
   letter
   (Or maybe just ignore it.)
3. Shop in Sedona with Kathy on
   Wednesday
   (It's a backyard wedding . . .
   absolutely no more than $500 for
   whole outfit!)
4. Call Mom and Dad
   (Maybe Tony and I can drive down
   next Saturday?)
5. Tony's booksigning in Flagstaff on
   Wednesday
   (7:30 P.M. University Club,
   Pregnancy Crisis Center Charity,

make sure he's not grumpy!)
6. Check with Dr. Icing
   (NO saguaro cactus on the cake!)
7. Invite Cooper Jarrett Shadowbrook
   to visit
   (Weekend of the 15th, his parents
   can come, too.)
8. Call doctor?
   (Hot flashes are really unbearable!)
9. Find out which house the actress
   Rosemary DeCamp lived in
   (What movies were filmed around
   Jerome?)

The most demanding crisis seldom is the most important.

"Tony, it's George Gossman on the phone." Price fanned herself with a 1917 copy of *The Verde Copper News*.

"Gossman? As in, editorial vice president at Atlantic-Hampton Publishing?" Wearing jeans and a black T-shirt, Tony scooted across the cool tile floor, barefoot.

"The one and only."

"Tell him to talk to Liz. That's why we have an agent."

"Eh . . . Tony . . . Liz told him he better call you directly because she couldn't get us to commit."

"The title thing?"

Price unfastened the simulated pearl button at the top of her pink cotton blouse and continued to fan herself. "Yes . . . come talk to George. . . ."

"I don't have anything to tell him . . . do I?"

"You can tell him we'll call it *Jerome.*"

"We are not . . ."

"Tell it to Gossman." Price laid down the phone. She bunched her hair into a short ponytail with a thick yellow rubber band.

Tony slunk over to the telephone and picked up the receiver. "Hi, George. Heard you saw the light and are wearing boots and a cowboy hat nowadays."

"Oh . . . why, eh, yes! Yes, I am. Listen, Tony, we've got production people sitting around twiddling their thumbs, waiting for the title in the next Hidden West book. What's this about you two being undecided?"

"Oh no, we're very decided."

"Splendid! What are we calling it?"

"The problem is, Price decided on one thing, and I've decided on another. So why don't we print the book with two different titles, throw them out on the market, and on the second printing we can go with whichever sells the best?"

"What?" Gossman gasped.

"That was a joke, George . . . relax. Look, the book's due out the first of May, right?"

"Yes."

"And your winter catalog goes to the printer about the first of October?"

"Yes, but with production time, we can't wait any longer for one of our featured books."

"We'll have something for you by the first of August."

"We can't wait that long!"

"Think about it . . . you've got the synopsis for the blurb. . . . You've got the location, so you can work on the cover. . . . All you need are those big block letters for the title. Put *Book Five* for a dummy title and we'll have the real one by August first."

"There's no way we can make it a featured book in the catalog if we. . . ."

"Oh, I'm sure Atlantic-Hampton doesn't want to break contract, George. You promised it would be a featured book and we promised to deliver it to you by October first. With any luck, the title will come in sooner."

"Oh . . . I . . . eh, wasn't insinuating that. . . ."

"George, I've got to get back to work. I think Price wants to talk to me about the title. Please give our regards to Carolyn."

"And you'll call me as soon as you've decided?"

"We'll call Liz immediately. She'll call you. Sorry it's taking a little extra time, but we want to get this right."

Tony spent the rest of the morning high up on Mingus Mountain, gazing over Jerome and the Verde Valley far below. A jet stream scraped the sky like chalk. In the distance three brightly colored hot air balloons coasted toward Cottonwood. He slipped off his glasses and rubbed the bridge of his slightly too large nose.

I don't know how they did it.

Morris and Sarah Ruffner hiked up here from their little ranch in the valley and spied copper outcroppings that the old Indian scout, Al Sieber, told them about. They filed a claim, convinced George and Angus McKinnon to grubstake them, then the three men hiked back over here from Prescott, dug a forty-foot shaft by hand, and the mining began. With the nearest railroad still in Kansas, and no smelter in the district, they fought the elements, hunger and hostiles. They bet their lives on the fact that there's something worth digging for under the rocks and dirt.

Not many left who would attempt such a thing.

Maybe old Vic's the last.

There's plenty who want to be rich. But only a

110

few will work hard labor for fifty years without pay just to strike it.

Must have been more trees then.

But some things haven't changed. Wildcat prospectors still need someone to bankroll them. Too bad old Vic can't talk to someone like Eugene Jerome's wife. She and her sister roused out that first two hundred thousand dollars in development money on their own. Price will want to research those two gals for sure.

Sisters.

I presume they weren't twins.

Lord, I always heard people say that daughters were tougher to raise than sons. There was a time I didn't believe them.

Not anymore.

Tony hopped down from his rock perch. He wandered over to a granite bluff that looked like a semi-circular pulpit. Every creature from the county line in the north to the interstate in the south served as the congregation. He picked up a golf ball-sized rock and hurled it down the slope as he teetered on the edge of the granite. The red-caked dirt was dry like powder, the grey sage short and stubby.

Sons go through rough times. But I could always just say . . . 'They have to learn this the hard way.' But daughters . . . Lord, there's something in a father's heart that tells him to hold them and protect them from hurt forever.

Someday both Kit and Kathy will find the right men, men who will cherish them forever. Lord, I want to meet those men. It would be real nice if you could, sort of, point them out ahead of time.

Tony tossed another rock off the cliff, then returned to his granite roost and his laptop.

By the time Spanish conquistador Antonio de Esperjo arrived in the Verde Valley in 1583, local Yavapai Indians were already active in mining the region. Wearing the full armor of the period, he hiked up the grueling mountain trail to reach the place where native miners worked the surface and tunnels. They chipped off magnificent colored blue and green rocks which were used for dyes and decorations, such as the crosses they made and tied in their hair. He followed them back down the hill, across the chaparral, and into the salt mines up to a hundred feet below the valley floor.

Esperjo, satisfied with only gold or silver, left the region to the Yavapais, but made mention in his notes of the copper that was discovered in a place that would one day be called Jerome.

A honk from the highway diverted Tony's

attention to a dust cloud rolling down the dirt road. As the airborne soil drifted down the mountain, Tony recognized the old, grey pickup of Clayton V. Gilette.

"Shadowbrook!" Gilette screamed as he rolled down the window.

Tony tipped his white straw cowboy hat and turned to save his screen.

"Shadowbrook, I'm talking to you!"

After running a backup copy of his document, Tony exited into DOS and shut down the laptop. Gilette crunched his way across the mountain.

"Shadowbrook!"

Tony closed the laptop, slipped it into the brown leather carrying case, and snapped it shut.

"Are you deaf? I've been calling you," Gilette announced, ten feet from Tony.

"Well, if it isn't the 'soon-to-be-late' Mr. Gilette. What brings you up here, Clayton?"

"You brought me up here. I saw you drive out of town this morning, and was waiting for you to drive back. But you didn't. So I came lookin'."

Tony thought Gilette's green golf shirt was new, but the rest of the outfit looked the same as he had worn for weeks. "What do you want?"

"I hear you've written a book."

"Yeah, I've written a few."

Gilette's large drooping mustache was almost lost in his bushy face. But it was his eyes that always caught Tony's attention. His eyes never focused on the same sight more than two seconds. "Well . . . I wouldn't make this offer to just anyone . . . but I'm looking for someone to ghost my autobiography."

"Oh?" *How many times in my life have I heard this line?*

"And I've got to write my memoirs *muy pronto*, because August fifteenth is coming."

"I presume you've led a fascinating life?" Tony pressed.

"Prophetic. My whole life's been prophetic."

Just don't give me "the Lord told me you are to write my life story" routine. "Well, I do want to encourage you to record your memoirs. But I don't ghostwrite, Gilette. Sorry about that."

"Yeah, that figures. I knew you'd want your name on the cover. But my name goes first. I'm going to call it, *Prediction of a Murder: The Life and Violent Death of Clayton Vincent Gilette by Clayton V. Gilette and Alfred Shadowbrook.*"

"Anthony," Tony corrected.

114

"Yeah . . . whatever. You'll do it, then?"

"Nope."

"Didn't you say I ought to get it all recorded?"

"That's right. If you can't write it, at least you can record it on cassette tape."

"Is it money? I'll give you fifteen percent of what I make off the book. That's fair, isn't it?"

"First of all . . . I really don't write biographies. And I don't co-author books, except . . . with my wife. Second, if you're dead, just who is going to split the royalties?"

"My brother. Everything I make will go to my brother, Layton. He's one year younger than me, but we look a lot alike."

Tony stared at the wild eyes and the unkempt, grey-streaked light brown hair and shaggy beard. *Someone else looks like this?* "Sorry, Gilette. I'm already swamped with book projects."

"It's the money, isn't it? OK, here's my last offer. You can have forty percent of the royalties."

"There are no royalties unless you have a publisher. It's a lot more difficult to get a book published than you might think." Tony swatted a horsefly off his arm.

"A story like this? You've got to be kidding. Publishers will be lined up from here to

Flagstaff wanting this one. OK . . . it doesn't seem fair, but I'll go fifty-fifty . . . what do you say?" Gilette's sandal-clad feet were caked with dirt and smelled like ancient dry sweat.

"Gilette, it's just not the kind of thing I do." Tony reached into a side pocket of the computer case and pulled out his sunglasses. "You just don't ask a cowman to raise sheep. He just won't do it. There are others in Jerome who write books. Check with them."

"But this thing could sell millions! Why, you could retire and never have to write that pulp again."

There were a dozen things Tony thought about saying. Most would have demanded repentance. He said nothing, as he slipped on the gold, wire-framed dark glasses.

"Surely you don't want to spend the rest of your life writing second-class westerns! That foxy wife of yours deserves better than that. This is a once-in-a-lifetime break!"

Tony jumped to his feet so quickly that the shorter, younger man stumbled back into the rocky hillside. Tony clenched his right fist, then took a deep breath and turned away. "I've got to be going." He stepped over to retrieve his laptop computer.

"Then you're turning me down?"

"That's a mild interpretation," Tony

growled, continuing to fight back rising impulses.

"You'll regret this, Shadowbrook!" Gilette screamed as he stumbled toward his pickup. "When the tourists are lined up to get their picture taken by my tombstone, when the book's on the bestsellers list, when a movie is made of my life . . . you'll regret turning me down!"

Tony, his face flushed and the back of his neck burning, glared at Gilette as he roared down the road. He took several deep breaths and found himself rubbing his chest. Sharp pains, like mini-cramps, tugged away in the region of his heart.

Lord, I'm sure these pains are nothing. But I sure wish they'd go away.

"He actually called me your 'foxy wife'?" Price fumed.

"Yeah, how's that make you feel?"

"Creepy." Price nervously fastened the top button of her white cotton blouse. "I don't mind a compliment, but somehow I don't even want a wacko like Gilette knowing I exist."

Tony stalked the glass-walled kitchen. "Maybe I'd better accompany you from now on around Jerome."

"It's not that big a deal. He just makes me

feel uncomfortable."

"Now I'm wondering if we ought to use him in the book," Tony moaned.

Price partially closed the mini-blinds on the west window. "Leave him in and use that scene this morning," she suggested.

"The foxy wife part?"

"No, the part where he wants you to write his story. Readers will relate to that. Half the people we meet think you ought to write their story for them."

"Well, I don't want you within fifty feet . . . a hundred feet of this guy, Gilette!" Tony announced.

Price's grey-green eyes sparkled.

"What'd I say?"

"Oh, nothing. But, my daddy was right."

"About what?"

"About marrying a cowboy. He'll put you on a pedestal and protect you like a mamma bear looking after her cubs."

"Did I do something wrong?"

She slipped her arms around his waist and laid her head on his chest. "Nope. I'd be insulted if you ever acted any other way."

They rocked back and forth, wrapped in each other's arms.

"Say, would this be a good time to talk about the title of a book?" he asked.

"I was just thinking the same thing."

"OK . . . grab a couple of sheets of paper," he suggested. "On one side we'll write *Deception Gulch*. Then we'll make a list of the positive features of using that name and another list of any negative features, if there are any. On the other side of the paper we'll write *Jerome*, then do the same. A negative list and a positive one."

"Why does *Jerome* have a negative list first?"

"What?"

"Nothing. Here's some paper. What do we do when we're finished?"

"We'll evaluate the lists. I think it will become clear when we see the pros and cons."

It didn't.

At 7:00 P.M. they stopped for supper. But by 9:00 the discussion reached the impasse level again.

"You're not even considering *Jerome*," Price protested.

"Of course I am."

"You are not. There is absolutely nothing I could say to convince you to use that name for a title. Nothing!"

"Hey, if it's the wrong title, it's the wrong title. No debate can change that."

"Then why in the world did we make up these lists?" She waved at the papers scattered across the kitchen table.

"Because I thought surely you'd see. . . ."

"I'd see? We did all of this in order that I might change my mind? You had no intention of any of this affecting you?" she raved. "I think you just wasted our whole afternoon and evening."

"I don't know why you're so stubborn about this! I have written lots of books in my lifetime, and I'm telling you. . . ."

"Here it goes, the old 'I'm the famous author' argument. I think I heard that one last summer at Fox Island."

"Experience counts for something. I have titled a few books in my day!"

"It's just possible that you might be wrong this time!"

"That's possible, of course . . . in theory!"

The telephone rang. Tony paced the living room floor while Price talked in hushed tones. He stopped when he sensed sadness in her voice. When she finally hung up, he hurried to her side.

"What's up, darlin'?"

"That was Mother. Uncle Harold died."

"Your dad's brother? I didn't know he was sick."

"Neither did anyone else. He and Dad were golfing, and Uncle Harold just keeled over on the tenth tee. I guess Daddy got him in an ambulance and rushed him to the hospital, but he didn't last long. Massive heart attack, they said."

Tony rubbed the ribcage on the left side of his chest. "How's Aunt Vera?"

"In shock, of course. Barry drove over from San Diego to be with his mother."

"How about your dad?"

Price's eyes were wet and swollen. "Mom said he's sitting out at his workbench in the garage and refuses to talk to anyone."

"They were close."

"Uncle Harold was three years younger than Dad. He never, ever thought he would outlive his brother."

"Makes those tests on your dad seem even more crucial, doesn't it?"

"That's what I was thinking." Price wiped back a tear. "That could have been Dad, Tony. I'm just not ready to lose him yet. He's only seventy-three. That's not very old anymore."

"I know, darlin'."

Price noticed Tony's eyes shone wet in his rugged face. "You thinking about your dad, honey?"

Tony took a big, deep breath and sighed, then wiped his eyes. "Yeah, I guess so. He was only fifty-five when he died. I'm going to be fifty-five in three years. Dad died twenty

121

years ago, right before the twins were born. I still miss him." Tony stared out the window into the starlit night. "It seems like everything I ever did when I was growing up was just to gain his approval."

"Everything you do now is still trying to gain his approval," she added.

"Well, it's wrong!"

"What's wrong?"

"Death is wrong. Mankind wasn't created to die. I knew that much even before I discovered Christ as my Savior. Life is supposed to go on . . . for my dad . . . for my mom . . . for your Uncle Harold . . . for your dad . . . for me . . . for all of us."

"You complaining about God's plan?"

"No, I'm just feeling the pain of mankind's sin."

"That's a big thought."

He continued to stare out the front window past the Douglas Mansion and the Powder Box Church.

"A little bigger and more important than the title of a book?" she asked.

"Yeah . . . sorry I flew off the handle, darlin'. It's crazy. It just doesn't matter that much."

"I know what you mean," she agreed. "But what are we going to do?"

"You make a list of five titles you could live

with. I'll make a similar list. We'll keep only the ones that are on both of our lists."

"Fair enough."

Price was brewing decaffeinated coffee when Tony let out a whoop at the kitchen table.

"We agreed on anything?" she asked.

"Yeah! There are two names the same on both lists."

"Which ones?"

"*Deception Gulch* and *Jerome.*"

"After all we've been through, I can't believe you'd put *Jerome* on your list," she mused.

"Me? How about you? You actually put down *Deception Gulch?*"

"So, where does that leave us, Mr. Shadowbrook?"

"Hey, we narrowed it down to one of two choices."

"If I remember right, those are the same two choices we started with."

"Yeah, but at least now we're not mad at each other anymore."

Price slipped her hand into Tony's. "Come on, Famous Author, we've had enough creative discussion for one night. You turn out the lights."

"Yes, ma'am!" Tony flipped the switch in

the kitchen and pulled her close to him, pressing his mouth against her soft and very warm lips.

Tony met Price at the carport. He reached in the Jeep for several heavy-laden brown paper sacks. "Everything go all right?"

Price pushed her designer sunglasses on top her head and brushed her hair out of her face. "Other than the blazing heat, everything went fine. I just drove down to get groceries."

"I know . . . but you didn't see anyone, did you?" Tony followed her up the stairs and into the Winslows' house.

"Well, yes, as a matter of fact . . ."

"Who? Was it Gilette? If it was Gilette, I'll call the police!" Tony snorted.

"Tony, there are thousands of people in Cottonwood. The supermarket was crowded. The only people I saw that I knew were Ms. Mangini who runs the Yavapai Pottery Gallery, and Mrs. Reingold of the Steep Sleep Bed & Breakfast."

"You didn't see Gilette?"

"Tony!"

"How about that Broussard woman?"

"Would you quit acting like a father with a fourteen-year-old daughter?"

"Gilette really ticked me off yesterday."

"Yes, I know." Price put away groceries while Tony leaned his backside against the sink. "Which ticked you off more . . . Gilette's words . . . or Anthony Shadowbrook letting someone get to him?" she asked.

"I don't like to think that some crazy man is wandering around town thinking my wife is a foxy woman."

Price's expression was somewhere between a wry smile and a pout. "Would it be more comforting to you if all men thought of me as a dumpy old lady?"

"I didn't like the leer in Gilette's eye."

Price folded the paper sacks. "Well, the trip was just fine. I don't think there's any problem when I drive down the hill. But I do have to decide how to answer Isabelle Broussard's letter."

"I don't think you have to write back, do you?"

"She said she was mulling over the things I told her and wanted to talk. Tony, what if God really wanted to help this woman?"

"You told me you never wanted to see her again."

"I was kind of . . . agitated. I don't know, Tony. How would I know if the Lord really wanted me to talk to her again?"

"If you're going to see her, I think we both

need to be there. And meet at a neutral spot
. . . like the supermarket in Cottonwood."

"She made it quite clear that she wanted to talk to me one-to-one."

"That sounds rather suspicious, doesn't it? If you really feel led to carry on the dialogue, why not drop her a note and say the two of us would be happy to meet with her some- time?"

"She won't like that."

"I will," Tony insisted.

Price gazed out the window, then turned to Tony. "I will too. That's what I'll tell her. I just want to make sure I'm not copping out on some spiritual responsibility."

"Darlin', if there were a head-to-head spir- itual battle between you and that Broussard lady . . . I'd put my money on you every time. But, maybe with the two of us meeting with her, there won't need to be that kind of bat- tle."

"I hope you're right."

"Hey, the Lord put us together to be a team. He must want us to do more than just . . . you know . . ."

"Write fantastic books?"

"Yeah," he grinned. "That, too."

"I might make her angry again."

Tony slipped his arms around her. "Well, you're not closing the door. You're just forcing her to decide how serious she is about continuing the conversation."

They could see Dillard's from their center booth at Enrique's. Kathy kept staring across the Sedona Restaurant. "Mother, the man at the table by the window is trying to get our attention."

Price didn't turn around. She studied Kathy's perfect complexion, vibrant blonde hair, and million-dollar smile instead. *Lord, may she never fully realize how you have blessed her with such incredible good looks.*

"Really, Mother," Kathy said under her breath, "he wants you to turn around."

Price stabbed a cherry tomato with a silver-plated fork, and debated whether to eat it whole or slice it in two. "Kath, if there's a man looking at this table, I can guarantee he's not looking at me."

"Me? You think he's interested in me?"

"Surprise, surprise. Ignore him."

"Really, Mom . . . he's . . . he's way too old for me."

"Just how old is too old for you?"

"Oh, you know, he must be in his thirties."

"I've got a son in his thirties. He's not looking at me."

"Yes, he is. What are we going to do?" Kathy whispered.

"Eat our lunch."

"Mom, he's coming over!" Kathy picked at her avocado salad.

"Excuse me, ladies," a deep, but mellow voice boomed. "I don't wish to appear rude or cavalier, but aren't you Dr. Priscilla Shadowbrook?" A tall, broad-shouldered man with a thick dark mustache, wearing a teal blue knit shirt and a thick gold chain around his neck, appeared.

"Yes, I am."

"And I'm her daughter!" Kathy quickly stuck out her hand. The man shook it lightly then turned back to Price.

"Do I know you?" Price asked.

"I attended a lecture of yours at UCLA a couple of years ago."

"Was that the cinema symposium?"

"You discussed how poorly motion pictures have treated the classic historical novels."

"Yes, if I remember right, it was not the most well-attended of the seminars."

"You had stiff competition," the brown-eyed man with thick eyebrows smoothly explained. "Robert Redford was speaking in the auditorium, and Michael Orvitz was down the hall. However, your lecture had a very strong influence on me."

The man had that perfectly balanced,

tanning salon-type tan. "How's that?" Price quizzed.

"It made me want to be more diligent about the author's intent when directing a film based on one of the classics."

"Oh? You're a film director?"

"Yes, I've had some success. By the way, I was sitting over there wondering . . . do you act?"

Price noticed the man glance down at her wedding ring.

"My mother?" Kathy croaked. "You've got to be kidding! But I've had quite a bit of experience myself."

"I'm afraid Kathy's right. I'm just a lecture hall critic." Price still held the tomato on the end of her folk. She finally laid it back down on the plate.

"That's too bad. I've got a made-for-TV movie coming up that cries out for a woman of your strength and beauty. Thanks again for that fine lecture . . . Priscilla."

"Thank you for stopping by and letting me know someone was actually listening. That was very encouraging."

Kathy stared, wide-eyed, as the man swept out the front door of the Sedona Restaurant.

"Who was that, Mother? Who was he?"

"He didn't really give his name, did he?"

"You don't know him? It's like he assumed

we knew who he was. I think he had a crush on you, Mother."

"What?"

" 'A woman of your strength and beauty.' Whoa . . . don't worry, I won't tell Dad."

"About what? He was just some young cinema student who. . . ."

"Who wanted my mother to act in his movie! This is incredible. I can't believe you didn't ask his name!"

"Why didn't you ask?"

"Because he was talking to you. He obviously thought of me as just some silly high schooler. I'm almost twenty," Kathy pouted.

"Well, that was very courteous of him to say those things about my lecture. That conference was about the worst experience of my life. Nobody seemed to care that I was there. No one really wanted my opinion on anything. I felt like the token Ph.D. in English."

"I can't believe some famous movie director came up to my mother and asked if she did any acting! This is so awesome."

"That's probably just the line he always uses. Besides, I'm not sure he's an acclaimed director."

"Mother, we just have to find out who he was!"

"No . . . what we have to find is a mother-of-the-groom dress."

"Mom, the blue one at Casa de Lujo was perfect for you, and you know it."

"It was seven hundred fifty dollars for the dress alone. I'm not spending that kind of money."

"But, Mother . . . Josh and Melody are worth it."

"There is nothing a seven-hundred-fifty-dollar dress can do for their wedding that a three-hundred-fifty-dollar one can't."

"But there aren't any three-hundred-fifty-dollar dresses in Sedona!"

"You're right, Kath. Why don't we just drive on back to Jerome after lunch? Maybe your father and I will go up to Flagstaff early tonight. I can check out a place or two there."

"Shopping with Daddy? Oh, sure, he'll give you six minutes to find an outfit . . . including accessories."

"I'll find something, sooner or later." Price sliced the tomato and baptized it in low-fat ranch dressing.

"Well, I've got to find out who that director was right now!" Kathy insisted.

Price watched her daughter saunter up to the restaurant manager and flash that knee-weakening smile of hers. In a moment, she scurried back to the table.

"Mother! That was none other than Richard DiNetero!"

"Who?"

"*The* Richard DiNetero!"

Price tilted her head to the side. "I don't believe I've ever heard of him."

Kathy began to giggle. "Yeah . . . me either."

"Pop, is Mom home?"

Tony laid his glasses on the table and leaned back in the leather and oak chair, the phone in his left hand. "Hi, Kit. No, Mom and Kathy are still shopping. What's up?"

"I wanted to talk to both of you at the same time . . . you know, about that deal with Lyle."

"What did you say about Lyle? I can't hear you too well."

"Oh, it's the phone. I'm using Mom's cellular."

"You are? Where are you, darlin'?"

"At a service station in Quartzsite."

"Quartzsite? What are you doing out there?"

"Thinking."

"About what?"

"Well, Mom said she'd stick with you even if you ran a service station at Quartzite. So I've been sitting out here trying to decide what kind of man it would take to get me to follow him here."

"What did you decide?"

"I decided that I haven't met the man yet."

"Does this mean you're going to talk to Lyle?"

"I already talked to him, Daddy."

"What did you tell him?"

"That's what I wanted to talk to both of you about."

"I respect that, darlin', but at the moment I'm kind of on pins and needles, worried about what you said."

"He cried when I told him, Daddy. He actually cried. I never had a man cry over me before . . . except for you."

"What did you tell him that made him cry?"

"He said it broke his heart to think that he could never have me . . . you know . . . as his wife? I think he really cares about me, Pop. Really."

"You feeling kind of low, kiddo?"

"Like a slug."

"What are you going to do now?"

"I was thinking about driving to Yellowknife." Kit's sigh turned into a slight giggle.

"What? And miss the big wedding?"

"Yellowknife is that far away?"

"It's a long drive."

"Lyle's going to come by tonight, Pop."

"Why?"

"He said he wanted to talk to me after he's had time to let it sink in."

"He's coming by the house?"

"Yeah, if I get home in time. He said maybe we can go for a ride and talk about it one last time."

"Beware of men wanting to take you for a ride."

"Why?"

"Because they just might take you for a ride," Tony cautioned.

"Pop?"

"Speaking as a man, I think this is not a good night to go for a ride with him. If you need to talk, talk on the telephone."

"You won't let me go with him?"

"Kit, you have to make that decision yourself. What I said was, I don't think it's a good idea."

"But he had to drive to Tucson to pick up some parts. He won't be back until this evening. I can't reach him."

"Doesn't he have an answering machine?"

"Yes, but I can't leave a message on it anymore."

"Why?"

"Oh, his wife has his security code and he's

afraid she'll phone up and listen to his calls."

"That tells you something, darlin'."

"It all sounds kind of dumb, doesn't it, Pop?"

"Yeah."

"I've got to talk to him, Pop."

"Well, kiddo, talk to him on your terms . . . in the way and in the place that's best for you. If he won't allow you that much, perhaps those tears weren't entirely sincere."

"Yeah . . . listen, Pop, I think my signal is fading. I'll hang up now. Tell Mom I called."

"Okay, darlin'. We'll be at a charity deal in Flagstaff tonight, but you can call us later, if you want to."

"Yeah . . . I'll see how it goes. Sometimes I wish I was still fourteen. Life was easier then . . . you know what I mean? Anyway, I love you, Pop."

"And I love you, Christina."

There is nothing particularly scenic on Highway 89A through world-famous Oak Creek Canyon . . . on a dark night. It's just another winding road. Tony took most of the corners wide.

"Well, Mr. Shadowbrook, you really shined tonight at the charity."

"You mean I was charming?"

"Maybe not exactly . . . charming. But very

135

friendly, witty, knowledgeable, relaxed."

"It was all a fake."

"You thinking about Kit?"

"Yep."

"She'll do it right. You know that."

"I know she wants to do right. I kind of wish we were home tonight."

"You want to just hop on the interstate and head to Scottsdale?" Price asked.

"No, let's go back to Jerome and wait for Kit's call."

"Did she say for sure that she'd call to-night?"

"Not exactly. But I strongly urged her to."

"Well, don't get in too big a hurry. I'd feel more comfortable if you remained on the correct side of the double yellow line."

They were silent through several curves.

"So I did OK tonight?"

"You did wonderful! I hear it was the most successful fundraiser the crisis pregnancy center ever had."

The streets of Sedona were almost empty as he followed 89A to the west toward Jerome. Neither had spoken for quite some time.

"What are you thinking about, Tony?"

"Just wondering whether the Shadow-brook family is going to need the services of a crisis pregnancy center before the night is out."

"She's on the pill . . . remember?"

"Somehow, that's not all that comforting."

Price was asleep on the couch. Tony's head and arms rested on the table next to a half-drunk cup of coffee as he dozed.

The ringing of the telephone brought both of them to their feet. Price grabbed the receiver in the kitchen. Tony plucked the one in the master bedroom.

"Mom?"

"Dad's on the other line."

"Hi, guys."

"Where are you, Kit? Is everything all right?"

"Yeah, Pop. Relax. I'm fine."

"Well, tell us what happened, honey," Price encouraged in her deep, still half-asleep voice.

"Lyle came by tonight."

"Did you go with him?" Tony quizzed.

"No, I told him if he wanted to talk he should come inside."

"You invited him into our home?" Price gulped.

"Melody, Josh, and Paul were all here. He said he needed to talk to me in private. I told him I didn't mind if my brother heard what he had to say."

"How did he react to that?"

"He kind of went ballistic."

"What does that mean?" Price prodded.

"I've never seen him that way before. Honest. He said I was acting very immature, then he grabbed my arm and tried to pull me out the door."

"He what?" Tony gasped.

"It was no big deal, Pop. I kicked him in the shin, and Paul and Josh escorted him to his car."

"They didn't . . . eh . . ."

"No, Mom. They didn't clobber him. Josh said they just politely mentioned that it would probably be healthiest for him if he didn't come back to the house ever again."

"Good for them."

"You still feeling like a slug?" Tony asked.

"No, I feel better than I thought I would. He called back about five minutes later to apologize for his rude behavior."

"You talked to him on the phone after all of that?"

"Nope. Mel talked to him."

"She did?"

"Yeah, I think 'married slime bag' was one of her more tame comments. Anyway, it's all over, and you guys don't have anything to worry about."

Tony could sense Price's thought. *That will be the day!*

"Anyway, I'll need to quit my job, Pop. I don't want to work around Lyle. I think the parts store will hire me on again."

"Why don't you relax for a few days?" Price suggested. "You don't have to go out and get a job tomorrow, do you?"

"Maybe I should."

"Listen, darlin' . . . in the mornin' call Debi Grayson at Travel Villa. Tell her to book you on the next flight to Yellowknife, Northwest Territories, in Canada."

"What?" Price choked.

"You're kiddin', Pop!"

"No way, kiddo. Tell her you want a week at Ernie's Thunder Lodge. Ask for the Caribou Room. You'll change airlines in Edmonton. Take your birth certificate, three hundred dollars cash, and your credit card. This trip's on me, darlin'."

"Are you serious, Pop?"

"You want me to drive home and make the arrangements for you?"

"No . . . no, you write your book. I'll do it. I can't believe you're telling me this. . . . This is totally awesome."

"Well, I can believe it," Price added. "Go relax, read, catch up on a few years' sleep."

"You two are going to make me cry."

"Good, that will make three of us," Tony added.

"I'm really going to do it, Pop."

"I'm counting on it."

"I'll call you in the morning after I've made the arrangements."

"That's great, Kit . . . now get some sleep."

"Did I ever tell you I've got the greatest parents in the world?"

Tony brushed back a tear from his cheek. "I heard that rumor, years ago."

He was still sitting on the edge of the bed when Price came in. "Do you know what you're doing, Mr. Shadowbrook?"

"I hope so."

"Can we afford to send her up there?"

"Can we afford not to?"

5

From the desk of Priscilla Carey Shadowbrook:

1. Write to Aunt Vera
   (Explain why Kit missed the funeral.)
2. Stop by ASU office on Saturday
   (Pick up final class schedule for fall.)
3. Search for Eugene Jerome's wife's maiden name
   (Where did she and her sister get the money?)
4. Check with Winslows . . .
   Bryce Lloyd, III?
   (Who is he, and why does he keep calling here?)
5. Get someone to fix fountain in Scottsdale front patio
   (Landscaper or plumber?)

6. Finish edit on Chapter Four
   (Good . . . good . . . good!)
7. Mark, Amanda & baby Coop
   11:00 A.M., Thursday
   (borrow crib from Copper Hill
   Bed & Breakfast.)
8. Call Doctor (I do not like these
   pills she prescribed!)
9. Have Melody & Kathy go check
   out the cake colors
   (Is mellow blue the same as
   dream blue?)
10. Visit Pedro Montoya's widow in
    Camp Verde on Wed.
    (Jerome . . . from the Mexican
    miner's viewpoint.)

The United Verde Apartments, on the high side of Clark Street, peer over downtown Jerome like a 1930s movie set, too big and massive for the present population, but a reminder of how things used to be. One almost expects to see Humphrey Bogart and Mary Astor ascending the stairs carrying a heavy brown paper-wrapped package . . . with Peter Lorre and Sydney Greenstreet lurking in the shadows.

The buildings were constructed for mine workers in 1918, and have been in use ever since. But not all the residents have opted to pay rent. And not all the activities have been legal.

From the front steps of the United Verde Apartments, Tony could survey most of the activity on Jerome's three central streets. In the summer, the town awakens at the same time every day. Those working in the valley below struggle down the hill a little after 7:00 A.M. A hospital administrator . . . a legal secretary . . . a clerk at the supermarket . . . two construction workers . . . and the others. Tony watched each car leave its cramped parking place and swoop down Cleopatra Hill. There were several local laborers, like Victor Lucero, who also kept early morning hours.

Then there were those who slept in the gulch, the deserted buildings, or their parked cars. They all seemed to know when it was time to show up at their favorite bench or street corner. Texas Annie . . . Incredible Bob Black . . . Pop McClure . . . Fanny Cae . . . Shuffles Kingman . . . the Nogales Kid . . . and Clayton V. Gilette. They all wandered out by 7:30 A.M., looking for free coffee and day-old doughnuts.

At 8:00 A.M. the service folks show up . . . waitresses, clerks, delivery truck drivers and real estate agents. The sidewalks get swept, the beer cans gathered and the chewing gum scraped off crumbling concrete sidewalks.

At 9:00 A.M., the gallery people appear like a tangent in a disconnected dream. Wishing they were in Santa Fe . . . or at least Sedona . . . they open their shops of art, pottery, sculpture and sketches, places where trends are established by price tags . . . not skill, demand, or beauty. The opening of the door is signalled by the tinkling bells of a genuine Tibetan spirit-chaser that can be purchased for only $212. That's the small one. The larger ones cost more.

And around 9:30 A.M. the first wave of tourists lap up on Jerome's sloping asphalt "beaches." These are the travel-home-and-trailer crowd that spend more time trying to park their rigs than they do buying souvenirs in the stores and shops.

About 1:00 P.M. the night people emerge, those who work the swing shift in the valley . . . the bartenders . . . and the want-to-be artists, writers, poets, photographers . . . and those like Isabelle Broussard, who seem to defy description.

Only then do the town . . . and the streets . . . really fill. By then, tourist families tromp the steep inclines looking for bargains, burgers and bathrooms.

Tony had only been in Jerome for four

weeks, but already he could tell the time of day by who was out and about. He glanced down and reread the last few lines in his notebook.

Summer in Jerome. The streets will remain crowded until the last visitors remember how far it is to their motel for the evening.

A few will stay at the bed and breakfast places that seem to have infected any building of size and stature in town. But most tourists see Jerome as an interesting excursion on their way somewhere else.

Just as a woman with a rumored shady past draws curious suitors from all levels of society, so also the rough, rugged, infamous cities of the West offer magnetic, though temporary, attraction to all. Perhaps in both cases some hope that casual contact will allow them to become a participant in something historical, or at least notorious.

"Oh . . . Tony, Tony, Tony," he mumbled out loud. "What in the world are you doing, writing things like this?"

I need to go write a western. Price always says I can't go six weeks without riding off into the sunset with six guns blazing.

That's not true.

It doesn't have to be a six gun. It might be a

145

Sharp's carbine converted to fire a .50 to .70 centerfire cartridge.

I could call it . . . Long Shot at Deception Gulch.

Tony flipped the notebook page over and began to scribble a few words.

Sweat poured down Lt. Karne's dusty, parched face as he climbed the final boulder to the spot where the dead man lay. He drew the sleeve of his dark blue wool shirt across his mount and stared at the .50 caliber hole in the chest of Heavy Noble.

Eight hundred and thirty-two yards from the brass to the body! There's no one in A.T. that shoots that good . . . except Junior Ruiz. But he's still in that Texas prison. Isn't he?

Lt. Karne's right hand slipped down slowly to his holstered .44. . . .

"All right, Shadowbrook . . . that's enough. Just a little western fix . . . now, get back to Jerome . . . where the sun always shines, the dogs always bark and the women should all wear hiking boots."

When the streets were empty it only took Tony fifteen minutes to walk down the steep hill to the Winslow house from the United

Verde Apartments.

But the streets weren't empty.

And everyone seemed to want to stop and talk.

By the time he reached Price, who was reading an old *Jerome Sun* while riding the stationary bike on the deck, he carried six almond biscotti, an autographed copy of Lady Harriet Fletcher's book, *The Yavapai County War* and an invitation to sign books at the Mining Museum's open house.

"You've been gone a long time, Mr. Shadowbrook." Price dropped the paper on the deck but kept pedaling.

"Oh, I got goin' on the book and time flew by. I just about used up my notebook, darlin'. You're startin' to sweat like a horse rode hard." He didn't look her in the eyes.

"Have you been cheating on me, Mr. Shadowbrook?"

His head shot up. "What?"

"I know that little boy grin and that excitement flashing in the eyes. You can't fool me. You've been working on a western, haven't you?"

His face flushed red. "Does it show?"

"Shadowbrook, even a preschooler could read you. What is it this time? Are you chasing off on another episode in the *River Breaks* Series?"

"Actually, I had this idea for a new series. Nothing serious, really . . . just a title . . . an opening line or two . . . some characterization."

"I don't know what I'm going to do with you! I just can't trust you," she grinned. "You say you just want some fresh air. You say you'll just go out and write a little non-fiction. But there you are . . . sneaking behind the barn . . . writing western novels again."

Tony laughed and shook his head. "I jist cain't hep myself, Miss Priscilla. Lord knows I've tried and I've tried. I'm hopeless, ain't I?"

"You're incredibly creative is what you are. How in the world can one man write fifty books and still come up with the enthusiasm for new ideas? It's a gift."

"Or a curse." Tony handed Price a towel as she climbed off the exercise machine. "Well, Dr. S., where did you go on your 'bike' ride today?"

"Yellowknife, Northwest Territories." She wiped the sweat off her neck and face.

"Did Kit call?"

"Yes. I think she was disappointed not to talk to you."

"Does she want me to call back?"

"Nope. She's going on a hike, if the flies

and mosquitoes don't carry her off."

"Is she miserable?"

"I haven't heard her this happy in years."

"Really?"

"Tony, she's having a ball."

"What did she say?"

"She said this is the first time in her life that no one's asked her if she's 'Anthony Shadowbrook's little girl'; 'Dr. Shadowbrook's daughter'; 'Mark and Josh's sister'; or 'the sister of that beautiful blonde girl.' "

"I take it that's good."

"She entered a golf tournament tonight."

"They have a golf course at Yellowknife?" Tony asked.

"She said they have concrete tee stands and wooden greens, and the tournament begins at midnight."

"The days are that long?"

"About fifteen minutes of twilight darkness, that's all. She's going on a caribou count this afternoon with a bush pilot she met."

"Oh?"

"A lady pilot." Price led Tony into the house. "Hey, I searched through the old United Verde annual reports and found a few pictures you might be interested in. I'll show them to you after I get a shower."

"Where are they? I'll look at them now."

"Why don't you fix us some lunch?"

"Me?"

She shook her head and gleamed. "Good looking and a quick mind! You're just a dream cowboy, Shadowbrook. There's some tuna in the cupboard. Just stir in some mayonnaise and pickle relish, smear it on bread, add lettuce. Then pull out a bag of chips and pour some Diet Cokes."

"Me?"

"You seem to be repeating yourself. Go for it. You can't ruin a tuna sandwich."

Price tried to act casual as she clutched the glass and let the cola cool her blazing throat.

"What do you think?" Tony quizzed.

"Well, eh, . . ." she stammered. "I've never thought about using hot green chili salsa and chunky blue cheese dressing with tuna before."

"I thought to myself, 'Hey, why have a boring tuna sandwich when we can jazz it up a bit?' "

Price took a deep breath and could feel the heat radiate all the way down her throat. *Did he do this on purpose just so I won't ask him to fix lunch again?*

Tony took about three bites to finish half a sandwich, then sorted through a stack of annual reports. "Which of these did you want me to look at?" he mumbled.

Price held an ice cube in her mouth a moment, then chewed and swallowed it. "That top one is interesting. . . . Look at that picture I marked on page twelve." She wiped the perspiration from her forehead.

"The engineering department of United Verde in 1928?"

"Yeah, who's the second guy from the right?"

"Vic! That's Victor Lucero. Wow, does he look young in that picture. He's just a kid."

"What does it say about him in the text under the picture?" she quizzed.

"Machinist?" Tony said. "Vic was a machinist?"

"A master machinist," she corrected.

Tony glanced up. "At age eighteen? What did he do, apprentice at twelve? I figured him for the old prospector type all his life."

"It says that after the underground blasts in the 1920s caused many of buildings to slide downhill, it was Victor Lucero who devised something called a 'blasting box' that allowed them to keep mining without ruining any more of the town," Price reported.

"I've talked with ol' Vic nearly every day for a month and he never mentioned any of this. Besides, I thought they stopped underground mining when the town began to slide."

"According to these annual reports they kept at it right up until the stock market crash of 1929."

"Well, that is fascinating. I'll have to ask Vic about that 'blasting box.' " Tony glanced at her plate. "Say, do you want the other half of that sandwich?"

"Oh . . . no. I'm stuffed. Why don't you eat it?"

"Thanks, darlin'," he plucked the tuna-salsa-blue-cheese-and-lettuce sandwich from her plate. "What else did you find in the annual reports?"

"I've marked some pages we might want to review."

"Hey, I did some work on the book this morning, too."

"Oh? When did the famous novelist have time?"

"Grab my notebook. Read those first six pages. I think it will be a good way to open Chapter Five."

Tony had finished eating and was pouring another Diet Coke into his glass when Price looked up. "What do you think?" he asked.

"Shadowbrook, I owe you an apology."

"How's that?"

"I insinuated that you were merely a terrific fiction writer. This is great, Tony. The scene with the city awakening each day. I love it! By all means, open Chapter Five with this. Whew! This guy can write!"

"Thank you, Dr. Shadowbrook. Can you imagine it? We agree on Chapter Five. You remember last year, don't you?"

"The infamous Chapter Five?"

"Hey, we worked it out."

"Oh, sure, after five months of what Melody calls 'artistic arguments.' It reminds me of a certain book title."

"I don't want to talk about it."

Price spent the afternoon in the house, alternating between wearing a sweatsuit and holding an ice pack on her forehead.

Tony, barefoot, wearing shorts and a "Cheyenne Frontier Days Rodeo" T-shirt, was glued to his laptop. "I've been thinking through these character sketches again. Maybe we can't use the street people ones. Those folks are so temporary . . . they might not be in Jerome next week, let alone when the book comes out."

"I was thinking the same thing," Price agreed. "Let's file those for a future project. Some of them are pretty interesting, but by next summer they could be living in Columbia Falls."

"There's a thought. We could have the same eccentric bum appear in every book. What a rip!"

"Sure . . . if we were writing fiction," Price reminded him. "Which we aren't."

Tony waved his hand. "Yeah . . . I know. . . ."

"How about Gilette? Are we still going to use him?"

"I'm still not sure. Did you know he petitioned the city council to allow him to have his tombstone erected at the Lower Park after his death?"

"Why?"

"He claims lots of people will want to have their pictures taken by it."

"Well . . . I think I'll go take a long bath. Only I can't decide whether to fill the tub with hot water or cold."

"A bath? You just had a shower a couple hours ago."

"So what? If I want a cold bath, I'll take a cold bath!"

"Eh, yes, ma'am!"

It was an hour before Tony saw Price. She wore pink satin short-shorts and a white, lacy, scooped-neck T-shirt. Her just-past-shoulder-length hair was pulled back into twin, diminutive ponytails, and she had on

154

hot pink loop earrings, with matching lip-stick.

"I cooled off," she announced. "Sorry I snapped at you, honey. This menopause thing is not my favorite season. Does this look all right to just wear around the house? Kathy left these shorts here. They looked cool. I couldn't think of any reason to dress up."

"Well," Tony grinned, "it looks okay — providing you want someone to mistake you for a twenty-year-old."

"That will be the day."

"I'm serious. You almost look like a teen-ager."

"In that case, I'll just wear this every day." Price shuffled over to the table and neatly or-ganized the papers she had been editing. "Did the phone ring while I was in the shower?"

"Yep. Some place called Casa de Lujo asked if you wanted them to hold some dress?"

"Did you tell them 'no'?"

"Nope. But they said if you didn't call by 6:00, they'd have to put it back out on dis-play."

"I told you I decided to wear the off-white dress you bought me when I was in Atlanta with you in April. That will look nice. I've hardly worn it more than once or twice. I can find some dream blue accessories . . . and we'll save several hundred dollars."

"And I told you, if you want a new dress . . . we ought to buy you one. This is your baby boy's wedding."

"My baby boy will do well to even remember I'm at the wedding. I'm sure he won't care what I wear. Besides, the money we save will pay for Kit's trip to Yellowknife."

"Honey, I told you we could. . . ."

"Tony, please! I think this was a super idea for Kit. She needed it. And I want to feel like I contributed something. You already told me this wedding would make things pretty tight for the next year. I want to do my part. Is that all right?"

"Well, darlin' . . . it makes me feel kind of cheap. Not buying my wife a dress and all."

"Cheap? Good grief, Tony . . . I'm the most spoiled woman in Scottsdale! Sometimes it gets I'm embarrassed to tell my friends at the University what you've bought me. They just shake their heads and say, 'Girl . . . are there any more like him around?' "

"What do you tell them?"

"I tell them, 'Nope, there was only one left and I got him.' So I am not going to buy a mother-of-the-groom dress."

"OK . . . you talked me into it."

"Good."

"Now . . ." Tony leaned back and laced his hands behind his head. "If I could just talk Melody and Josh into serving Twinkies at the wedding, I'd save another thousand dollars."

"Forget it, Shadowbrook."

"Whoa . . . I did forget. . . . There was another call."

"Oh?"

"An old friend of yours," Tony teased.

"Who?"

"A movie director."

"Movie director?" Price picked up a tea towel and draped it over her shoulders like a shawl. "I don't know any . . . wait! DiNetero? Was it Richard DiNetero?"

"That's what he said."

"What did he want?"

"He said he was interested in picking up an option on a Shadowbrook western. Said he was leaving Sedona in the morning and wanted to stop by and talk to us this evening."

Price's hands shot up to her little ponytails. "He what? When?" She reached behind her and tugged down on the back of the pink shorts. "Here?"

"I told him he'd have to talk to Terrance Davidian."

"What'd he say?"

"He said he'd 'do lunch' with Terry next week."

"Did he actually say, 'do lunch'? Do they really talk that way?"

"Richard DiNetero does."

Price stood and began to stroll toward the bedroom. "I think I'll go comb my hair out and put on some slacks."

"Why?"

"You never know who might stop by for a visit."

"I told you DiNetero wasn't coming by."

"I know . . . but someone else might."

"Darlin' . . . if you change that outfit you'll break my heart."

Price folded her hands under her chin and tilted her head. " 'I want to be a cowboy's sweetheart . . . I want to learn to rope and to ride . . .' to quote Patsy Montana."

"Are you funnin' me, ma'am?" Tony drawled.

Price winked. "Maybe . . . maybe not. I won't go change if you promise we won't have any company tonight."

"Trust me."

Tony sorted through a stack of loose newspapers on the coffee table. "Who was on the phone?" he called.

"Honey B. Goode."

"What did you say?"

"I said, her name is Honey B. Goode. G-O-O-D-E."

"That's someone's name?"

"Yes, she owns the Copper Hill Bed & Breakfast."

"You're telling me the truth? This isn't some campus joke, right?"

"She's a good friend of Natalie Winslow's. She's been sending us all those vegetables out of her garden."

"Someone on this mountainside has a garden?"

"A greenhouse, actually. Everyone calls her Honey. She's really a nice gal, about our age . . . probably. If we ever need to recommend a B & B, hers would be a good one."

"OK . . . Honey B. Goode with an 'e' called. What for?"

"She wants to bring over the crib tonight."

"Crib?"

"Remember? Cooper Jarrett and his parents are coming for a visit tomorrow."

"Right . . . I knew that." Tony continued to shuffle through the papers.

"Anyway, why don't you help Honey unload the crib when she gets here? I think she's anxious to meet you."

"Me?"

" 'Oh,' " Price batted her eyes, " 'I've read all your husband's books! Tell me, is Anthony like the heroes he writes about?' "

"She said that?"

"Something to that effect."

"And what did you tell her?"

"I told her you were a couch potato wimp computer nerd."

"What?"

"Relax, Shadowbrook . . . I get asked those questions all the time. I just tell them there's a lot of you in every protagonist, but if they make one move at you I'll rip their lips out. Anyway, Honey will be over in a minute or two. You get the door."

"Yeah . . . eh, sure," Tony mumbled. "I wonder if her husband calls her 'Honey, honey'? Hey, have you seen my latest issue of *ProRodeo Sports News*?"

"Have you checked the bathroom?"

Tony shuffled out of the living room. "Oh . . . yeah, it's probably in there."

Price dove back into the manuscript pages that covered the table. *"Eccentric"* . . . *Tony, you just can't keep using that to describe every person who ever lived in Jerome.* She thumbed through a dark green reference book. *"Eccentric" means bizarre, odd, peculiar, weird, er-*

160

ratic, *idiosyncratic, whimsical, unconventional, unorthodox, outlandish, and unique.*

She had settled on *idiosyncratic* when the doorbell jarred her. "Oh!" Price jumped up and scooted toward the back of the house while the doorbell rang again. "Tony! She's here with the crib. Come get the door!"

I should have changed clothes!

"Tony?"

The doorbell persisted.

"Oh, brother. . . ." Still barefoot, Price plodded over to the front door and tugged on the door handle. "Honey, I'm sorry I took so loooooo. . . ."

With perfectly straight white teeth Richard DiNetero sported a wide smile and surprised expression as he eyed Price from ponytails to pink satin short-shorts.

"I'm not . . . it's just. . . ." Price croaked. The front door, recently flung open, had bounced off the door stop and now returned, slapping her on the backside. Price lurched forward, desperately throwing her arms around DiNetero's neck to keep from falling down the concrete steps.

DiNetero held her tightly for a moment, then quickly released her. "Eh . . . excuse me," he mumbled, ". . . is your father home?"

"I'll go get him!" she blurted out, then ran

161

inside and slammed the door in DiNetero's face.

Racing to the bedroom she cried out, "Tony! Get out here!"

He stumbled out of the bathroom. "What's wrong?"

"What's wrong? I look like this and you say 'what's wrong?' "

"But . . . but . . . but. . . ."

"DiNetero's at the door!" she groaned.

"Who?"

"Mr. White Teeth, big hands, and a gleam in his eye . . . Richard DiNetero!"

"Here?"

"I just slammed the door in his face. Go talk to him!"

"Why did you do that?"

"I don't want to talk about it . . . ever!"

Tony sauntered toward the front of the house.

"Don't let him in!" she called out.

"What's going on?"

"I told you, don't invite him in. . . . You are not going to let him make a movie out of one of your books . . . and I never want to see that man ever again!"

"Good grief, what did he do?"

"It wasn't him . . . it was me."

"You? What did you do?"

"What did I do? Look at me!" she bawled.

"Send him away, Tony!"

Honey B. Goode drove up while Tony and Richard DiNetero were still talking on the deck. Within a few minutes DiNetero hopped in his dark green Mercedes convertible and headed down the mountain. Honey flooded Tony with a dozen questions about writing. It was almost an hour before she returned to her Bed and Breakfast. And Tony toted the crib into the house. He was surprised to find Price wearing a dress, hose, heels, necklace, and matching earrings. Her hair was combed out.

"Wow! Where are you going?" Tony asked.

"Going? I just thought this might be more appropriate for company."

"Company's all gone. It's just you and me, babe."

"Yeah, Shadowbrook . . . I've heard that before. I've never been so humiliated in my life!"

"It's OK . . . DiNetero thought you were one of the girls."

"You didn't tell him differently?"

"Nope."

"Did you tell him you didn't want him directing a movie based on one of your books?"

"Eh . . . no . . . I told him I had nothing to

talk about until he checked with Terry Davidian."

"Tony, let's get this straight. I do not want to ever have anything to do with Richard DiNetero again!"

"You're serious about that, aren't you?"

"You better believe it, buster!" Price scooped up a stack of manuscript papers and began to fan herself. "Is the air conditioner working? It's hot in here."

"It's just a blush burn," he teased.

"Yeah . . . well, I'm going to take a cold shower," she announced.

"Again? But you already . . ."

The glare from her eyes silenced him.

On Friday morning Tony grabbed his grey cowboy hat, jammed it on his head, and scooped up the keys to the Cherokee.

"You going to get the mail?" Price quizzed from the manuscript-littered table.

"Yeah. Anything you need in town?"

"How about taking the crib back to Honey? That way we won't have to do it when we take off for home this afternoon."

Tony stared at the empty, dark-walnut wooden crib. "He's very active for his age, isn't he?"

"Who?"

"Cooper Jarrett."

"Tony, he's exactly like Mark. Don't you remember?"

"He's a Shadowbrook, all right."

"Did you see that killer smile?"

Tony nodded. "Yeah, he'll knock 'em dead some day, Grandma Price. Just like his daddy and his Uncle Josh."

"And his Grandpa Tony." Price leaned back in the director's chair and stretched her arms. "There were four adults here yesterday and one kid. . . . How can I feel so worn out? I don't know how Amanda can keep up day after day."

"Did I hear her say they want to have another one next spring?"

"That's what she said."

"Did you tell her she ought to wait a year or two?"

"Tony Shadowbrook . . . I am never going to tell my daughter-in-law how many children she should have and how many years there should be between them!"

"Eh . . . yeah . . . you're right."

"Of course, I wanted to tell her!" Price sighed. "It makes me tired just thinking about next year."

Tony opened the front door, but looked back at Price. His six-foot-two, square-shouldered frame filled the doorway. "If I find Vic Lucero . . . I'm going to try to find out a little more about this 'blasting box' thing . . . and I'm going to try to find what Gilette's up to this week. He was offering mining stock shares to tourists last week."

"Couldn't they arrest him, or force him to stop, or something?"

"Nope . . . Jerome has a law that says it's legal to sell mining certificates on the streets and sidewalks. Besides, Gilette says the authorities can't arrest him for peddling . . . because no one has purchased any yet."

"Now, there is one strange man."

"Eccentric," Tony concurred.

Price pulled off her reading glasses and waved them at Tony. "Gilette is bizarre, odd, peculiar, weird, erratic, idiosyncratic, whimsical, unconventional, unorthodox, outlandish and unique . . . but he's not eccentric."

Tony just shook his head. "English teachers. They're all the same." He closed the door behind him, then immediately opened it again. "Except that some English professors are a whole lot cuter than others!"

"Go to work, Shadowbrook."

"Yes, ma'am."

All the stools at the Ireland Cafe were empty when Tony slid up and nodded for owner and operator Pete Caldron to bring him a cup of coffee.

"It's a quiet morning, Pete."

"You're late. The place was hoppin' an hour ago." Caldron, white canvas apron tied around his midsection, sat the coffee pot on the counter, then brought two cups around and settled in next to Tony.

Tony grabbed the steaming black mug. "Seen Vic? I wanted to talk to him."

"Nope. Come to think of it, I didn't see him yesterday. Did you?"

"No, I stayed at the house and played with my grandson."

"Well . . . he must have been the only one of the regulars missing. They all got hepped up this morning trying to explain what they figured would happen to this Gilette fellow come the fifteenth of August."

"What do you think, Pete?"

"I reckon he'll leave town, just drive off with his tombstone."

"And maybe someone's money?"

"Well," Pete refilled Tony's cup. "There's bound to be some profit in it for him."

"Anyone catch him suckerin' tourists yet?"

"Nope. Who's going to buy phony mining certificates from a guy who hasn't had a bath in a month and carries his own tombstone around with him?"

"So, what's the general consensus from the others?"

"He's a loony. Heard you had a run-in with him."

"He wanted me to write his autobiography. Claims it will be a best-seller."

"What'd you tell him?"

"Nope."

"He probably didn't take that too well."

"You can say that again," Tony agreed. "Gilette's got a pretty high idea of himself."

Pete swung around on the green stool, leaned his back on the counter, and sipped his coffee as he stared at the empty cafe. "Well, somebody thought Gilette was a psycho planning to commit suicide. Figured he was doin' all of this so he'd have a big crowd to watch him."

"He's been claiming he's going to get murdered."

"Yeah, but how to get someone to murder you on schedule? Old Raymond Till thinks he's hired a Mafia hit man to come do it."

"Why?"

"Just for fame. To live in the history books. If you're going to take yourself out, why be boring about it?"

"What if . . . what if he did something so despicable on August fifteenth that the town was incensed to the point of someone actually murdering him?" Tony posed.

"Like Jack Ruby shootin' Oswald?"

"Yeah . . . I suppose," Tony rolled his stool around until he, too, sat with his back on the counter. "Here's my prediction. I say that Gilette doesn't die, and, second, he will try to make money out of the thing."

"I'm with you on that. But what's he sellin' other than fake mining certificates? He'd better make his play soon. Boy, I'll tell you . . . ever' summer it's a different set of crazies that come driftin' in. Nobody in this town ever heard of Gilette until he moved in a few weeks ago. Now, everbody knows him. Say, he came about the same time as you and the missus, didn't he?"

"Three crazies on the same day."

"Oh, no sir . . . it's a privilege to have you and Dr. Shadowbrook in the community. Why, just the other day after you left, I had a lady and gent from Carefree sittin' in that booth right over there," Pete pointed to the window, "come up and ask, 'Wasn't that tall, distinguished gentleman Anthony Shadowbrook, the famous author who writes westerns?' "

"What did you tell them?"

Pete's dark brown eyes danced. "I told 'em, 'shoot, no, lady . . . that was just Tony.' "

"Thanks, Pete. . . ."

"That's the thing. You're too ordinary to be famous."

"I take that as a sincere compliment."

"Good . . . now, if you want to talk crazies . . . here's the queen." Pete nodded at the woman who burst through the swinging screen door at the front of the cafe.

Her long black hair cascaded in waves down her back. Her dark, full skirt dragged the concrete. Her off-white peasant blouse was pulled to one shoulder in such a way as to show a tan line on her neck. Stopping at the doorway, she waved a hand at Tony.

"I'm not talking to you!" she shouted. Then she left the building.

"What did you do to tick off Broussard?" Pete asked.

"That's Isabelle Broussard?"

"You haven't ever met her before?"

"This is my first time. But I've heard lots about her."

"Well, if she ain't speakin' to you, consider yourself lucky."

"Is she new this year, Pete?"

"She drifted in last fall. Said she was attracted by the Spook Convention."

"But I thought that's just an annual city reunion for former residents." Tony commented.

"You're right. I do believe she was disappointed. But she's been around ever since."

An elderly man and woman carrying a large genuine Tibetan spirit chaser pushed their way into the sparsely lit cafe. "Are you open for business?" the lady asked.

"Yep." Pete got up from a stool and led the couple to one of six tables.

"I've got to get home, Pete. If you see Vic, tell him I'm looking for him."

Tony dug through the zucchini in the vegetable drawer of the refrigerator looking for a slice of Swiss cheese. Price wandered into the kitchen carrying a long stream of paper.

"Was there a fax?" he asked. "I didn't hear anything."

"You never do, Grandpa. Here, it's from your friend Marty Lawington."

Tony leaned his elbows on the white-tiled kitchen counter and scanned the letter.

"Did he find anything else on Gilette?" she asked.

"Nothing about him during the past two years. But he did find out Gilette grew up near Canyon City, Oregon."

"Where's that?"

"Out in the eastern part of the state, north

171

of Burns. His mother took off, and he was raised by his dad who was a prospector and fortune hunter."

"That doesn't surprise me. Anything else?"

"He claims Gilette was an only child."

"What's surprising about that?"

"Good old Clayton told me he had a brother, one year younger, named Layton. He said this brother would get the royalties from his autobiography after his death."

"Do-to-do-to-do . . . now it's getting weird. Why don't you ask Marty to see if he can find a Layton Gilette over the past two years?"

"But Marty said Clayton was an only child."

"I know."

"Whoa! You're right! You think maybe the reason we can't trace Clayton is because he's been passing himself off as Layton!"

"The thought occurred to me."

"You are one smart cookie, Dr. Shadowbrook. That reminds me of an old cowboy proverb."

"Oh?"

"Always marry a woman with brains enough for two. That way you'll at least break even."

6

From the desk of Priscilla Carey Shadowbrook:

1. Mail doggie pacifier and rubber sheet to Amanda
   (Search guest room for other Coop things.)
2. Barbara Mason arrives Wednesday
   (3:08 P.M. . . . . Melody will pick her mother up.)
3. Monday, Tony & I visit all the galleries
   (He may NOT give his public opinion on any piece!)
4. Tuesday, 9:00 A.M.
   Mr. J's Salon
   (Chic? Youthful? Cool!!!)
5. Double check with Valley of the Sun Caterers
   (Why haven't they sent final menu yet?)

6. Edit Chapter Five
   (Best chapter in the whole series?)
7. Make Josh go in for tux measurements
   (Call Mark to see that he gets there.)
8. Look for Dream Blue accessories in Sedona
   (Earrings, necklace, belt, shoes . . . ring?)
9. Call Dr. Icing
   (Sheet cake does NOT have to be shaped like the Superstition Mountains!)
10. Research Clarkdale Museum back files
    (What do they have on Yavapai Cowbelles?)

Tony stood staring at the ice skate that was welded to the top of an old Ford carburetor. The entire turquoise-and-peach painted object was poised in the lap of a headless, naked black mannequin.

Price tugged at his sleeve. "Don't say it, Shadowbrook," she mumbled under her breath.

He chewed on his tongue. "Wasn't it Ovid who said *'ars est celare artem'*?"

Price pushed her finger to her mouth. "He said, 'It is art to conceal art.' "

"Well, this old boy did a mighty fine job," he blurted out. "Yes, sir . . . I believe the art is concealed to such a degree that no one on earth could discover it!"

Suddenly the gallery felt extremely warm to Price. "Tony, you promised not to embarrass me!"

"Did you see those prices? Seventeen thousand dollars for that?"

"Tony!"

"This is criminal!"

"OK, Shadowbrook . . . that's it. You're leaving."

"What about the upstairs?"

"I'll check it out by myself." She dug in her purse and pulled out a dollar bill. "Here . . . go buy yourself a cup of coffee and wait for me at the Ireland Cafe."

"Yes, ma'am."

Price thought she caught a sparkle in his grey-blue eyes.

A thin, six-foot-tall woman with a long, tight skirt floated over to Price. "He calls it 'Denver, 1973.' Isn't that piece unbelievable?" the woman cooed.

"That's exactly what my husband said," Price concurred. "How about a personal tour of your upstairs gallery?"

"I'd be delighted. Is Anthony coming with us?"

"Oh, no . . . Anthony said he wanted to go off and meditate on that last piece."

"I know just how he feels. It's utterly breathtaking. But wait until you see the others. I'm afraid they will make 'Denver' look rather pedestrian."

The chipped and faded four-by-six-foot painting on the wall behind the lunch counter at the Ireland Cafe showed Charles Lindbergh at attention beside his *Spirit of St. Louis.*

"Pete, how long's that picture been hanging there?"

"Since Christmas Eve of 1927. Some say Lindy stopped by Jerome in the early '30s . . . but I doubt it. He was too busy for a place like this. But it's a powerful picture, ain't it?"

"Probably the most intelligent artwork I've looked at all day. Pete, have you seen Vic Lucero?"

"Not all week, Tony. Kind of worried about the old man. He wasn't going off to Vegas, was he?"

"He didn't tell me anything about it. Does he sometimes go there?"

Pete poured the thick ceramic mug full and slid it over to Tony. "I tease him about

176

the ladies, but I think he likes the slots. Actually, he always says he's going to see his banker about a loan."

"I think I'll check his place. He lives over at the old Nevada Hotel, doesn't he?"

"Yep . . . in that little add-on, in the back," Pete reported. "They tell me it used to be the hotel laundry."

"I thought he lived in the basement of the hotel."

"Nah . . . the basement's been closed since the slide in '27. 'Course, the whole hotel's been shut down since '53. Except for squatters like ol' Vic. Last I heard, there's nothing left in the basement but boulders and dirt."

A cottonwood tree seemed to be the main support for the east wall of the slant-roofed addition that jutted out behind the flat-iron-and-brick Hotel Nevada. Years of grime opaqued the few windows. A faded green screen door sagged half open, wedged against the crumbling concrete step. The mountainside behind the hotel dropped so steeply that the addition was actually two floors beneath the hotel's lobby.

Vic would have to climb stairs from this place to get to the basement!

Tony knocked on the unpainted wooden door and tried to peer through the window.

"Vic? It's me . . . Tony Shadowbrook. Hey, I've been worried about you, partner. Is everything all right?"

He waited for a response, then turned to study the hill. *The Powder Box Church . . . the Little Daisy Mine . . . the Douglas Museum . . . the Little Daisy Hotel . . . the Honeymoon House . . . and behind the trees, the Winslows'. You can see it all from Vic's front step . . . or back step . . . the only step. 'Course, the whole town's a flight of steps. Twentieth-century cliff dwellers is what they are. From the back of your house you can look down your neighbor's chimney.*

Tony knocked again.

"Vic?" he shouted.

He tested the loosely attached brass door handle. The warped door popped open when the catch released.

"Vic?"

The room smelled musty, like a cave. Tony stepped inside. A heavy wooden table in the middle was filled with packages, papers, utensils, food remnants and assorted miner's hats, lanterns and handpicks.

Against the south wall was an unmade brass-framed bed piled high with olive green army blankets and a well-worn bear rug. Rustic wooden shelves lined two walls, crammed with tools and ore samples, arranged in no apparent order. Some of the tools had enough dust on them to qualify as ore samples. The floor was rough concrete that looked like it had been swept at least once in the past ten years.

Three stair steps in the back of the twelve-by-twenty-four-foot room led up to a big, green, faded door.

I presume that leads to the hotel . . . or the basement.

Tony's boot heels ground dirt into the concrete as he climbed the steps and tried the door. It was locked tight. He retreated from the room. Even though it was well over ninety degrees outside, with very little breeze, the air tasted fresh and cool in comparison.

Holding onto the wild bushes growing at the base of the abandoned hotel to keep from sliding downhill, Tony tramped along the basement, trying to peer through the boarded-up windows.

"Vic?" he called out again.

Hiking to the north edge of the building, he looked back at Vic's shack.

Not exactly where I'd expect a master machinist to end up. By the time he tramped back around to the sidewalk in front of the building, he was sweating profusely. Tony pushed his straw cowboy hat to the back of his head.

"Well, Vic . . . hope you're doing all right, and didn't have a heart attack down in the mountain or something."

On the other hand, Lord, it wouldn't be a bad way for an old sourdough like Vic to pass on.

Tony was at his computer, staring out the window overlooking the Verde Valley, when Price came in. "I guess I flunked the gallery tour."

"You missed the best pieces," Price grinned as she pulled off her sunglasses and lay them on the counter. Even though she wore pastel shorts, sandals and white cotton blouse, the house felt stuffy. She pushed the thermostat lower. The air conditioner rose to the pitch of a dull roar. "You'd better take your checkbook if you go into the gallery where the old drugstore used to be. They've got a bronze calf roper that will make you want to start carrying a piggin' string in your mouth again."

"How much?"

"Three times the cost of a certain wedding cake."

"Oh, well . . . maybe I'd better not look at it."

Price sorted through a stack of mail on the coffee table. "How'd your morning go?"

"I'm worried about Vic. No one's seen

180

him around town. I checked his place, but he's not home."

"You mean, no one knows where he's been prospecting?"

"Not that I can tell. He never leaves town . . . so it must be within walking distance."

"Maybe he went to see relatives, or something."

"I've never heard him speak of kin . . . but there's bound to be someone, somewhere."

The phone rang. Tony listened to one side of the conversation.

"Oh, hi, Bryce. . . . No, Dick and Natalie aren't here this week, either. I don't suppose you want to call them in Scottsdale? I didn't think so. Sure, I'll tell him. You too, Bryce!" Price looked at Tony.

"Bryce Lloyd III?" he asked.

"Yes, he said to tell you 'hello.' "

"Well, that's nice. I wish I knew who he was."

"I wish he'd stop calling every Monday morning. The Winslows said they've never heard of him."

"And yet he refuses to leave a message or a phone number."

Price shrugged, "He always seems very pleasant."

"Tony, I had a really weird dream," Price

reported the next morning as she wandered into the kitchen, wrapped in a yellow terry cloth robe.

"What made it weird?"

"Well, I couldn't tell if it was a good dream or a nightmare."

"What was the subject?"

"I dreamt we had five grandchildren under the age of four years old and we were taking care of all of them at once."

"That was definitely a nightmare," Tony laughed. "Is that a possible scenario?"

"If the girls married young it could be."

"Don't think about it. Anyway, the girls aren't going to get married until they're thirty."

"If you believe that, Mr. Shadowbrook, you've been writing fiction too long."

"So, Mamma, what's your prediction about the girls?"

"They'll never see twenty-four . . . still single."

"What makes you so sure? There aren't even any possibilities on the horizon. . . ." Tony had a sudden panicked glance. "Are there?"

"Not that I know of this week, but they are marrying girls, Shadowbrook. They want their own homes . . . and their own men to take care of."

"But what's the hurry? They know they can stay with us."

"Well, Kath summed it up one time last spring: 'You and Daddy always seem to have all the fun!' I think we've succeeded in presenting a positive view of marriage."

Tony shook his head. "Good thing none of them remember the first ten years."

"There were some good times back then, Mr. Shadowbrook."

"Sure . . . but some dumb decisions. Like the time I was going to learn to be a saddlemaker and we moved into that smelly, dirty, cockroach-infested place above the saddle shop. I think we made it a month."

"Thirty-four days and six hours, but who's counting?" Price grinned. "But even that made sense at the time. Where should a saddle maker spend his time . . . but in a saddle shop?"

"Shop!" Tony blurted out. "And where should a chief machinist spend his time?"

"Eh . . . in a machine shop?" Price's puzzled look faded to a nod. "You mean, Victor Lucero?"

"Maybe he's at the machine shop."

"The machine shop's been closed for years, Tony."

"Yeah, and so's the Nevada Hotel. Someone told me they shut down the shop and left all the equipment right where it stood. If Vic was making something, that's where he'd be. Think I'll go uptown."

"Well, I have a hair appointment with 'Mr. J.' He promised to make me beautiful."

"Whoa . . . talk about easy work."

The old machine shop of the United Verde Copper Company was shut down in 1932. When Phelps-Dodge resumed production, they built their own facility on Sunshine Hill.

The beige stucco and corrugated tin building roosted on the side of the mountain above the town on a road with a pipe gate and a sign marked "Private Property."

The padlock was so rusted Tony figured it hadn't been unlocked in twenty years. The "No Trespassing" sign was faded almost beyond reading and shot full of holes. The thin, extremely old asphalt topping on the roadway was cracked wide and filled with weeds as brown and dry as the mountainside. But leading from the side of the gate to the machine shop was a worn foot path.

"Well, Vic . . . someone's been trespassing on a regular basis. I guess I'm going to follow suit."

As he approached the old machine shop, Tony stepped across concrete foundations of buildings long gone. *This was quite a complex in its day — welding shops, equipment storage. Nothing left but a rusty fence . . . weeds . . . and an abandoned machine shop.*

The padlock on the door was locked, but the hasp had been unbolted from the door jam, making it look locked at a distance. Tony swung the corrugated iron door open with a loud squeak.

"Anyone home?" Tony stepped inside the dark, stale building.

Idle and slightly rusting antique screw machines, lathes, drill presses and giant band saws lined the wall. Wooden bins were filled with bolts, parts and tools. The air was dry, dusty. But it was the aroma of fresh dust, metal dust . . . dust that had been heated, machined . . . case hardened.

Two things caught Tony's eye.

The clean concrete floor.

And the portable generator.

That's how someone can use this equipment. But it's all so old . . . not many around who could operate this stuff. Except . . . maybe a master machinist of the 1920s.

"Vic? It's me, Tony Shadowbrook."

Tony trudged toward the far corner of the building. A half wall signaled a likely place for the shop foreman's office. The papers on the desk were not yellowed with age.

185

And the body on the bare army cot was not moving.

"Vic!" Tony hollered at the reclining old man wearing worn khakis and a dirty hat. He scooted over to Lucero and instantly ran his fingers over the stubble of a two-week beard and a dirty neck.

Searching for a pulse, Tony was surprised when Lucero's eyes popped open. He was stunned when he felt the .45 revolver poke him in the ribs.

"Vic, it's me . . . Tony!"

The .45 disappeared back under the covers and Lucero rubbed his eyes and scratched his beard. "You shouldn't come sneakin' up on me!"

"Sneaking? I've been pounding on the door and shouting your name for ten minutes."

"What are you doin' here?"

"Looking for you. I was worried about you, Vic. Didn't have anyone to buy sugar doughnuts for."

The old man sat up on the cot. He shook his head and yawned. "How did you find me here?"

"When you weren't at your house, I had to ponder where a master machinist would hang out."

"A master machinist, eh? You must have

found the old annuals."

"Yep. Are you doin' all right? Folks around town are askin' about you."

"Which ones?"

"Eh . . . me and Pete Caldron, to name a couple."

"That's all?"

"I didn't check with any others. Are you hiding out from someone?"

"Nope. But it don't hurt to know who's scoutin' your tracks."

"So you've been cached down here for a week, working on some secret project?"

Lucero's eyes flitted around the shop. "Anyone come with you?"

"No."

"Well, I'll be much obliged if you don't tell folks where I am. I'm kind of busy here for a while. The company ever finds out I'm back in here, they'll run me off to the county jail again."

"Again?"

"Trespassin'. But I think as long as I don't mess things up, they don't pay much mind. You know what the crime is, Shadowbrook? The crime is neglecting all of this equipment. Ever' tool in this shop still works and there ain't three men in the state of Arizona who know how to run them." Lucero set his hat straight and limped over to the door.

"Thanks for wakin' me up. I better get to work."

"Vic, I've got an idea." Tony reached in his wallet and pulled out a twenty dollar bill. "Hike out with me and I'll drop you off at your place. Get yourself a bath, shave, and I'll buy you Pete's biggest steak. Then come on back here to work and you'll get a lot more done."

The old man scratched his chin. "You might be right. But I'll stop to eat first. Bathin' could kill a man, and I wouldn't want to die with an empty stomach. You're the first writer I ever met with horse sense."

"Maybe because I spent the first thirty years of my life horseback."

"You don't say?"

"Come on, I'll give you a lift."

Lucero carefully closed the door behind them. As they approached the pipe gate across the drive, Tony turned to him. "Vic, how's that prototype 'blasting box' coming along?"

The old man didn't slow down or look up.

"Those cussed Annual Reports. You're the only one in seventy years that's ever read 'em. In fact, nobody read 'em when they came out."

The men piled into Tony's Cherokee and he pulled back out into the highway. "I surmise you're wonderin' what I'm buildin'?"

"Vic . . . whatever a 'blasting box' is . . . that's between you, the Lord, and Phelps-Dodge. I won't tell a soul, and I won't mention it in the book. I'm just curious . . . and would like to see it sometime . . . that's up to you, partner. But here's the thing that really interests me. Four or five weeks ago you wanted to borrow some money to build a scale model of some boon to mining. I presume your fortunes have changed?"

"Yes and no," Vic admitted.

"What do you mean?"

"I ain't got the financing yet . . . but I'll have it in two weeks."

"In the meantime?"

"A credit card."

"A what?"

"The fool bank sent me a credit card. A gold 'Visa,' they did. Said my excellent credit rating entitled me to a pre-approved limit of eight thousand dollars. Can you believe that? And I don't have to start paying until November. By then, I'll be sittin' in one of them Victorian houses in Prescott, drinkin' lemonade and hirin' twenty-year-old girls to do my laundry."

Tony pulled the rig over in front of the Ireland Cafe. "Vic . . . you better start thinking about how to make some payments, just in case the financing falls through. You could be paying on that the rest of your life."

"That's where I got 'em beat! Just how long do they think I'm goin' to live? In fact, I could just charge my dinner. You want this twenty back?"

"Nope. The treat's on me."

"Shadowbrook, I like you. When it's time for a demonstration, you get yourself one of them little video cameras and record the whole thing!"

"I'll do it, partner."

"You ain't afraid of close quarters underground, are ya?"

"Well . . . I guess we'll just have to find out." Tony glanced in at the cafe. "Looks like you get to have dinner with none other than Clayton V. Gilette."

Lucero slammed the door on the dark blue Cherokee and leaned in through the open window. "I'll get him to buy me some sugar doughnuts."

"If he has any money."

"He's a lot better heeled than he lets on," Vic guffawed and headed inside the cafe.

Tony drove slowly through town. The streets were filled with tourists, regulars and kids on skateboards and rollerblades. It was downhill from the machine shop all the way to the Winslows'.

Price called from the deck. "I'm out here, honey."

"Oh, excuse me. . . . Is your mother home?"

"Give me a break, Shadowbrook."

"Your hair really looks nice. How was this 'Mr. J' character?"

"He swished around a little too much, if you know what I mean. But he did a good job. You should definitely not go there for a haircut."

"How's the chapter?"

"Going great. I have no idea what the name of this book is, but it's sure flowing right along. Did you find Victor?"

"Yeah . . . he's been busy working on an invention that's going to open up mining all over this copper hill. Vic's amazing. Sun City's full of people his age who have been retired for twenty . . . twenty-five years. He's squeezed in a whole generation of living while they were at the clubhouse learning to line dance and enjoying the early bird special at Denny's."

"Well . . . we certainly don't have to worry about Anthony 'Don't-stop-'til-you-drop' Shadowbrook ever retiring, do we?" she teased.

"There are too many things in life to do.

Why would anyone want to retire?"

"Maybe they get tired?"

"Maybe I'll get tired . . . but I won't ever change."

"Speaking of change . . . you want to get the latest report from your daughters?"

"What's wrong now?"

"Nothing. Kathy called and hinted around that she wished her daddy would let her try out for the Miss Arizona contest this year."

"I thought we got over that stage."

"Apparently not. And she's wondering what to do about Kit."

"Kit? But I thought . . ."

"Now, relax, Daddy . . . I'll explain. Ever since Kit came home from Yellowknife, she's been much easier to get along with. Rested and relaxed . . . Kathy says she's mellowed out."

"Sounds good to me. What's wrong with that?"

"It's just going to take some getting used to. Last night the girls were cleaning because Melody's mother arrives today. Kit vacuumed the entire house without Kathy mentioning a thing."

"I didn't even know she knew how to operate a vacuum."

"She's a bright girl . . . with a mechanical mind. But the big news was, this morning before she went to work, Kit announced to Melody and Kathy that she really wanted to walk down the aisle with Mark. She said Kathy should walk with Mr. Soon-to-be-Hollywood-Star."

"Did she give a reason?"

"She told Kath she thought they had the two neatest brothers in the whole world and she hoped someday to find someone of their caliber herself. She said until she gets to walk with her pop . . . Mark would do just fine."

"Whoa . . . she *is* making some changes. How's Kathy adjusting?"

"At first she was delighted to get to be paired with Mr. Hollywood, but now she's wondering why she made such a big deal over it. She met him once over at Josh and Paul's place, and he acted like a snob."

"Has Kit talked to Lyle since she came back from Yellowknife?"

"Kathy said he called once. Kit told him that if he called again she'd have to refer the matter to his wife's divorce attorney."

"Whoa! That ought to end things."

"Mr. Shadowbrook, that little trip might have been the second best idea you ever had."

"Second best? What was the best idea?"

"Marrying me, of course."

Price headed for the kitchen door. Tony

trailed quickly behind.

Anthony Shadowbrook spent most of the afternoon looking around town for Clayton V. Gilette. He hoped to discover something about his whereabouts for the past two years. But for the first time all summer, Gilette was not loitering around Upper Park, and no one had seen him all day. Tony did discover a crudely printed cardboard sign at the parking lot of the Lower Park that read, "Future site of Clayton V. Gilette tombstone."

At 4:00 P.M. he jammed his hat on a hook near the Winslows' front door and plodded to the kitchen in search of a cold drink.

Price had one ready for him. "You got a fax from Lawington."

"About Gilette? What did he say?"

"A Layton Gilette has been a surveyor for a mine engineering firm in Las Vegas for almost two years. He quit his job the second week in June."

Tony glanced over the fax. "Sounds like a description of our Gilette, doesn't it?"

"Yes, but medium height, medium weight, and medium brown hair could fit lots of people. This Gilette is fastidiously neat, even to the point of wearing a tie when he's out in the field."

"Like the old-time surveyors? That's not

the Gilette we know . . . but he could have been putting on around here. . . ."

"Or in Vegas."

"So he left the second week in June. . . . That's the same week Clayton showed up in Jerome."

"According to Lawington's report, Layton took a job with some big Canadian mining consortium and moved to Alberta. But that can't be confirmed. What do you plan to do with all this?"

"Makes an interesting anecdote in our book, I suppose. If he wants to quit his job, move to a different city, go by a different name . . . that's his business. In less than two weeks, maybe we'll find out something more."

"Adding the scenes with Gilette does give our book a hint of mystery. I like the way we trail it along through the chapters."

"There are lots of mysteries in this book."

"Oh . . . ?" she said.

"Sure . . . there's a mystery about Gilette . . . a mystery about Vic Lucero . . . and the greatest of all mysteries . . . what's the name of this book, anyway?"

"You promised Atlantic-Hampton a title by this week."

"With the continuing revelations of Gilette's deceptions . . . I'm sure you've realized my idea looks good."

"And . . ." she insisted, "if you go out to the city limits sign, what do you see? What's the name on the sign?"

"But, darlin' . . . we've never done one of these series strictly limited to the city limits. *Fox Island* covered the whole island. *Promontory* covered most of northwest Utah. This book stretches from Clarkdale all the way up to Jerome Junction and the narrow gauge railroad."

"Are you trying to tell me that *Deception Gulch* is more inclusive than *Jerome*?" she stormed.

"No, it's just. . . ."

Price fanned herself with a photocopied replica of a United Verde Extension mining certificate. "If you want it to be inclusive, call it *The Black Hills*."

"Readers would confuse that with South Dakota."

"Then why not call it *Cleopatra Hill*?"

"Come on, Priscilla . . . that sounds like one of the girls in the crib district."

"How about *Mingus Mountain*?"

Tony shook his head. "Would you want the word *Mingus* on the cover of your book?"

Price leaned her head back and wiped the perspiration off her neck. "Well, Shadowbrook, we have to have some words on the front of the book!"

The phone rang. "Saved by the bell." Tony stepped toward the kitchen.

"It's only Round Five. . . ." she warned. "And I think I'm ahead on points."

Price had finished her first edit of the opening pages of Chapter Six by the time Tony returned. He was rolling up the sleeves of his red, white, and blue western shirt.

"You were in there a long time."

"That was Davidian."

"Anything new?"

"Here's the deal. He actually sold an option on *Shotgun Creek*. They want to use the story for a TV movie. That means they can't make it as raunchy as they would for the theaters. It's pretty good money for a TV deal, and they've asked if I want to work on the screenplay. But it's just an option. That doesn't mean it will actually be made."

"But that's where it begins! Tony, it's wonderful! I knew you could do it, babe! This is the one you've been waiting for!" She scooted over and threw her arms around his neck.

He tugged her arms loose and held her at a distance. "I told him we'd have to think about it."

"You don't like the deal?"

He took a deep breath and let it out

quickly. "*You* might not like the deal."

"Me?"

"It's your buddy Richard DiNetero and his production company that want to buy the option."

"DiNetero? No . . . no way! You are not going to sell it to him. That's impossible!"

"Whoa, darlin'. . . . Aren't you carrying this a little too far? I know you were a little embarrassed."

"Anthony! I was considerably more than a little embarrassed. I'm going to carry that humiliation to my grave. But it's more than that. There was something . . . something at the restaurant . . . something at the door . . . not DiNetero. Not now. Not next year. Not ever. Don't you understand?" Price burst into tears and ran off to the bedroom.

Tony sauntered toward the refrigerator.

Understand? Lord, I don't even understand three cold showers a day. I love her, and I cherish her . . . but I don't know if I'll ever understand her.

Wednesday was productive. Tony and Price didn't talk much. They pounded computer keyboards between cups of coffee and tea and piles of research papers. They scratched out their own lunches and worked until mid-afternoon. Tony was describing the grandeur of Jerome's famed Montana Hotel when Price slipped up behind him and began rubbing his neck. He pulled off his glasses and relaxed his shoulders.

"Sorry, I've been kind of grouchy lately."

He scrunched his eyes. "Forget it, kid. . . . I get too intense. You know how it is. The books just consume me. I need a break. How about you and me hopping on a plane and flying to Cabo San Lucas for a two-week R and R?"

"Sounds wonderful," she sighed. "Of course, we'll miss the wedding."

"Is that the good news or the bad news?" he laughed.

"Maybe in September we can get away for a few days. When do you need to start that new western?"

"Yesterday."

"Really?"

"It's going to be tight. Besides, after the wedding I won't be able to afford to go to Nogales . . . let alone Cabo."

"Well, that movie deal will add a few funds to the bank account, won't it?"

"I'm afraid not."

"But don't you get some of that option money now?"

"Nope."

"But what is an option if you don't get . . . ?"

"I called Davidian right before lunch, when you were in the shower. I turned the deal down, darlin'."

"You did what?"

"I told Davidian we didn't want to work with DiNetero, not now, nor in the future. I didn't explain. I just said there was something about him that didn't click with us."

"You really turned down a movie contract?"

"Yeah."

She stopped rubbing his neck and Tony thought he heard a sniffle. He stood up and lifted her head until their eyes met. Tears streamed down her face. "What's the matter, darlin'?"

Price wiped her nose with the back of her hand and tried to take a deep breath. "Your whole life you wanted to see one of your westerns made into a movie. Then the first chance you get you turn it down because your wife pitched a fit."

"Seems like a good reason to me. Why are you crying, babe?"

"I just can't believe you did that. You just told them no?"

"Hey . . . it's no big thing. It just wasn't the right guy. My daddy always told me not to trust a man who wears Italian patent leather shoes and no socks. Don't worry. Something else will come along."

"Do you believe that?"

"Well . . . it won't come along for a while. Terrance Davidian quit."

"Really?"

"He was counting on his cut of this deal. Said I should seek other representation."

Price began to bawl. "I ruined everything! Tony, I'm sorry I. . . ."

He held her against his chest and rocked her back and forth. "Darlin', you didn't ruin it. It was just not to be. The only thing you're going to ruin is your makeup. We aren't in this for the money . . . or the fame. If that's all we wanted we should have bought that McDonald's franchise years ago. We write because the Lord wants us to write. He's in charge of sales and promotion. You know that."

Price sought refuge near a box of Kleenex and began to wipe her eyes. "I don't know why I got so emotional. It just hit me all at once that there's no other man in America who would do what you just did."

He sauntered up to her from behind and slipped his arms around her waist. "There's no other man in America married to a woman like you."

She leaned back. "I like your style, Shadowbrook. You know . . . I'm glad I married you. Have I ever told you that before?"

"You might have mentioned it once or twice."

Price pulled loose and headed to the back of the house.

"Time for another shower?" he asked.

"Nope . . . I just need to wash my face."

"How about an early supper at Dos Hermanas in Sedona?"

"Really? It sounds wonderful. What's the occasion?"

"I don't have to get any more phone calls from Terry Davidian!"

It was just past seven when they returned to the Winslows' Jerome house. Tony was changing clothes when Price came in.

"You might want to keep those things on," she suggested. "The message on the machine was from Melody. She said she couldn't really talk, but that she and her mother were going to pick up Josh at Rawhide, then drive up here."

"Tonight?"

"She said they'd get here around 8:00, and if we were gone they'd wait because this was a pretty big deal."

"What's a pretty big deal?"

"Whatever they need to talk about, it must

have something to do with Barbara."

"Maybe she doesn't like the cake."

"Melody was almost in tears . . . I think this is serious."

"Well . . . that sort of changes an evening of writing, doesn't it?"

"I'll stir up some lemonade. Maybe it will be pleasant enough to sit out on the deck."

Josh hugged his mother and dad, then headed for the kitchen, leaving Melody and her mother on the deck.

"Barbara . . . it's so good to see you again," Price began. "These two kids of ours have been busy since we saw you last summer."

Barbara Mason's short black hair had a slight wave in it. Contrary to the summer before, she wore absolutely no makeup. Her beige and green dress looked comfortable for Puget Sound, but a little too heavy for August in Arizona. After a moment of small talk and greetings, they perched on the deck.

Returning with a Coke and bag of potato chips, Josh kicked off his shoes then leaned back in a deep blue chaise with his stocking feet in Melody's lap. Price, Tony and Barbara Mason sat around a white enamel, circular deck table.

"Now, Melody . . . what do we need to talk about?" Price asked.

"My daughter is going to get married in a church!" Barbara Mason blurted out.

"But . . . I thought . . . that was decided back in February," Tony blustered.

"Well . . . no one consulted me!" Mason huffed.

"Mother, I did tell you that's what we decided. You didn't say anything."

"Well, I'm saying something now. It's been eating away at me." She pointed at Price. "It's your doing, you know."

"Mine?"

"Last summer you turned my life around. You pointed out my spiritual poverty. Well, when I decided to give my life to the Lord, I meant it. What a year! I found out who my father was, and got to be at his bedside when he passed away, rest his soul. I lost thirty pounds, stopped drinking and managed to get in twenty-one college units."

"You have had a remarkable year," Price agreed.

"And I'm not going to let it be ruined now! Melody's a Christian girl, and Joshua's a Christian boy. They should be married in the church. Anything else will be making a mockery of God. There, I've said it . . . but that's the way I feel!"

Tony glanced over at Josh and Melody. They were expectant, looking straight at him. "Well . . . Barbara," he began, "I'm glad you were able to express what's on your heart. We do need to be open about all of this. Let me give you a little background from my point of view. I believe all of us have a great desire, like you do, to be obedient to the Lord in this matter. Isn't that right, kids?"

"Yeah," Melody added. "I thought we were doing everything right. Pastor Wayne didn't say anything was wrong with a backyard wedding."

Barbara leaned forward, her face taut. "What kind of church do you belong to?"

"It's a community church that we helped start about fifteen years ago. . . ."

"Doesn't it believe in the Bible?" Mason demanded.

Price felt the back of her neck heat up.

Tony stayed calm, relaxed. "Barbara, here was our reasoning. Our sanctuary holds eighteen hundred people. We don't have a chapel yet, so all the weddings have to be done in the sanctuary. Since the kids wanted this to be a fairly small wedding . . . well, even if all two hundred show up, it will seem like no one showed up in that big building. So Melody and Josh thought our backyard would be a good location."

"Mel and I do so many things together

outside," Josh explained. "It seemed like a good choice, Mrs. Mason."

"As far as I can tell, the Bible doesn't specify where a wedding commitment should be made," Price added.

"The important thing is that all is done in a way that honors God and includes a recognition of the seriousness of the vows to be said," Tony offered.

"Are you trying to tell me that the New Testament church had weddings in people's backyards?"

"Mother . . . in New Testament times they neither had backyards . . . nor church buildings!"

Barbara Mason looked out over the Verde Valley as the streetlights began to blink on.

"Melody, I've thought about your wedding since the day you were born and I held you in my arms." This time Barbara Mason's voice was much softer. "And in every one of those daydreams, the wedding took place in a church. Don't let your mother down now."

7

From the desk of Priscilla Carey Shadowbrook:

1. Monday, pray for Melody & Barbara (They meet with Pastor Wayne at 11:00 A.M.)
2. Call Mom and Dad before they leave for Texas (Has Aunt Vera decided to go with them or not?)
3. Check out You've-Got-Your-Health Store in Flagstaff (Honey said licorice root tea helps hot flashes!)
4. Clean up Chapter Six (Sunset scene needs more drama . . . more zip.)
5. Interview Mrs. Gwyndalyn Burkett, Wed. 9:30 A.M. (Father was last administrator at U.V. hospital.)

6. Meet with Isabelle Broussard
   on Wednesday
   (2:00 P.M. Upper Park . . . Tony?)
7. Thursday lunch with girls
   (Del Monico's in Prescott . . .
   reservations?)
8. Check with Winslows about care
   of red tile floors
   (Ask Tony about hiring house
   cleaner?)
9. Call Dr. Icing
   (Don't start any other work on
   cake until I call!)
10. Tell Tony about title decision
    (Then call Liz . . . or Atlantic
    Hampton?)

Confession might help the soul, but it's tough on the ego.

Price sat out on the deck sipping Earl Grey tea and gazing at the sprawling Verde Valley twenty-one hundred feet below. She could hear the lilting sounds of a flute solo from one of Jerome's street corner musicians drift down the mountainside. She was anxious to talk to Tony, but he was running. The dry air seemed to combine the aroma of diesel smoke, sage and a touch of something like garlic.

It was time for them to settle on the title of the book and she had a new plan. It couldn't fail.

"Mornin', babe!" came the shout from a sweaty, middle-aged man with dark brown hair and streaks of gray. "You're up early."

Tony tromped up the wooden stairs to the raised deck and stretched his legs on the railing. "Did you ever notice how flat Scottsdale is? Every morning I start thinking about how wonderfully, wonderfully flat it is at home."

"I don't suppose you'd consider just using the exercise bike instead?"

"Nope."

"Someday, Mr. Shadowbrook, you'll be too old for a six-mile run every morning."

"I know." He grabbed a towel from a deck chair and wiped his head and neck. "In twenty-five, thirty years I'll probably slow down to only four or five miles a day."

"Yes, I can see it now . . . some shriveled up, grey-haired man plodding around the clubhouse circle at Sun City, with knobby bowlegs and a black cowboy hat."

"Never! No Sun City . . . no clubhouse . . . no shuffleboard. We'll go live with Kit in Yellowknife before Sun City."

"Relax, Shadowbrook. You're getting a little touchy about retirement communities. Grab on to your saddlehorn, buckaroo. I've got some staggering news for you."

"The girls? The wedding? What's happened now?"

"It's even more shocking than that. I've been sitting out here reading my summer verse from Isaiah. . . ."

"The one about peace?"

"Lord, you establish peace for us; all that we have accomplished you have done for us."

"What peaceful thought did you have today?"

"Well . . . I, eh . . . I don't think we should call this book *Jerome*. I've decided to agree to . . . *Deception Gulch*."

"That's the big stunning news?"

"It is to me."

"No . . . no, you're right! It is a big deal." Then Tony began to chuckle like a prospector with color in his pan. "I can hardly believe it!"

"Are you laughing at me, Anthony Shadowbrook?"

"Darlin' . . . I'm laughing at this famous husband and wife writing team! It's a wonder we ever get anything done."

"What's so funny?"

"OK . . . I'm out running this morning. And I'm thinking about this area around Jerome. So I decide that when I finish The River Breaks series of westerns, I'll start a

210

new series called Arizona Untamed."

"I like the sound of that."

"And book number one in the series will be *Long Shot at Deception Gulch*."

"*Deception Gulch?*"

"You were right all along. It's a better name for a western. And I'm sure not going to have two books with 'Deception Gulch' in the title. So I'm running down the mountain this morning and I said, 'Shadowbrook, that woman you married has a literary eye for poetry, symmetry and impact. If she says *Jerome* is a good title, chances are, she's right.' "

"Wait a minute . . . wait a minute . . . are you telling me at the same time I am deciding on *Deception Gulch*, you are deciding on *Jerome?*"

"Mamma . . . what a pair we are."

They both roared.

"What are we going to do now?" she snickered, tears streaming.

"*Deception Gulch* is out . . . so let's go with *Jerome*," he suggested.

"I don't like it," she announced.

"What? But you've insisted all along. . . ."

"I've been wrong. You're completely right. . . . It doesn't have the ring of the other books, and our text includes more than just the town anyway. I've really been thinking this over. I don't want to use *Jerome*, Tony."

"Are you sure?"

"Positive."

They stared at each other for a minute, then doubled up with laughter.

The rest of the day they crafted dynamic texts and discussed the project. Not another word was mentioned about the title.

"We've covered *The Jerome Chronicle*, *The Jerome Mining News*, *The Jerome News*, *The Verde Copper News*, *The Jerome Reporter*, *The Jerome Daily News*, *The Jerome Copper Bell*, *The Jerome Sun* and *The Verde News*. . . . That's got to be enough about the newspapers," Tony announced.

"It's getting dark. . . . I'll turn on some lights."

"Did you get hold of Melody?" Tony asked.

"Yes, I talked to Melody and to Barbara and to Josh and to Kit and to Kathy."

"Whoa . . . the whole gang."

"They were going out to *Rustler's Roost* for supper."

"Did Josh promise not to ride the bull they have corralled by the front door this time?"

"I don't think he actually promised."

"How did the session with Pastor Wayne go? Is Barbara still insistent on a church wedding?"

"She said Pastor Wayne was convincing. He went over the whole service with her. I think Barbara was imagining some sort of extemporaneous happening, rather than a traditional structure."

"I'm glad she takes her commitment to the Lord seriously."

"Did you hear Melody say her mother got kicked out of the biology class she took at the college last spring?"

"A fifty-five-year-old woman got kicked out of class?"

"She kept arguing against evolution, so the professor dismissed her."

"Can they do that?"

"Until Barbara's attorney called and threatened a lawsuit."

"She's a feisty gal, isn't she?"

"I enjoy her," Price added. "She's extremely opinionated . . . but willing to change. You don't always see both those qualities in a woman."

"Or a man," Tony added. "Then everything's back on course for the wedding?"

"I wouldn't say completely on course," Price sighed. "Barbara doesn't like Melody's dress."

"The wedding dress? But . . . I thought . . . you don't decide ten days before the wedding that you don't like the dress . . . do you?"

"Apparently, Barbara does. She was so busy in the spring with Mr. Bennington's death and her mother's stroke and twenty units at college . . . I don't think she paid any attention to what Melody picked out."

"Well, what's wrong with the dress? Is the neckline too low, or what?"

"The problem is the train."

"As I remember," Tony pondered, "it's a short dress. It doesn't have any train."

"That's the problem. Barbara said, 'A chaste young woman like Melody always has a train on her dress.' She insists a short dress signifies loose living and stated that she would be humiliated if Melody wore a short dress."

"But you can't drag a long train through the rocks and cactus of our backyard!"

"Barbara says she'll pay for the alterations and rent a satin runner for Melody to walk on."

"Alterations? How do you add several feet to a dress?"

"You can't."

"Eh . . . is there a pattern developing here?" Tony questioned. "Every time a crisis in the wedding is solved, is Barbara going to find another?"

"Probably."

"What's her problem, anyway?"

"I think it's Barbara's way of holding on just a little longer. Melody's all she's ever had. Her father took off . . . her husband left her . . . her mother lived over fifty years in seclusion and deception . . . Melody's held her life together. Now the daughter is a grown woman. . . . She's getting married and going to live fifteen hundred miles away. It's tough, Tony. . . . Give her some slack."

"Yeah . . . I think you're right, babe. Can you imagine how I'd feel if one of our girls were getting married and moving away?"

"You'd be beyond depression," she agreed. "And it's not if . . . but when . . . it will happen, Daddy."

"The girls like Arizona . . . I'm sure of that. . . ."

"The question is, what about their husbands? You just coached Kit to follow her man to the end of the earth. She's not going to hesitate to move, if that's what Mr. Wonderful wants."

"I don't want to think about it," Tony insisted. "Now, give me the report from the rest of the gang."

"Kit said the air conditioner broke down this afternoon, but she fixed it when she got home from work. It was just a busted belt."

"Why is it I have a hard time imagining the kind of guy who would marry that girl?"

"He'd better be a special guy . . . because she's a unique, special girl," Price submitted. "Oh, yes . . . Kathy met a young man last night at church who works in the front office for the Phoenix Suns. He thought she ought to try out for one of their cheerleaders."

"Cheerleader for an NBA team?" Tony groaned. "All they do is shake and wiggle in skimpy costumes!"

"How would you know, Mr. Shadowbrook?"

"Eh, well . . . that's what I've heard. I won't let her do it!"

"She didn't ask you."

"Well . . . what did she tell the fast-talking, slick character?"

"Tony! He's a nice young man she met at church. Anyway, Kathy turned him down."

"She did! That's my girl. All right!"

"She said she thought being a professional cheerleader would disqualify her from the Miss Arizona contest."

"But I didn't say she could, . . ." Tony stammered. "Eh . . . am I being asked about that one?"

"I don't think so."

"The rules are changing, babe."

"Yes . . . they are. But some things are the same. Your youngest son wants to come up Wednesday and talk with his father."

"What about? Does he need a loan?"

"I wouldn't know. It's a father and son thing. That's the day the girls and I are going out to lunch in Prescott . . . so you have the place all to yourself."

"Let's see, over the years Josh and I have already had the how-to-treat-girls talk . . . the personal-hygiene talk . . . the how-to-make-Jesus-Lord-of-everyday-life talk . . . the staying-sexually-pure talk . . . the alcohol-tobacco-and-substance-abuse talk . . . the what-shall-I-major-in-college talk . . . the how-to-choose-a-political-party talk . . . the how-to-find-a-life-vocation talk . . . the how-to-keep-from-going-into-debt talk . . . and the how-do-you-know-who-you-should-marry talk. . . . What's left?"

"I'm sure you'll find out on Wednesday. Are you ready for some dinner?"

"Supper," he corrected.

Jerome's Upper Park stretches between Main Street and Clark Street in the center of town. Although it's only a hundred feet deep and a few lots wide, it offers one of the few level spots in town . . . an excellent place to sit and watch the world go by.

And it provides a very public location to meet people.

Isabelle Broussard wore her customary

long broomstick skirt. This one was solid black. Her legs were crossed as she leaned forward, elbows resting on knees, head in her hands. Her peasant-style white cotton blouse was slipped to one side of her shoulder, revealing a bra strap. As Price approached she had the urge to adjust the woman's clothing, especially since Tony trudged along beside her.

"I don't know why he had to come!" Broussard whined.

Tony and Price sat down on the wooden park bench next to her, but Broussard jumped to her sandal-clad feet and paced in front of them.

"Because we both wanted to talk to you," Tony offered.

"I don't like talking to men. Especially you."

"Why do you think that is?" Price quizzed.

"You mean, other than the fact that most men are morons and only have one thing on their minds?"

"Yeah," Tony continued, "other than those obvious things . . . why don't you like talking to men?"

A wide smile broke across her heavily made-up face. "OK, Shadowbrook . . . you passed the first test," she asserted. "You didn't try to punch me out when I called you a moronic sex fiend. So far, so good. But I still don't know why you had to come along."

Price folded her hands in her lap. Her legs felt cool. She was glad she'd worn her beige pants. "Ms. Broussard . . . the last conversation you and I had weeks ago was not too cordial. I didn't want that to happen again. I thought maybe it would be better to have Tony along . . . to mediate."

"It's like you're trying to gang up on me."

Tony pulled off his sunglasses, folded them, and shoved them into his shirt pocket. "Ms. Broussard . . ."

"You can call me Isabelle."

"Isabelle," Tony continued, "we were led to believe you might be interested in discussing spiritual matters. Price and I quite often do that sort of thing together."

"Why?"

"Because we feel we can be of more help that way. The Lord's given us complementary gifts. Neither of us is all that wise by ourself, but together we've managed to be of some help to others over the years," Tony tried to explain.

"So you don't claim to know everything?"

"That's for sure," Tony insisted.

"Okay, Shadowbrook, there's another quality in your favor."

"Isabelle, what exactly did Price say to you

that day that made you stop and think?"

"She said something like, 'You're experimenting with something far beyond your understanding. It's a deadly game you are playing.' Then she said I should pull away while I have the power to do so."

"Does that trouble you?" Price asked.

"At the time, I thought you were the one that had no idea what you were talking about. But right after that I started having dreams about . . . killing myself. I don't like the dreams, but they are always there. . . . I can't stop them. That's when your words about not having the power to pull away kept coming back."

"Tell me about one of the dreams, Isabelle," Tony encouraged.

"Well, last night I dreamt I was giving a, you know, ghost tour of one of the mine shafts. . . ."

"Does your tour include mine shafts?" Tony interrupted.

"No, but I wish it did." She continued to pace as she talked, never looking either of them in the eyes. "Anyway, in my dream I'm leading some people into a tunnel, and we come upon a big vertical shaft. It's so deep that when a stone is thrown into it, we never hear it hit bottom. Well, all of a sudden this ghost comes floating out of the hole."

"What's it look like?" Tony asked.

"Like a woman in a long dress, only she's very pale-skinned. I can almost see right through her. She's calling to me to join her. She says if I'll just jump into the dark hole, I will be painlessly transformed into a ghost like her and the two of us will be able to live together in the mountain forever. She says it's my destiny to be a wandering spirit, and I will be much happier with her."

"What did you do?" Price asked.

"In my dream, I tried to hold back . . . but it was like she was dragging me. I couldn't hold up, so I jumped into the hole."

"And then you woke up?" Tony asked.

"Yeah, and I couldn't get back to sleep."

"Do you really want the dreams to stop?" Price asked.

Broussard tugged her blouse up on her shoulders. "The ghost thing is a rush . . . you know what I mean?"

"Not really," Price replied.

"Here's the thing. . . ." Broussard stopped prowling back and forth in front of the bench and looked straight at Price. "The spook tours are a diversion . . . a hobby . . . a business, not a fixation. I don't want to join any ghosts or phantoms or apparitions or demons. But when I go to sleep I seem to have no ability to back away."

"Can you back away when you're awake?" Tony asked.

Broussard held her thin arms tightly against her chest. "Not always. I used to. . . . A couple years ago it was just like flipping a switch . . . but now, I'm losing it."

Tony leaned forward and spoke softly. "And you want to be free?"

Broussard didn't move or say anything. Her face twisted. A frightened expression flashed across her eyes.

"Tell them to be gone, Isabelle!" Tony commanded firmly.

Her face knotted up with obvious anxiety. "I don't have to stand here and take this!" she cried out, in an almost animal-sounding grunt.

"Isabelle!" Tony called out. "Tell them in the name of Jesus to be gone!"

Instead, Broussard spun around in a circle three times, then bolted across the park.

"Isabelle!" Tony jumped to his feet and shouted so loudly that everyone within a block turned in unison to stare at them.

Extreme terror bulged the eyes of the woman with long, wavy black hair. She looked like a woman helplessly falling over a cliff. She clutched the neck of her scooped blouse as if to tear it.

"Please!" Tony yelled again.

"Be gone! Be gone! Be gone!" Broussard yelled, each word louder than the one before. "In the name of Jesus . . . be gone!"

Suddenly she collapsed on the dirt in the middle of the park. Tony looked back toward Price. "Help me get her to the bench," he called out. By the time they reached Isabelle Broussard, a couple of other park regulars were approaching.

"Is she all right?" one called out.

"She'll be fine," Tony assured. "We'll take care of her."

"Should I call 911?" another shouted.

"I'll let you know."

Tony lifted the upper part of Isabelle's body, and Price struggled to carry her feet. They toted her to a park bench. "Tony, do we really know what we're doing?" Price quizzed as they laid her down.

"I don't know, darlin'. . . ."

"What do we do now?"

"Wait until she comes to."

"And then what?"

"Well, we've got to encourage her to trust Christ as Lord and Savior. Anything less than that and she'll be in worse shape than she was before."

It took only a couple of minutes for Isabelle Broussard to come around. But it took over two hours of prayers, tears and dialogue before they felt comfortable about leaving her.

When they finally reached the Winslow house, Price went straight in to take a cold shower. Tony slipped on shorts and a T-shirt and camped out on the deck with a glass of unsweetened iced tea.

He was still sitting there looking down at the valley when Price joined him. "What are you thinking about, Shadowbrook?"

"Just wondering if we did the right thing with Ms. Broussard."

"You're allowed to call her Isabelle, re-member?"

"Whatever. Man, I was wishing Pastor Wayne had been there. Remember his series last fall on spiritual warfare? That deal in the park was not my element. I'm not comfort-able with this occult kind of thing," Tony ad-mitted.

"You aren't? What about me? I was scared spitless most of the time."

"You were? You didn't seem to be."

"Tony, you were the strong one. I was just sitting there praying we wouldn't do any-thing dumb."

"Me? I was just trying to remember all those things I've learned over the years and dismissed as information I'll never need."

"You were wonderful. Sensitive . . . yet firm."

"Wonderful? My mind went blank on half the Bible verses I was trying to remember."

"Well, I thought you had a calm, reasoned presentation. She certainly heard all she needs to hear at this point. Do you think she's ready to make a decision about the Lord?"

"I suppose we'll find out soon enough. She'll either wind up saved . . . or dead."

Price ran her hands through her hair. "Yes . . . but that's true of every one of us, isn't it?"

"How'd we get into this, Dr. Shadowbrook?" he asked. "All we wanted to do is come up here for the summer and write our little book. We're supposed to be observers, not participants, right?"

"It seems like we've had this discussion before," she chided.

"You mean, like last year?"

"And the year before, and the year before, and the year before. Sometimes it seems like The Hidden West Series is just a tool to move us around where God wants us to be."

"But we planned all year on being in Columbia Falls, Montana."

"That doesn't mean the Lord planned on us being there."

Tony laced his hand into Price's. "You

know, I have noticed a pattern over the last five years."

"You mean, that we always get in at least one big wingding argument?"

"No! Here's what I've observed. Our life gets hectic around the house. You're busy teaching . . . the girls are going to college and involved in every activity within a hundred-mile radius . . . I'm in my office plunking away at a novel . . . then finally things get so frenzied that we take off for the summer to get some rest."

"And?"

"By the end of summer we can hardly wait to get home where it's peaceful and relaxed."

"Are you saying the grass is always greener?"

"I'm saying it's our lives . . . you and me together . . . that are chaotic. It doesn't matter where we are, it's always the same. This divinely reckless lifestyle seems to follow us around like a wounded rhino."

"That's a comforting thought."

"The scene with Ms. Broussard was definitely not boring."

"Ms. Broussard? 'Why, you can call me Isabelle, you big hunk of a famous author, you!' " Price mimicked.

Tony held her tight. "Darlin', if that's your best competition, you have absolutely nothing to worry about."

"Maybe not Ms. Broussard . . . but who is my best competition?"

"Well, babe . . . I have to be honest with you. Ever since Sophia Loren married that Italian dude, there just hasn't been a woman in your league at all!"

"Loren's loss is my gain. By the way," she teased, "when was the last time you talked to Sophia?"

"Darlin', I want you to know I'm tellin' the truth. . . . I can't remember the last time she called me."

He winked. Then he kissed her.

Full, on the lips.

Tony grabbed the video camera and headed out the door just as Price shuffled into the kitchen the next morning. "Have you already run and had your shower?"

"Yeah. I saw Vic Lucero. He wants me to videotape this great invention of his."

"At the machine shop?"

"No. We're actually going into the mine."

"He's going to show you his diggings?"

"Apparently."

"It's amazing he trusts you."

"Well, he's afraid this new financial backer he's found might try to steal the design of his invention. He figures if he has a witness and a dated video, it will be some protection."

"Who's the backer?"

"I don't know. Someone from out of town, I suppose. I can't imagine anyone in town having much money for such a project."

"You'll be back by 11:00, won't you?" she asked.

"Eleven?"

"Kit and Kathy both have today off. I'm taking them to lunch at *Del Monico's* in Prescott."

"Sure . . . but I'm not going, am I?"

"Remember your youngest son, Joshua Shadowbrook? The one who's getting married next week?"

"Oh, yeah! . . . the mysterious talk! Right! I'll be home before eleven." He searched the wall for a clock. "What time is it now?"

"7:30."

"No problem. I'll be back no later than 9:30 or 10:00."

Tony parked in front of the Nevada Hotel and hiked around back to Lucero's shack. Victor sat on the porch.

"Jist about gave up on you," he remarked. "Is that the camera?"

"Yep."

"You going inside the tunnels dressed like that?"

Tony stared down at his outfit. "Jeans,

packer boots, T-shirt . . . what am I missing?"

"Well, you cain't wear that J.B. Stetson."

Tony grabbed his cowboy hat. "Eh . . . Resistol."

"And you'll need a hard hat and light." Vic motioned him inside. Tony laid his hat, crown down, on the cleanest shelf he could find. He scrunched on the miner's hat Lucero handed him.

"Where we going, Vic?"

"To my diggin's."

"And how are we going to get there?" Tony prodded.

"Through the tomatoes."

"The what?"

Lucero pointed at a rack of shelves lined with one-gallon tin cans filled with ore samples. The cans all sported faded tomato sauce labels. "I got them at the school cafeteria years ago."

Victor Lucero latched onto a handle on the stack of shelves and swung it open like a big door. He reached inside and flipped an electric switch. Dimly lit twenty-five-watt bulbs spaced about fifty feet apart illuminated a tunnel that went back under the Nevada Hotel basement and straight into the side of the mountain.

"Close that tomato door, then watch your

step," Lucero called back as he led the way. "Stay on the timbers, 'cause some of them puddles is deeper than they look."

Twelve-by-twelve-inch rough-cut timbers ran down the middle of the tunnel floor. As they got back into the mountain Tony's eyes adjusted to the dimness of the tunnel. Water stood along the sides of the beams and dripped down from the rock walls above them. He could feel the sweat in his collar and socks.

"When do we need to drop lower?" Tony called out, trying to stay up with the scampering Vic Lucero.

"Here's the beauty of it, Shadowbrook. I worked this out so the diggin's is completely level. We just keep going deeper into the mountain."

"But that makes this back in United Verde Copper Company claims. I thought you said you were exploring the land between the UVCC and the United Verde Extension?"

"Nope, that's what you said. You were wrong. The Little Daisy Mine stripped all the pickin's clean out of the hill there. The good stuff that is left is too deep into the mountain for open pit. It's right in the heart of the mountain. Good ore, too. I've had it tested. Mainly copper. Ain't no way for one man to salvage that. It takes a good market and a big company to go after the copper. But there's just enough gold and silver to set a man up awfully nice."

The air was getting heavy, warm, and moist as they continued the trek into the mountain. "Where's the blasting box, Vic?"

"The original is probably stuck in somebody's barn or a dump. I built a unit in 1927 and we used it until 1929. Then the mine shut down for a couple of years. When things opened back up, the box and all the engineering papers were missing. Watch your head. . . . I'm shorter than you, and I decided not to dig this any deeper than needed."

The tunnel now was no wider than four feet, and barely six feet high. Water dripped like through a slow sieve as Tony lurched along behind the old man.

"Where does this water end up, Vic?"

"About the six thousand-foot level, I reckon. I've got it drained off to one of the vertical shafts."

"It's awful stuffy back in here, Vic. How long a shift do you work?"

"I run two wheelbarrow loads of good stuff to the outside, then go take a little siesta or walk uptown . . . or somethin'. I can keep that pace up for several days in a row without end."

"Vic, there's no doubt that you're workin'

hard. But you don't seem to be haulin' in the gold or silver. Are you sure this is worth it?"

"I hope to high heavens it's worth it, or I've been wastin' my life away. If I didn't believe in this, I'd be down there in the valley at one of them nursing homes staring at my teeth soaking in a glass jar. I still got my own teeth, did you know that?"

"So you've been working sixty years to rebuild what you had back in 1929?"

"Yes and no." Lucero continued to lead Tony into the heart of the mountain. "Phelps-Dodge held the patent on the blasting box for fifty-two years. That expired in 1981. But explosives have changed. Metals have changed. This new one is built out of titanium. Course, it's just a model. The real one would be a lot bigger."

"How big's the prototype?" Tony longed to stand up straight and stretch his back. Sweat poured from his head and plunged onto his already soaked shirt.

"You'll see, soon enough," Lucero's voice crackled. "We're just about here."

Tony strained at the darkness of the tunnel. "These lights go out and it would be mighty black back here."

"The lights go out and you have to crawl on your knees on those floor beams. It takes two and a half hours to crawl out . . . if you're going the correct direction. If you ain't . . . well . . . your bones will be buried deep, that's for sure."

Lucero led Tony Shadowbrook around a corner to the right and into a large cavern. The ceiling rose up to about ten feet, but the room was about twenty by twenty feet, and braced by railroad ties. A half-dozen twenty-five watt bulbs gave the room an eerie glow. Every stitch of Tony's clothing was soaked. The air was thick. His lungs ached. He had a powerful urge to bolt back out to fresh air.

"Vic, I'm not breathing too well down here. Let's make this video, if the camera isn't fogged up, and hightail it on out."

"Some men ain't made to work in the mines. Let me turn on my motor."

In a wooden box hanging from a beam was a canister style vacuum cleaner. The attachment end of the hose was taped to an expandable plastic clothes dryer hose that ran straight up a wooden ladder that ascended into the dark. "It ain't much, but it sucks down some fresh air for me."

Tony pointed toward the dark hole leading out of the ceiling. "It goes all the way up to daylight?"

"The dryer hose does. Comes out behind the hospital. But I ain't sure that ladder still goes all the way to the surface. It used to in the old days. One bear of a thing to climb, but once in a while the winch would need repairs and we'd have to climb out."

Tony looked around at the set-up. "You've been just chipping out a couple of wheelbarrow loads a day? Where did you say you panned them out?"

"I didn't say I chipped out a couple loads. I wheel 'em right to the back step and haul the tailing into the hotel basement. I get by with a little gold or silver now and then. The pickin's are slow. But that's not the point. This is mainly just a proving ground for my invention. The real money will be this!"

Lucero pulled back a dirty canvas tarp to reveal a football-shaped metal object about three feet long and a foot and a half high. "Here's my baby. . . ."

Tony turned on the camera. "It's kind of dark in here, but I think we can get it all on tape. Go ahead."

A heavy-jacketed electrical cable supplied the machine with power. When Victor punched a red switch on a remote-control box, the front half of the football-shaped blasting box began to spin counterclockwise. Lucero had it running on a narrow steel track right up against the solid rock of the mountain. With a high-pitched screech, it began to grind a hole into the rock. Within ten minutes the machine had buried itself into the rock, filling in behind itself as it went. Now Tony could only see the electric cable running into the rock.

"The big one will run in six to ten feet. But I stop this one at two. Now, it's time to blast."

"What do you mean, blast?"

"I've got explosives in that unit. I can blast, and we're perfectly safe right here. The backfill is packed so tight that the blast will shatter a ten-foot radius of rock. Well, the big one can at full blast. This one is set for around two feet. That will make me two wheelbarrow loads."

"You mean, you blow up the machine each time you use it?"

"Nope . . . it sustains the blast. Actually, the big one will be more durable than this little model . . . although the modifications of the past two weeks should make it work better."

"Do I need to stand back or anything?"

"Nope . . . but listen careful and watch the rock wall."

Victor Lucero pressed several buttons on the remote control. There was a dull "thwump . . ." and the wall cracked like a shattered windshield. Small pieces tumbled to the floor of the cavern.

"Partner . . . that's amazing!"

"You ready to invest?"

"I still don't have the money." Tony tried to get a close-up on the shattered rock. Sweat was rolling off his wrists and across the camera. "Does it eat its way back out?"

"The big one will . . . but with this one I just dig out my two loads of rock and haul it home."

Tony flipped off the video camera. "I'm impressed, Vic, but I really do need a little fresh air."

"Well, sir, I'm not going to let two loads of rock go to waste. I think I'll work a while. Let yourself out and close the tomato door behind you."

"How about this videotape? It belongs to you. You want me to leave it out on the table?"

"Shoot, no. You take it home with you and don't tell anyone you have it. That way, if I get in a pinch and need a witness, I'll have the video."

"You got it, partner. Thanks for the tour . . . but I'm going to get a shower and some dry clothes on."

Lucero shook his head and muttered, "You ought to see it when it's really miserable in here!"

★ ★ ★

Showered, wearing shorts, sandals and T-shirt . . . drinking a Diet Coke in the living room of the Winslow home . . . Tony thought it was the freshest, cleanest air he'd ever breathed. He tried to explain the scene to Price as she hurried in and out of the bedroom, dressing for her luncheon date with the girls.

"What about these copper spur earrings?"

"Stunning!" he replied.

"Good, it's always nice to get an unbiased opinion." She fumbled to stab the earrings into the holes in her ears. "So you don't think you want to become a deep-shaft miner?"

"It was horrible . . . I just knew I would suffocate before I found my way back out."

"Can we use any of that scene in our book?"

"Not until Vic sells his invention. I don't want to jeopardize any deal. But he seemed to think something would happen by next week."

"Lots of things happening next week." Price pulled a small, thick glass bottle out of her travel bag and splashed some perfume behind each ear.

"Whoa," Tony called out, "I believe that stuff is illegal in Arizona."

"Only for old geezers with weak hearts."

"Too bad the girls and Josh are coming over," he challenged.

"It's a good thing. . . ."

The ringing of the telephone drove Tony to the kitchen.

"Hey, Dad . . . it's Josh."

"Where are you, bud?"

"At Rawhide. . . . A couple of guys quit this morning and I had to work after all."

"How about the girls?"

"I thought they'd be there by now. They left about three hours ago. Look, Dad . . . here's the deal. I have ten minutes before I need to get back to the stunts. So maybe you can tell me over the phone."

"Josh, is this the I-have-no-idea-what-I'm-getting-into-getting-married talk?"

Josh howled. "Yeah. . . . Did you hear this same thing from Mark a few years ago?"

"Sure did. I also heard it from my own lips over thirty years ago."

"You did?"

"Yep. You didn't really think you're the first man on earth to feel that way, did you? I can give you an answer in a lot less than ten minutes."

"Oh yeah?"

"First, you are not ready to be a husband because you have little idea what you're getting into. And second . . . you're as ready as you'll ever be. Go for it."

There was silence. Then Josh's voice came on softly. "You're right, Dad. This is it, isn't it? Thanks. Tell Mom hello."

8

From the desk of Priscilla Carey Shadowbrook:

1. Pray for Isabelle Broussard
   (Find out where she lives and take
   her a Bible.)
2. Get Tony to call plumber
   (Fix back bathroom tub drain
   at home!)
3. Decide what to write about Jerome's
   "soiled doves"(Is there any way to
   trace one of the crib district girls
   who married?)
4. Edit Chapter Seven
   (Lead off with "inside the
   mountain" scene?)
5. Pick up Tony's tux on our way
   home Wednesday
   (Check out Metro Mall for
   Dream Blue earrings.)
6. Read "Apache Life in the Black

Hills" (Check to see if Tony's already read it.)

7. Call Mrs. Nathan S. Blake about next Tuesday
(secretary, Yavapai County Historical Society)

8. Pick up Mom, Dad and Aunt Vera (Friday, 10:10 A.M., SouthWest Airlines.)

9. Have the girls drive by Dr. Icing's (Why is his telephone disconnected?)

10. Talk to Barbara Mason about old/new, borrowed/blue
(Not a superstition . . . just a fun tradition.)

The voice was masculine and had a slight New Jersey twang. "Anthony Shadowbrook, please."

Tony tucked the phone between his shoulder and his cheek and searched the refrigerator. "Speaking."

"Is this the Anthony Shadowbrook that writes books?"

"Yes."

"Wow . . . I got right to you! Do you always answer the telephone?"

"Only when it rings."

"I mean . . . I expected you to have a secretary . . . or some staff person answer the phone."

"Sorry to disappoint you."

"Oh . . . that's right!" the man bubbled. "You're on location, working on a new book. I forgot. Your research assistant, Melody, is the one who gave me this number."

"What can I do to help you, sir?"

"My name is Jackson . . . Lance Jackson. I've read all your books. You and Hillerman and Clancy and Grisham . . . do you know those guys?"

"I've met a couple of them, but I don't know them well."

"I figured all you types hung together."

"Writing can be a lonely occupation at times."

"You're telling me! I'm a writer, too. Not that I've got anything published, yet. But one of these days. . . ."

"Can I help you with something, Mr. Jackson?"

"Well, now, here's the situation, Tony. I can call you Tony, can't I?"

"Sure."

"See, I've been meaning to write to you for some time and today I said to myself . . . why put it off? Just phone him. So here I am."

"And . . . ?"

"Oh, I thought I'd help you out by letting you know about the errors in your book."

"Which book is that, Mr. Jackson?"

"*Shotgun Creek,* of course."

"Well, which errors do you wish to point out?"

"The first one is on page nineteen."

"What's the problem?"

"You have your copy open?"

"I remember the text."

"Well, there on the fourteenth line, you say, 'Stevens' carriage. . . .' "

"Yes?"

"You put the apostrophe after the s, but it should be between the n and the s . . . to show possession."

"Mr. Jackson, the people's name was Stevens, remember? Since the noun ends in an s, I believe you put the apostrophe after the s to show possession, but don't add an additional s."

"You do?"

"Yep."

"Oh. Well, how about that? Now the other error is on page 186. There you are talking about Jake's rifle. You mention it being a '73 Winchester, and the cartridge was just forty grains. That's way too light. I've read all about those guns and the bullet actually weighs over one hundred fifty grains. You'll probably want to change that in the second printing."

"Mr. Jackson, thanks for your concern. But what I said was the cartridge had forty grains of black powder. The lead bullet is two hundred grains. I know . . . because the rifle is in my guncase and I often go out and shoot it myself. When you read about a .44-40, that means a .44 caliber bullet, with forty grains of powder."

"It does?"

"Yep. Anything else I can do for you?"

"Eh . . . no, I guess not. Bye, Shadowbrook."

Price scooted into the kitchen and straight to the teapot. "Who was on the phone?"

"A critic."

"Were you polite?"

"I was charming," he grumped. "From now on, you answer the phone."

The bright Arizona sunlight reflected through the front window, warming the room rapidly. Sitting at the laptop, Price slipped off her sweater, tennis shoes and socks, and pulled her hair into a ponytail. She leaned back and extended her arms. She found it a delight for once to have to get up and answer the phone. Any excuse to stretch her legs.

The woman on the phone was in tears.

"Melody, what's wrong?"

"It's my mother!" she sobbed.

"OK honey, what is it?"

"Is a gold wedding band a pagan symbol?"

"A what?"

"You know, is it just a superstitious symbol held over from fortune tellers of the Middle Ages?"

"Your mother told you that?"

"Yeah. She says if we were sincere about our faith we wouldn't have wedding rings. Is that true about the Middle Ages and all?"

"Melody, I have no idea about the origin of the wedding rings. But there is nowhere in the Bible that says not to wear a ring. What's important is what it means to you and Josh, and what it means to the society in which you live."

"It means we're married . . . that's all it means."

"I agree with you on that. Would you like me to talk to your mother again?"

"She's not here. She went over to Dr. Icing's to check out the cake."

"I hope she checks out his phone. I can't get through to him."

"Are you sure it's all right to have the wedding rings?"

"I'm sure." Price nonchalantly twisted the

diamond and gold ring on her finger.

"Thanks, Dr. S."

"You're welcome, honey. Just hang in there this week. We'll be home Wednesday afternoon, and by Saturday night, you'll be a Shadowbrook."

"Sometimes it feels all tingly, like I'm marrying into royalty or something, you know what I mean?"

"The tingly part . . . yes. The royalty part . . . no."

"Kath wants to talk to you."

"Hi, babe . . . what's up?"

"Mother, why is it that Kit gets to walk down the aisle with Mark? I don't think it's fair!"

"What?" Price gasped. "I thought you wanted to walk with Mr. Hollywood."

"He's an egocentric bore! This is a family deal, and I want to walk with family."

"But we just don't have enough brothers. You both can't walk with Mark."

"Why not? Kit could be on one side and I could be on the other."

"Are you serious?"

"Yes!"

"Eh . . . let's talk about it at the rehearsal on Friday night."

"Good, I'll tell Kit that's what we're going to do."

"Tell her we'll talk about it. . . . We haven't decided anything."

"Are you nervous about the wedding, Mother? I think everyone here at the house is coming apart."

"That, my daughter, sounds like a mild understatement."

Tony had his cowboy boots pulled off, his sleeves rolled up on his western print shirt and the shirttail pulled out of the Wranglers as he pounded on the keyboard in front of him. Price, with beaded and fringed T-shirt, waited for the inkjet printer to crank out her edited chapter and contemplated changing from blue jeans to shorts.

"Tony, is it getting warm in here again?"

"Nope . . . the air conditioner's working just fine. I set it lower right after lunch."

"Well, I'm getting warm!"

"Surprise, surprise," he mumbled. "Go take a cold shower."

"I wish we had a swimming pool up here. . . ."

The telephone interrupted her.

"I wish we didn't have a phone," Tony groused. "You want to answer that?"

"It's your turn," she complained. "I got the last one."

"Just let it ring. We're not home."

Price scooted toward the kitchen. "Oh, I'll get it. Another catastrophe with the girls, I presume."

Within two minutes, she was back in the living room.

"Is it for me?" Tony asked.

"It was Paul."

"Well, how's the Best Man handling the week?"

Price rubbed her chin and stared out the front window at the letter "J" made up of white painted rock, above Jerome.

"What is it?" Tony pressed.

"It was kind of strange. Paul said he was calling for Josh, and we were to be at the helicopter pad at the Sedona airport at 5:30."

"5:30 P.M.? This evening?"

"Yes."

"But that's only an hour from now! What's going on?"

"Paul said it was a surprise . . . just be ready for a short helicopter ride."

"A ride to where?"

"I don't know, but we'd better hurry. With traffic down in the valley at this time of the day, it could take us a little while."

"That's it? That's all we know?"

"Oh, you know Josh and Paul. They never know what they are doing three hours in advance."

"Stunts!" Tony blurted out. "They probably have some big stunt thing and want us to see it. I bet it has to do with hot air balloons. They've been launching a lot of them that way lately."

"I don't know why they have to keep it a secret," Price mused.

"Josh knows how you worry. . . ."

"That's nice . . . I can have a massive, quick heart attack when I get there, rather than worrying myself to death slowly."

"Well, come on, darlin'. . . . Let's shut down the laptops and take a break. How about supper at *Dos Hermanas* after the stunt show?"

"That would be nice . . . but it's always kind of crowded and noisy," Price cautioned.

"Good. It will get us ready for going home on Wednesday! It's a zoo down there."

"Should we change? I don't know if we have time to change. Why couldn't they give us more notice? Why didn't Josh call us?"

"Forget changing," Tony insisted. "Grab some lipstick and a windbreaker, in case this place is the boonies. I'm not even going to bother shaving."

"Well, I'm going to put on some earrings at least. How about the gold ones with the wild horses? Do you think they would look appropriate with jeans and boots?"

"I'm sure they'll be stunning."

Tony turned the Jeep Cherokee west at the junction in Cottonwood. With the declining mid-August Arizona sun at their backs, they drove toward Sedona. The early evening light reflected off the red cliffs and rocks ahead of them.

"Whoa . . . that's a dramatic view, Mamma. If the kid has to scare us to death with another stunt, he picked a mighty pretty place."

Price started to giggle. "Do you know what I was thinking about?"

"About our daredevil son?"

"Remember that time when we lived in that little rental in Mesa? The boys were only ten and seven, I think. The girls were about two."

"Was that the 'two-bedroom house with swimming pool'?"

"Yeah, but the ad in the paper didn't happen to mention that the pool was broken, empty, and they had no intention of fixing it. Anyway, I was standing at the kitchen sink, looking out the back window . . . and there goes Josh out on that old wooden diving board. I opened the window and yelled for him to get down before he hurt himself, but he said 'Don't worry, Mom, I know how to dive.' He did a perfect somersault and disappeared out of view. I ran out of the house screaming for Marky to call an ambulance, and there . . . in the bottom of the empty pool . . . was Josh . . . flopped on two mattresses and howling with laughter."

"How did the boys pull their mattresses out of the house without you knowing it?"

"I was trying to learn how to raise very demanding, unidentical twin girls and get my master's at the time. I think I was a little distracted."

"Do you think Melody will ever get him to stop doing stunts?"

"I don't think she'll even try." Price watched the increasingly bright sunlight bounce off and over the red rock and buttes. "I just don't know why, at his age, he has to stage such a drama."

Tony slammed his hand on the steering wheel. "That's it! He's not going to do a stunt. Do you remember Paul and Josh's friend from Flagstaff? B . . . B . . . it starts with a B."

"Bryan?"

"Yeah . . . the helicopter pilot!"

"But he's in Flagstaff. . . . What does that have to do with us?"

"In the summer, he flies one of those Red Rock dinner flights."

"The ones where they fly a couple to the top of the mountain, and provide a private dinner . . . table, linen, crystal . . . prime rib . . . everything?"

"Yeah. I remember Josh said we ought to do that while we're spending the summer up here! I'll bet he's got that deal lined up! I can't believe he'd really do that! And in the middle of wedding hassles and all."

Price pulled down the vanity mirror to check out her hair. "Maybe we should have dressed up a little. I wish Josh had told us what to expect."

"No, darlin' . . . we don't need to dress up. There won't be another soul for fifty miles. That's the fun part about it. It will be just you and me."

"But . . . but . . . what if they take photos, or something?"

"With your ravishing smile? You haven't taken a bad picture since you were a freshman in high school."

She closed the mirror and pushed the sun visor back up. "Just what was wrong with my freshman picture?"

Tony pointed toward the jagged, colored mountains ahead. "This is really great, babe. I've always wanted to do this. Those kids come through when you least expect it, don't they?"

"We haven't made it there yet."

"Hey . . . be sure and act surprised. Let's not spoil their fun."

They parked the car in the lot and walked toward the charter terminal. Paul's smiling face greeted them.

"Mr. and Mrs. S. . . . over here! Come on!" He led them out of the one-story glass and steel waiting room toward the slowly circling rotors of a dark blue helicopter.

"Where's Josh?" Tony asked.

"Oh . . . you know. . . ." Paul stalled. "He, eh . . . is already there. . . . He wanted to get things ready."

Price glanced over at Tony. He mouthed the words, *I told you!*

"You know Bryan, don't you?" Paul shouted and waved toward the pilot.

Both Tony and Price nodded and smiled, but didn't speak. The rotors revolved in a roar. They lifted off smoothly. Soon all of Sedona was within view. Tony was surprised that instead of flying southwest toward Red Rock, they swerved southeast.

Bryan flew low past Cathedral Rock toward Oak Creek, then he turned toward towering Courthouse Rock. Parallel to the sheer cliffs of the red mountain, the helicopter slowly rose until it crested and swooped across the top. A cluster of people gathered at the west side of the flat-top mountain.

Tony looked at Price, then back to the crowd on the mountain. *What is this? What have they got cooked up?*

They left the helicopter on the east side of the mesa. The others seemed to be waiting for them to hike over to the western edge. Bryan departed in a roar and a cloud of red dust.

"Kit and Kathy?" Tony sputtered.

"Barbara?" Price said tentatively.

"Melody and Josh?"

"Cooper? Good grief, Tony . . . Mark and Amanda brought the baby up here!"

Tony and Price repeated in unison. "Pastor Wayne?"

"Mom and Dad!" Josh shouted, "Hey, is this great up here, or what?"

"Joshua Carey Shadowbrook, you've got some explaining to do," his mother lectured.

"All right . . . all right," Josh called out. "Everyone come over here. You've all got it figured out . . . but let me explain." He wore jeans, cowboy boots and a crisp white long-sleeved western shirt. Melody stood at his side, clutching his arm, dressed in a prairie skirt and white lacy blouse with a western yoke. Three white daisies were just behind her right ear, contrasting with her long, dark, straight hair.

"Here's the deal. This morning, a couple of things happened. First, Melody and I finished the last session of premarital counseling with Pastor Wayne. We had a very good, long talk about the wedding service. Then a few minutes later I got a phone call from Hawaii."

"They want Josh and Paul to do stunts for the next Harrison Ford movie!" Melody blurted out.

"I'll explain that in a minute. As all of you know, not everything has been going exactly well as far as wedding plans are concerned."

Melody looked at Price. "Did you know Dr. Icing closed down?"

"Closed?"

"The bank foreclosed last Friday," Barbara reported.

"But . . . what about the deposit?" Price stammered.

"And," Josh continued, ". . . the plumber had to tear up half the backyard this morning to fix the plumbing at the house."

"He did what?" Tony gasped. "The new landscaping?"

"He said the mesquite trees had damaged the sewer pipe and it all had to be replaced. Plus, there were several arguments over the service itself. . . ."

"Why's everyone looking at me?" Barbara Mason protested.

"It was all of us," Kit offered. "Me and Kath have sort of been jerks, haven't we?" Price noticed she wore old jeans, hiking boots and a Daytona 500 T-shirt as she threw her arm around her sister's shoulder.

Wearing a crisp pink blouse, pink shorts, pink earrings, pink tennies and a pink ribbon in her hair, Kath slipped her arm around Kit's waist. "Yeah . . . we're sorry, Josh and Mel. . . . I guess we didn't help things out much."

Price tried not to stare. *Kit and Kathy arm in arm? They haven't posed that way since the Christmas photograph when they were three!*

"So," Josh continued, "we asked Pastor Wayne if we could have the wedding early, with just family present. He said as long as we make serious vows, before God and witnesses. . . ."

"And have a marriage license," Melody added.

". . . that there's no biblical reason not to proceed."

"So," Melody explained, "while we had lunch at Burger King, we came up with this idea. Paul, Bryan and Pastor Wayne helped us put it together. The rest of you were kidnapped, I know. Kim couldn't make a flight, and Brock's committed to the studio until Thursday."

"Are you telling me the wedding is right now . . . right here?" Barbara Mason gasped.

"Yep, Mom . . . that's the way it's going to be!" Melody managed a wide, closed-lip smile.

"So, why tonight?" Tony asked.

"We didn't want anyone to have time to try to talk us out of it," Josh justified. "And . . . the stunt job in Hawaii starts Wednesday. They've agreed to pay for Melody's way too . . . so we'll have a Hawaiian honeymoon."

"But shouldn't we have a reception . . . or something?" Price offered.

"We'll talk about that when we get back from Hawaii, Mom."

"But . . . but . . . what about all the people coming in? Your grandparents are flying home from Texas," Price reasoned.

"Nope. I called them this afternoon. They're going to stay another week."

"Grandma Carey said it sounded terribly romantic," Melody beamed.

"She did? But . . . all the invitations? What will. . . ." Price stammered.

"Hey, we'll call everyone in the next couple of days," Kathy suggested. "Won't we, Kit?"

"Don't worry, Mom and Pop . . . we'll take

care of it." Kit's short, permed hair bounced with every word.

"But . . ." Tony stammered, "this is so . . ."

"Melody's the right one, Dad," Josh insisted. "You told me to do it! And I'm going to. Now, here's the way this thing is going down. Pastor Wayne, you stand over here with your back to the sunset. Paul, you're the best man, so you stand over here."

Melody positioned her mother. "Mom, I want you to be my matron of honor."

"You do?" Barbara Mason gulped.

"Now, Melody and I will stand here, of course," Josh continued. "Mom, you and Dad stand right over there, and you'll have to hold Coop. . . ."

"Now, that's something I can do!" Price took the four-month-old sleeping baby from his mother.

Josh nudged the young parents toward Pastor Wayne. "Mark and Amanda . . . we want you to stand right here . . . and sing 'Wind Beneath My Wings.' I know you don't have your guitars . . . but you two sound really, really good *a capella*."

"How about us?" Kathy asked, nodding at Kit.

"Stand over by Mom and Dad," Josh commanded, then softened. "But first, I want everyone to turn around and look. Look at Kit and Kathy."

Suddenly, the girls dropped their arms down to their sides.

"What?" Kit gasped. "What is it? Have I got dirt on my face?"

"Look at them," Josh repeated. "Mark and I were blessed to have the two prettiest sisters on the face of the earth . . . and then, we both found wives just as beautiful. What are the chances of that happening?"

Tony thought perhaps it was just the setting sun reflecting off the red barren mesa, but he had never seen Kit and Kathy's faces glow like that.

Still holding the baby, Price leaned toward him and whispered, "That kid is one smooth talker . . . just like his old man."

Senior Pastor Robert T. Wayne, D.Min., cleared his throat. "This just might be the most beautifully decorated sanctuary in which I have done a wedding. Let's proceed. Dearly beloved, we are assembled here on the top of this majestic mountain in the presence of Almighty God to join this man and this woman in holy marriage. . . ."

The baby slept.
Mark and Amanda sang.
Pastor Wayne officiated.

Price and Barbara cried.

Commitments, vows, and rings were exchanged.

Tony teared up.

Josh prayed for his wife, his marriage and his family.

Everyone cried.

The groom kissed the bride.

Everyone hugged . . . and laughed. Really laughed.

It was after dark by the time everyone was ferried back to the airport and returned to their homes. Barbara went back to Scottsdale with Kit and Kathy. Paul flew off with Bryan to Flagstaff. Mark, Amanda and little Cooper Jarrett flew back to Tucson. Josh and Melody headed for the bridal suite at the Oak Creek Resort.

And Price and Tony drove back to Jerome.

It was 10:30 by the time they carried their bowls of cold cereal out to the deck, and looked down at the lights of the Verde Valley.

"What a day, Mamma. When life is about over on earth and we decide to pick the ten most memorable days of our lives . . . this will be toward the very top of the list."

"I keep thinking I'll wake up and it will have been a dream. Did our youngest son just get married on top of a mountain?"

"I don't know why we ever thought Josh's wedding would be any different. At least he didn't ask us to sky dive."

"It was beautiful!" she spoke softly. "I stood there and listened to Mark and Amanda sing . . . little Cooper asleep in my arms, you by my side, the girls radiant in the sunset, Josh and Melody pledging their love before the Lord. . . ." She brushed back a few more tears from her eyes. "Life doesn't get any better than that, cowboy!"

"Maybe some things get over-organized . . . some of the wonder is lost," Tony added.

"I think I'll stay up a while and write down that whole wedding scene while it's fresh in my mind. All the relatives will want to hear about it."

"Yeah . . . maybe one of us can use it in a book sometime."

"I don't know, babe, do you think anyone would believe it?"

Tony was reading a copy of the "Arizona Mine Production Statistics for Fiscal Year 1952-53" out on the deck by the time Price made it to the kitchen the next morning.

"I slept in," she called out from the sliding screen door.

"You needed it. Yesterday wore us all out!"

Price grabbed some orange juice out of the fridge, poured a small glassful, tossed two vitamin pills in her mouth, took a big swig and grimaced at the bitter taste. Wearing tennis shoes, grey sweatpants, one of Tony's rodeo T-shirts and a bandanna around her hair, she plodded out to the exercise bike and began to pedal.

"Well, Mamma . . . did we go to a wedding late yesterday afternoon?"

"I woke up wondering if we had just seen it in a movie or something."

Tony lay down his reports and strolled near the stationary bike. He leaned against the deck railing. "I suppose it will take all day trying to cancel everything."

"I'll call the caterers, florist, photographer, sound technician . . . and the others," Price offered. "Kit and Kathy don't have to go to work until this afternoon, so they're going down the guest list. I'll call the immediate family."

"I'm glad Paul took some pictures."

"I hope he got some good ones."

"Josh and Melody have the two most natural smiles in Arizona. The pictures will be dynamite," Tony boasted.

"I meant good pictures of the rest of us.

There are nine of us now, Daddy."

"I suppose we're going to lose all those deposits."

"Yes, but think of all the money you saved."

"Sure . . . what will I do with all of it, anyway?"

"Better put it in the bank. The girls were huddled yesterday, planning their weddings. They won't let you off so easily."

"But they don't even have steady boyfriends."

"Mere detail. Did you hear them mention how cool it would be to get married at the same time?"

"You're kidding? They've sworn for nineteen years that they wanted separate weddings!"

"Well, opinions do seem to change from day to day." Price stopped pedaling and motioned for Tony to hand her a towel. She dried off her forehead and face, then tossed it back to him. "How's everything uptown this morning?"

"Well, the boys at the Ireland Cafe are taking bets on what happens to Gilette on Friday."

"Did you see Victor?"

"Only for a minute. Said he had to meet with his new backer."

"He still didn't tell you who it was?"

"I didn't ask, but it's someone with at least sixty thousand dollars lying around."

"Well, I hope both stories have a printable ending in the next couple weeks. We're almost through with this book."

"We've got plenty of drama this time. . . . We just need a punch line." Tony wandered back into the kitchen as the telephone rang.

He came back out carrying a half-empty coffee cup.

"Guess who that was?"

"Josh?"

"Not hardly. That was none other than T.H. Hampton IV."

"The publisher himself?"

"Calling from Martha's Vineyard."

"Let me guess," Price puffed as she continued to pedal. "He wants us to fly out to New England for a week this fall?"

"He wants to know if we have a title."

"That was my second guess. What did you tell him?"

"I told him we were making good progress and should have an answer for him in two or three weeks."

"He bought that?"

"Well, I also told him that Sedona is beautiful and that he and Mrs. Hampton might enjoy a trip out here sometime."

"He's remarried, you know."

"Oh, yeah . . . you don't forget a gal whose name is Spunky."

"But what I want to know is . . . are we going to have a title by the time we finish this book?"

"Trust me."

Dynamite Vic Lucero, with wide toothy grin and wrinkled eyes squinted in the sun, waved Tony down with both gnarled hands.

"Hop in, Vic, I'm going to get my mail."

"Yes sir, I believe I will . . . and I'm buyin' the coffee and doughnuts today." His smile slanted crooked, but open, like he cached a gold nugget in his left cheek.

"You celebrating?"

"Yep."

"Well, let me guess," Tony grinned back. "You either struck a rich vein, talked some twenty-year-old into marrying you, or got a backer for the blasting box."

"Shadowbrook, you surely know how to deflate a man's pleasure. Me gettin' stuck with the lesser of the three."

"So your new backer came through?"

"Yeah . . . I'm goin' to sign the papers in the morning, and I should be able to draw on the account by Monday."

Tony parked near the post office and both

men walked along the pitted concrete of an empty sidewalk.

"Just how much is he buying?"

"Fifty percent, fair and square. He puts up the money . . . I seen his letter of credit for sixty thousand dollars . . . and I do the work. We split the profits."

"He understands there might not be a profit?"

"Yep. He knows that. It's all in the contract."

After retrieving his mail, Tony joined Lucero on a chipped and peeling green-painted park bench across the street.

"Vic, you got a copy of that contract on you?"

"No, he didn't have it completed. Said it would be ready in the mornin'."

"He wants you to read it and sign it at the same time?"

"I reckon. What difference does that make?"

"Sometimes you don't read things too carefully when you're in a hurry. I never sign a contract on the day I receive it."

"You get contracts much?"

"Every book has a contract. I've read a lot of them."

"Well . . . well," Vic sputtered. "How about if I nabbed me a copy of the contract and had you read it over?"

"I'll be happy to look at it."

"By golly, I'll do that! I'll go find him right now." Lucero stood up as if to leave.

"Vic, let me give you two suggestions. . . . Don't tell this backer you're going to have someone else read it. Second, ask to take another glance at the letter of credit. Don't tell him what you're doing, but remember which bank the letter is from. It never hurts to check things out."

"You saying this fellow might kite me?"

"Unless you've known him for years . . . it never hurts to have it checked out."

"Well, sir . . . you're right! I never thought of that. I'll git that contract and hike on down to your place." He started to walk away, then turned back. "I'm glad you come along, Shadowbrook. Too bad you can't be the backer. I like you. This other fella . . . well, he's a little strange."

Vic shuffled down the sidewalk leaving Tony staring at the Jerome Fire Station.

Tony napped right after lunch.

It wasn't something he had planned. It just seemed to be a good idea at the time. He had finished roughing out Chapter Eight, except for a description of Jerome's galleries and artists. Price had insisted on writing that part herself.

So Tony plopped down on the chaise lounge in a shady spot on the deck with a copy of the *Federal Writer's Project on Arizona's Copper Mining Communities, 1929-1935*. He was asleep by page three.

He was lying in the sun, wringing wet with sweat, when Price poked him awake. "You'll get sunburned out here, Mr. Shadowbrook!"

"What time is it?"

"Wednesday . . . and you've got company."

"What? Who?"

"I believe it's Mr. Victor Lucero, although we haven't been formally introduced."

"Where is he?"

"At the front door. I'm going back to work." She retreated through the sliding glass door.

"Vic, I'm around here!" he hollered.

Lucero shuffled around to the deck. He carried a brown manila envelope in his hand. Tony pulled out a chair in the shade of the umbrella-covered patio table and motioned for Vic to join him.

Dynamite Vic rubbed his unshaven chin. "You're sweatin' like a stuck pig, Shadowbrook. I didn't know writin' them books was such hard work."

"Oh, well, some of it's tougher than others."

"Say . . . that daughter of yours is a purdy thing."

"Daughter?"

"The one that met me at the door. You got two daughters, don't ya? Is that one married?"

Tony laughed. "I've got two daughters, Vic . . . but they're at home in Scottsdale. That was my wife at the door."

"Your wife? Well, I'll be . . . a fine, handsome woman. Never figured you for that type, Shadowbrook."

"What type's that?"

"You know . . . robbin' the crib like that."

"It keeps a man young," Tony laughed.

"Well, my lucky day is just around the corner. I got a copy of that contract. Not that Gilette was real tickled to give it to me."

"Gilette?"

"Yes, sir. . . ." Vic leaned close. His breath smelled of sweet tobacco. "Don't that beat all?"

"He's a strange one, Vic."

"But he wants to spend some money before Friday. I figure it might as well be my blastin' box."

"This guy who's been living in his truck and trying to peddle phony mining stock to tourists has sixty thousand in the bank? Doesn't that seem a little odd?" Tony challenged.

"Look, up here you learn quick that a person can do whatever they want, and live however they like. When ol' man Barton died in the UV Apartments they found over one hundred thousand dollars under his mattress. I guess it helped him to sleep easier at night."

"When are you planning to sign this?"

"Tomorrow mornin' at 9:00 A.M. right there at the parking lot next to the old sliding jail."

"I've been meaning to ask you, Vic. Were you around town when the jail tipped over and slid down the hill?"

"Around town?" Again Vic leaned close to Tony. "I was the one who set off the blast in the mine that toppled her. Jist don't you tell 'em that."

"You got it, partner." Tony glanced down at six pages of small print. "Vic, how about letting me make a copy of this? I'll read it over this afternoon, then you and I can meet at the Ireland Cafe in the morning about 7:00 and talk about it."

"Sounds good to me."

"Has Gilette seen your machine work?"

"Yep . . . I took him down into the shaft

yesterday. Now there's two of you who's seen my diggin's. He got real excited about the prospects. Said he knew some Canadian company up at Goldfield, Nevada, that would be interested in bidding on it. Shoot, I didn't even know there was any mining left up in Goldfield."

"Did you see that letter of credit again?"

"It was from Clark County Savings and Loan."

"In Nevada?"

"Yep."

The conversation bounced from big mining companies to eccentric prospectors, understanding contracts and marrying younger women. Finally, Tony copied the contract using the fax machine and gave the original back to Lucero. Vic declined when Tony offered to give him a ride back to town.

By 5:00, Tony's copy of the contract had been heavily marked, and a phone call had been made to Martin Lawington.

Price scooted out on the deck carrying two glasses of iced tea. "Need a break, counselor?"

"Counselor?"

"You're representing Vic Lucero in this deal, aren't you? Maybe you should collect legal fees!"

"This contract is a crock. There are a dozen different conditions that favor Gilette. Where did he get this thing? Did he come to town with a contract in his back pocket?"

"Are you going to tell Vic not to sign?"

"I don't know. Vic sees this as his last big hurrah. He's got to get the backing soon. He knows he doesn't have many years left."

"What makes an eighty-six-year-old man push himself like this?"

"Well, darlin' . . . Vic's from the old prospector school. And I think he wants to walk into the Ireland Cafe just one time in his life and say, 'Boys, I struck her rich today. Let's celebrate, I'm buyin'.' "

"That's his life's goal?"

"That would be my guess."

"What happens to him after that?"

"Then he can finally move on."

Price sat down next to Tony. "A man would work hard for eighty-some years just for that?"

"Many a man's worked for a whole lot less."

"Well, Mr. Contract Attorney, what are the weak parts of the deal?"

"Here's one. . . . Gilette becomes a partner not only in this invention, but with any others Lucero may have in the future . . . or any he had in the past."

"Is that a real problem?"

"What if the master machinist, Mr. Lucero, invented a few helpful items back in the old days that he wasn't properly compensated for? If someone pressured Phelps-Dodge to settle up, Gilette would get half the money."

"That obnoxious man with the tombstone in his pickup wrote a contract like that?"

"Kind of has the feel of a setup, doesn't it?"

"What else did you find?"

"If Vic needs over sixty thousand dollars, additional money will be loaned in relationship to percentage of the partnership."

"So Gilette could gain total control of the inventions?"

"Exactly."

"Why does a man who claims he's going to be dead by Friday want to gain control of anything?"

"And here's another thing . . . it's sort of a moral turpitude clause. If either party is found guilty of deception, fraud, swindle, or any felonious crime punishable by law, ownership of the entire partnership reverts to the other party."

"Any other crime . . . ?" Price questioned. "You mean, if Vic gets a drunk and disorderly, then Gilette gets everything?"

"Only if he's convicted of a felony. But here's another strange feature. This contract will hold true for all heirs and assigns, and Gilette lists his brother, Layton, as heir."

"You said he was an only child."

"That's what Marty told me. This is crazy. Vic even has to agree to place a flower wreath on Gilette's tombstone every Memorial Day. There's something way wrong in all this . . . but it's going to be mighty hard for Vic to turn the money down. I'm going to try to get him to stall until later in the day tomorrow. Lawington wouldn't be able to reach Clark County Savings and Loan until 9:00 A.M. tomorrow. At the least, I'd like to know if that letter of credit is any good or not. That's about the only thing that might convince Vic not to go through with the deal."

Tony jogged by Vic's place during his morning run, but no one was at home.

He sat in the Ireland Cafe from 6:45 A.M. until 8:15, but Lucero didn't show up.

He checked out the machine shop, and walked the streets and alleys until noon. Neither Gilette nor Lucero had been seen all morning.

Price was peeling potatoes at the sink when he returned to the house.

"What happened? You've been gone all morning."

"I can't find Vic or Gilette."

"So you didn't give him your opinion on that contract?"

Tony stretched his shoulders and back. "I'm getting too involved in this deal. Maybe I ought to just sit at home and write."

"You did everything you could. Vic will have to live with whatever deal he makes with Gilette."

"But there's something grinding at me about this."

"Kind of like the Holy Spirit shoving you along?" Price asked.

"Perhaps. . . . It's just that I don't feel like a detached observer. Characters like Gilette make me mad."

"Good. . . . Why don't you go in there and start writing Chapter Nine? . . . A little fury might just be the zing that we need."

"I will, as soon as I call that bank in Las Vegas."

Clark County Savings and Loan would not give out any information about Layton . . . or Clayton V. Gilette. Tony stormed through the rest of the afternoon splitting his time between driving uptown to look for Lucero . . . and pounding the keyboard of his laptop.

It was after midnight, Friday, August fifteenth, when he finally went to sleep. He woke up about 2:30 A.M. and tried to read. He was out for a morning run at 5:00 A.M. The first thing Tony noticed different in the streets of Jerome was that Clayton V. Gilette's truck was parked at the Y where Main Street swings back down to Hull Avenue. The tombstone was standing straight up so everyone who drove by could read it.

The second thing he noticed was a long span of bright yellow police tape stretched around Vic Lucero's shack at the back of the Nevada Hotel.

"Crime scene tape?" Tony blurted out, as he stopped jogging in the middle of the street and marched toward the plastic barricade.

9

From the desk of Priscilla Carey Shadowbrook:

1. Go with Tony to Prescott
   (Visit Vic Lucero at the Yavapai County Jail.)
2. Decide what to do with wedding cake
   (Call Rescue Mission or attorney?)
3. Finish restaurant section
   (Do we really need to eat at the Slide On Inn?)
4. Add section to Chapter Eight
   (Jerome from Courthouse Butte, minus wedding!)
5. Help Tony with correspondence
   (Talk him into individually printed form letters!)
6. Faculty meeting, Thursday, 10:00 A.M.
   (Meet Dr. Calandria, new

department head.)

7. Write to Josh and Melody
   (Call Barbara Mason for the kids'
   Hawaii address.)
8. Friday, take Kit shopping for
   dresses
   (What is going on here???)
9. Look for house gift for Winslows
   (Maybe the Southwest Galeria
   in Oak Creek Village?)
10. Check on Isabelle Broussard
    (Haven't seen her since last
    Wednesday.)

"This ain't good, Shadowbrook!"

The visitation room at the Yavapai County Jail was solid concrete and steel. A windowed door and two video cameras were the only link to the outside world. A six-foot metal table was bolted to the grey painted concrete floor. There was a single metal chair on each side of the table. They, too, were bolted to the floor.

"Vic, I came over three times during the weekend but they wouldn't let me see you," Tony explained.

"Yeah, they ain't real friendly to murderers. You didn't pack me in any sugar doughnuts, did you?"

"Actually, I did. They won't let me give them to you. They're watching the monitor right now. They said if I hand you anything, the visit is immediately over and they'll strip search both of us."

"Thanks for thinking of me. I don't know how I got into this fix, Shadowbrook, I surely don't."

Tony tried not to look up toward the video camera. He stared into Lucero's troubled brown eyes instead. His thin grey hair was neatly combed and he was clean-shaven for the first time all summer. The bright orange short-sleeved coveralls hung three sizes too big.

"Tell me what you remember, Vic."

"Well . . . like I told the police . . . I only remember a little bit about Thursday morning, and nothing about Thursday night. Anyway . . . I was woke up early Thursday by Gilette knockin' on the door. He says he's been thinkin' it over and is willing to up the ante with some cash. He flashes a roll of them new Ben Franklin hundreds. But he wants to see another demonstration. Well, I get my boots on and we go right back into the cave. Shoot, I plum forgot about meetin' you at the cafe. We must have been back in there for two hours.

"When we get out, we're sweating like a

couple skunks in a steam bath, but he's dancin' a jig 'cause this is going to make us both rich. While I change into some dry duds he goes out and gets us something cold to drink to celebrate.

"He brings back three big old bottles of champagne. Now, I don't drink often anymore . . . but this does seem like a time to whoop it up. Before long my head's gettin' kind of light and he says we ought to sign them contracts before we both pass out.

"Well, we signed them papers and he plopped down that wad of bills, and we commenced to drink."

"Did you count the bills?"

"I didn't reckon it was polite. I think we drunk a couple of bottles of that stuff and I was gettin' sleepy. Gilette says he's going to take my papers and drawin's uptown and photocopy them. Since he's a partner, he wanted a set of plans himself."

"What did you tell him?"

"I told him that wasn't part of the deal. All he bought was half the profits after it's sold."

"What did he do?"

"He said I better read the contract better, then grabbed my schematic drawin's and headed out the door."

"What did you do then, Vic?"

"I grabbed my .45, I did, and took chase. I

caught up with him about halfway across the mountain to the sliding jail."

"I presume you had a little argument? You didn't threaten to kill him, did you?"

"Yes, sir . . . I did. Them papers is my life. You know that. I've been workin' on them over sixty years."

"Were there folks around who heard you threaten him?"

"Shoot . . . tourists is standin' up on that sidewalk ever' day and you know it. Anyway, we had a pretty good screamin' match, but I got my papers back."

"And then?"

"I went back and ripped up that contract."

"How about the wad of bills?"

"It turned out to be one hundred dollar bill and the rest was only ones. I was goin' to throw it out the door, but figured some kid would spot it and tumble down the mountain trying to retrieve it."

"So you stayed in your place all Thursday afternoon?"

"Yep. I was so mad I drank that third bottle of champagne. Must have passed out on the cot. Well, the next thing I know one cop is shining a light in my eyes, and another pointing a gun at my head. They had the tomato door open and wanted to know what was back there. I didn't figure I had anything to hide at that point, so I took 'em."

"What was there?"

"Back in the big room, they found Gilette's cap. It was lying in the dirt, had a hole shot in it, so they said I was under arrest. I've been here ever since, talking to everyone in the world except the governor."

"Well, let me give you the story that is circulating on the outside," Tony began. "Witnesses say you chased Gilette down Thursday with a gun around 2:00 P.M. They didn't call the cops because they figured Gilette would. There were two people who were on the street Friday morning about 2:30 A.M. The bars had just closed and they heard an argument down at the sliding jail. It was a dark night but both of them claim to have seen you and Gilette down there."

"Me? I was passed out in my cabin."

"Well, someone was wearing an old khaki hat and shirt, and waving a gun and screaming. The two witnesses admit to having had a drink or two themselves, but they both claim they saw you . . . that is, the one in khaki . . . shoot Gilette in the back of the head. One of 'em went to call the cops while the other watched you drag Gilette over to your cabin."

"Me drag Gilette? Them witnesses have a fanciful idea of my strength."

"When the police arrived they found a champagne bottle in your hand, the .45 lying on the bed and the tomato door open. Then, they claim, you led them back to the diggings. That is where they saw evidence of a body being dragged across the ground, and Gilette's bloody cap. They said you won't tell them which shaft you shoved the body into."

"I didn't do it, Shadowbrook. I can get madder than Hades, but I could never shoot any man, let alone an unarmed one, in the back of the head. No sir . . . that ain't the code. I would never do that. Not even drunk."

"I believe you, Vic. But it doesn't look good. I'm going to look around and see what I can find out. Have they appointed a public defender for you?"

"Yeah . . . some twenty-five-year-old girl fresh out of law school. Cain't trust a lawyer that giggles!"

"Is she purdy?"

A smile and a blush broke across the old man's face. "As purdy as a two-ounce nugget in the bottom of a pan of black sand!"

"Well, I'm glad something is going good for you. If they'll let me snoop around, I want to see if they found that wad of bills . . . and the torn-up contract."

"Forget them. Just retrieve my schematics and my machine. Take 'em home with you and keep 'em until we get this settled. At least, if I did kill Gilette, he cain't steal the plans or my machine, can he?"

"That's true. . . . Here comes the guard. I guess my time's up. Vic, I'll do what I can for you."

The blue uniformed jailer tapped Tony on the shoulder as Victor blurted out, "And next time smuggle me some of Paul's sugar doughnuts! The ones they have around here taste like used socks!"

Tony spent the entire trip from Prescott back to Jerome reporting on what he learned from Victor Lucero.

"Well, I did a little nosing around in the sheriff's office while I was waiting for you," Price announced.

"What did you find out?"

"The rumor around the office is they have enough evidence to take Victor to trial, even if they can't recover the body. They say there are so many deep vertical shafts in that area they hardly know where to begin. Most all of them are filled with water. If the body sank, it would be almost impossible to ever find."

"But they have to search for the body, don't they?"

"Apparently not."

"Could they explain how an eighty-six-year-old man could drag a one hundred seventy-pound man over one hundred yards across the mountain side, and then another mile or two into the heart of the mountain?"

"Adrenalin."

"Are you serious?"

"They say when a man kills someone it's sometimes a rush that gives you temporary strength."

"They actually said that?" Tony pressed.

"Yes, they did."

"So they're sure they got their man?"

"So it seems."

"Well, they're wrong."

"Tony, as much as you like Vic, he does admit to being drunk and threatening Gilette."

"But he wouldn't shoot a man in the back of the head. It goes against the grain of everything he stands for."

"You sound like one of your westerns."

"What's that suppose to mean?" he snapped.

"Relax, dear . . . I'm on your side. Remember?"

"Right . . . sorry . . . it's just that this is starting to snowball on Vic and I'm not convinced he committed murder. I wonder what kind of evidence they have."

"I did get to look at the list of items they've removed from Mr. Lucero's place."

"You did? Wasn't that classified?"

"That sergeant was such a sweetheart!" she purred.

"A sweetheart? You flirted with him?"

"Oh, just a wink and a wiggle. . . . It wasn't much."

Tony pulled the rig off the road and slammed on the brakes. "You did what!" he shouted.

"Oh, my . . . there is a little fire left in the old man, isn't there? Relax . . . I was teasing you."

"You were?"

"Yes. I didn't think you'd actually believe that line. What I did was get him talking about his favorite western writer."

"Anyone I know?"

"I had to promise to bring him some autographed Anthony Shadowbrooks. While we were talking books, I glanced over his shoulder and read the list of items taken from Lucero's."

"Are you sure that's all you did?" he demanded. Tony pulled the Cherokee back onto the highway and continued toward Jerome.

"Do you want to rant and rave, or do you

want to know what was on the list?"

"You memorized the list?"

"No . . . but ask me what you're looking for, and I can tell you if it was on the list or not."

"Money . . . did they bring any money?"

"I believe the figure was $11.26."

"No one-hundred-dollar bill and a roll of ones?"

"It was less than twelve dollars."

"How about papers? Any charts, graphs, drawings?"

"No."

"Torn-up contract?"

"No papers were mentioned at all."

"How about his blasting box? It was back where they found the hat. Did they haul it out?"

"Not according to that report."

"All right! They're still there! Good work, darlin'!"

"Then I'm forgiven?"

Tony glanced over at her and then back to the road. "For what?"

"For teasing a very uptight Tony Shadowbrook?"

"Oh, yeah . . . sure . . . no big deal. Sorry I got a little testy."

"Testy? You were close to jealous rage."

"I was not."

"You were, too."

"Nope."

"Yep."

"OK," he admitted. "So I was about to explode. You shouldn't tease me like that."

"I know. But sometimes . . . it sort of feels good to find out you're still that wildly jealous over me. Do you know what I mean?"

Tony was silent for several miles.

"Yeah," he finally replied softly, "I know what you mean."

It was after 1:00 P.M. by the time they got back from Prescott. Price warmed up some leftover Calabacetas Especial while Tony paced the kitchen.

"I've got to get into Vic's place, and they have the police barrier all around it."

"What will you be looking for?"

"If I can retrieve the machine or the plans or the torn contract, it would help establish Vic's story."

"But it's against the law to cross that line, isn't it?"

"Yeah . . . and unless I'm his attorney they won't let me in there. There's got to be a way!"

"You mean, there's got to be a legal way. . . ." she corrected.

"But I can't cross the . . . wait . . . wait a minute! I've got it! That will work!"

"You figured out a way to search Vic's cabin?"

"Yeah."

"Is it legal?"

"I think so."

"What do you mean, you think so? What do you plan on doing?"

"I'd better not say."

"Why?"

"Just in case it's not legal."

"Tony, what are you going to do?"

"I'm going to find a dynamic, dramatic way to end our book, that's what!"

"Are you starting to live like your heroes, Shadowbrook?"

"Did I ever tell you about the time me and Stuart Brannon held off fifty well-armed banditos down on the border?"

"Oh, brother . . . like father, like son." Price brushed her hair back. "I don't think I like this thing you're planning. Am I going to need bail money?"

Tony spent the afternoon pounding away at the laptop, working on the opening of Chapter Nine. Price kept her appointed rounds visiting each eating establishment in the area. She made it back to the house a little after six.

"We are not having dinner!" she announced as she burst through the front door.

"Supper," Tony corrected.

"Yeah, we're not having that either. I've been eating samples all afternoon," she groaned. "Maybe if I rode the exercise bike all night . . . for the next three days. . . ."

"Well, if I were home, I could eat a four-foot wedding cake. I got a call from Kathy."

"What's the latest?" Price pulled off a blue silk scarf and fanned herself with the front page section of *The Wall Street Journal*.

"Dr. Icing showed up again and demanded his money . . . in cash!"

"What did Kathy tell him?"

"Just what Mel said. She told him to contact our attorney, Wade Jefferson, and to please remove the cake from our premises. If it was not removed by 5:00 P.M. it would be disposed of in any way we chose."

"And what did Dr. Icing say?"

"Kath said she'd rather not repeat the exact words, but needless to say he was not a happy camper."

"The whole thing is crazy. He was not supposed to proceed until I called. He closed up shop and went out of business."

"With my three hundred dollar deposit

290

. . . ," Tony added.

"Then he shows up at 8:00 P.M. Saturday, anyway."

"Four hours after the wedding was to take place. . . ."

"And," Price bemoaned, "delivers a cake in the shape of a giant cowboy hat and demands the rest of his money."

"In cash," Tony added.

"The man's a loony. The wrong cake, four hours late, after going out of business."

"Kath said he finally said he would split the costs and we'd only have to give him four hundred fifty dollars more."

"So . . . what was your advice to Kathy?"

"I told her to take a picture of the cake, freeze a small portion, and call the Rescue Mission to come get the rest."

"They'll have a nice dessert on South Central tonight."

"How did we ever get lined up with someone called Dr. Icing, anyway?"

"Gloria Reimers said he did a wonderful job with Pepe's birthday cake," Price reported.

"They buy a birthday cake for their dog?"

"I guess they have a little party each year and give Pepe gifts."

"That's weird . . . really weird."

"Anyway, Gloria said this Dr. Icing fellow

was engaged to Irv's first wife's daughter . . . and that he needed the business. . . ."

Tony threw up his hands. "Oh, well . . . that explains it."

Price glanced down at his computer screen. "What page are you on?"

"Two hundred fifty-five."

"Are we aiming for three hundred again?"

"Yep."

"I think I'm ready to bid a fond farewell to Jerome."

"The professor is missing her classroom?"

"Yes. You know I love to teach. How about you, Anthony Shadowbrook? Are you ready to ride the high line with your slightly shady, but thoroughly straight-shooting heroes?"

"It will be nice to get back to fiction. I wish I could clear up this deal with Victor Lucero first."

"Have you executed your nefarious endeavors?"

"Whoa . . . it's tough being married to a Ph.D.!"

"Oh . . . I wouldn't know. . . ." she teased. "My husband majored in agriculture."

"Scientific Farm Animal Production."

"Whatever. You didn't answer my question."

"I'm going down to look at Vic's cabin

about daybreak tomorrow. Town's mighty quiet then, and there's no reason to have to do it all in the dark. That makes it look like criminal intent."

"I don't know why you just can't go to the police and have them search."

"Because I promised Vic I'd do it myself."

"And everyone knows a Tony Shadowbrook promise is as good as gold."

"Or, at least, as good as silver and copper."

Jerome's late summer night was turning grey in the east above the Mogollon Rim when Tony left the house. He wore his normal early morning running ensemble: black shorts, black T-shirt, running shoes, and thin white cotton "roping" gloves. He carried a small black flashlight in his left hand. The usually tough climb up the "Company Road" to the highway went by quickly. Even the grueling grade up the paved highway and the hairpin turn at the old Crist-Sahlor house seemed manageable.

By the time Tony reached the front of the abandoned Nevada Hotel, he no longer needed the flashlight. With no one in sight, he tried the front and side doors of the boarded up hotel. Both were locked.

He knew that Vic's place in the back was still cordoned off with yellow crime-scene tape, so he avoided even going in that direction. Instead, he checked the boarded-up basement windows on the south side of the building.

Squatters have lived in this building from time to time. . . . They had to get in somehow.

The unpainted plywood that covered the windows was so old that it was beginning to separate and curl in places, but all seemed secure. The slope of the hill made the furthest piece to the east shoulder-high. It was held in place by a one-inch bolt and a rusted hex nut.

In spite of the seeming security, Tony twisted the nut. The entire bolt pulled easily from the concrete wall. The plywood swung away from the building at the bottom, revealing a large window with all the glass broken out.

So, here's the front door! There had to be some way.

Tony laid the bolt on the windowsill and struggled to pull himself up into the room, which turned out to be the basement of the old hotel. He carefully repositioned the plywood cover, then flipped on his flashlight to examine the semi-dark room. The otherwise barren, cracked, concrete room was three-quarters filled, almost to the ceiling, with neatly piled rocks and dirt.

This is actually Vic's tailings pile, but anyone looking in here would assume this filled up when the building shifted during the mine explosions of the 1920s.

The room smelled like a fairly dry cave. He brushed back cobwebs as he hiked around the dirt to the green door in the back of the room. He could feel his shoes grind dirt into the concrete floor. After the uphill run, and in a room with absolutely no ventilation, Tony sweated profusely.

The wide green wooden door with opaque glass at the top sported an old brass deadbolt.

"Oh, great. . . ." Tony mumbled. "It's keyed on both sides. I figured it for a throw lock on the inside."

He tugged and pounded with white-gloved hands for a few moments, then stepped back and examined the whole door.

Well, Shadowbrook . . . maybe you just aren't supposed to be here. You didn't even bring a pin to try to pick the lock.

He searched the floor for a wire to use on the lock, but found only a slightly bent, galvanized sixteen-penny nail.

"End of the line, sport, . . ." he grumbled, "unless those hinge pins kept from rusting even after sixty years of neglect."

To Tony's amazement, the bottom and

middle hinge pins slipped straight out. But the top one was jammed tight. He searched the rock pile and found a piece of quartz about the size of his fist to use for a hammer. Using the nail for a punch, he drove the hinge pin out of its socket. Tony pried open the door into Vic Lucero's shack.

There's no way to close that door while I'm in the tunnel . . . so I'll just have to trust no one comes in this early in the morning.

Lucero's room was just as messy as before. The table was cluttered . . . the bunk unmade . . . the shelves crammed with ore samples and tools.

Vic said the money would be on the table, on top of the White Owl cigar box. Well, the box is here. But the money's gone. Somehow, that doesn't surprise me.

There were no papers scattered in the dirt and dried mud of the floor of the room, and the shallow, long drawer that Lucero said contained his calculations, schematics and drawings was empty.

Well, Vic, someone ripped off your paperwork. But who knew what you had here? If Gilette and me are the only two you told . . . and Gilette's at the bottom of a mine shaft . . . who's got your papers?

Tony pulled open the tomato door and flipped on the lights in the tunnel. *If I'm go-*

*ing to be caught back here, it might as well be
with the lights on.* He pulled the door shut behind him and hiked into the mountain.

It seemed to be further and hotter than the
previous jaunt. Sweat rolled off his body and
splashed to the tunnel floor as rapidly as the
water dripped off the ceiling.

When he finally reached Vic's diggings, he
noticed that several footprint casts had been
made by the sheriff's investigators. He stayed
on the floor beams, trying not to add his own
prints to the others.

The second thing he noticed was that the
Lucero Blasting Box had been removed. The
thick coaxial electric cable had been sawn in
two.

*Well, Victor . . . someone knew what he was
after.*

Tony flashed his light over the entire underground room, looking for anything the
police might have missed.

Gasping for breath, Tony flipped on the
switch in the vacuum. He gulped the fresh air
pumped in from the mountainside straight
above, then pulled off his running shoes.

*Sock prints are harder to trace than shoe prints
. . . so I've heard.*

He hiked across the floor of the room in
stocking feet, avoiding existing tracks. At
least six lateral tunnels branched off from the

room. Three of them revealed, in addition, the tops of vertical shafts.

Tony tossed a pebble into one shaft and counted slowly. He reached nine before he heard a distant water splash. In the other two holes he couldn't hear the pebble hit at all.

I don't blame them for not wanting to search for a body!

Tony hiked back for his shoes and turned off the vacuum air pump. He flashed the light straight up the vertical shaft that carried the fresh air hose to the surface.

Vic said he didn't think that the ladder still went all the way up. But what if it did?

Staring up the black hole that was illuminated by the narrow beam of his little flashlight, Tony spotted something red and green, just a tiny speck caught on a rung of the wooden ladder.

That shouldn't be there.

He could reach the bottom rung with both hands extended. He held the flashlight in his mouth like a fat peppermint stick and pulled himself up the ladder.

You're too old for this, Shadowbrook! Too weak.

There were no rungs for his feet, so he pulled himself up by his arms a couple more steps. His muscles burned. The flashlight, still in his mouth, pointed at the colored object only one rung above him.

That's part of the electrical coaxial cable! Someone . . . someone strong . . . carried the blasting box right up this ladder! And he put his hand over on that muddy wall to brace himself. Tony stared at the indented print of a left hand.

I don't remember Clayton wearing a ring. But he's left its outline in the mud. One thing's for sure, he's in better shape than I am. . . .

Tony dropped to the cave floor below. His arm muscles throbbed. He retreated to the vacuum pump and sucked up some more fresh air.

Well, Vic . . . I don't know if you killed Gilette or not . . . but someone ripped off your machine, and they carried it up that shaft.

Tony was just closing the tomato door inside Lucero's shack when he heard voices outside the back door.

"Fellas, let's take down the tape and double check inside!" a deep voice commanded.

Oh, great! I am going to need that bail money!
He scampered up the steps and jammed the basement door back on the hinges just as someone entered the shack. The bottom two pins slipped quietly back into the hinge, but the top one wouldn't go without banging. Tony laid it in the dirt pile and slinked over

to the broken window.

If they're in the back . . . they won't see me. If they're along this side . . . I don't even want to think about it!

Tony eased himself down to the ground. No one was in sight. He shoved the bolt back in its concrete socket and jogged around to the front of the hotel where two sheriff's cars were parked. He trotted by the front of the hotel intending to head up the street toward Lower Park.

"Hey, you . . . stop!" a voice called from beside the building.

Tony's heart sank. A uniformed deputy sheriff waved at him.

"Yes?"

"Say . . . aren't you Anthony Shadowbrook? I didn't get to talk to you much yesterday over at the jail, but that wife of yours surely seemed friendly."

Tony walked over next to the officer and held out his hand. "Are you the sergeant who likes my books?"

"Yes, sir. And she promised me some autographed copies. Boy, you're drippin' like a mineshaft, Shadowbrook!"

"It's mighty tough running up this hill," Tony explained. "I'll bring you those books next time I go see Vic."

"You and the old man friends?"

"We drank coffee and swapped stories all summer."

"I suppose you don't think he killed that crazy Gilette?"

"I have serious doubts."

"Well, normally I would, too. But every time there's gold or silver mining involved, folks do the stupidest things. It drives 'em mad. That's my theory. I've seen it before. You'd be shocked at the kinds of things otherwise-sensible folks end up doing."

"I'm sure I would. Say . . ." Tony asked, "Vic liked to tinker with inventions, and he was worried about some drawings he had in a drawer in his place. Would it be all right if I stepped in and got the drawings so I could take them to him?"

"He's arrested for murder and he's worried about drawings?"

"I suppose it's that gold fever thing you mentioned," Tony offered.

"No problem. We're all through here. We just came over to take down the barricade. You can look around all you want."

Tony's head felt light. *You mean if I had waited, I could have just walked in the front door?*

"Tell Lucero I'm boarding up this door only to keep the tourists from ripping everything off. But if you or the old man's lawyer need to come in, just pull down these braces."

"You're not going to search for the body?"

"I'm leaving that up to the DA. We'd have to bring in a search team from South Dakota if we did. None of us wants to go down there. Now, what was it you were looking for?"

"Eh . . . he said there were some papers in a drawer."

"The drawer under that shop bench?"

"Yes, that's the one."

"It's empty," the sergeant reported. "I came in the next morning after the murder and helped them search. Here's a room that is as cluttered as a rat's nest and he leaves a whole drawer empty. Maybe those papers were some other place?"

"That could be." Tony stepped back out the doorway. "I'll check with Vic next time I see him."

"And don't forget my books."

"You got it, partner!" Tony hiked back to the street and continued his run up Hull Avenue.

Out on the chaise lounge on the deck, even the eighty-eight degree weather felt comfortable. A slight breeze tumbled down the mountain as Tony related the morning's story to Price, who sat in the shade of the big umbrella.

"So . . . Mr. Amateur Detective . . . where does this lead?"

"Someone could have stolen the machine and the papers . . ."

"And the money," she added.

" . . . during the afternoon Vic passed out. But there wouldn't have been any reason to take it up that shaft."

"So you figure someone snuck it at night?"

"Someone strong. That's a bear of a climb carrying a hundred-and-fifty-pound machine. But Vic has been so secretive . . . not more than two people on earth knew what he was up to . . . I think."

"What are your plans?" she asked.

"A long, cold shower."

Price raised her eyebrows. "You, too?"

"Hey . . . you didn't use all the cold water, did you?"

Tony emerged in jeans and T-shirt still drying his hair with a large brown towel.

"You were in there a long time," Price challenged.

"I was a grimy mess. I don't know how they did it in the old days . . . working eight-, ten-, twelve-hour shifts down in the mines."

"Some still do."

"They're better men than I am. After fifteen minutes I'm running for fresh air and wide-open spaces."

"Yes, that's about the average length of time you like to spend in big cities."

"I want to see the skies, and the trees . . . the sage and mesquite . . . the cactus and greasewood . . . the coyotes and the hawks . . . hear the creak of a wagon wheel . . . smell the new leather. . . ."

"Oh, brother," she sighed. "I'll be happy when you get back to writing your beloved westerns."

"Me, too."

"You had a phone call," she announced as Tony ran a black comb through his dark-brown-and-grey streaked hair.

"Oh?"

"It was your old buddy, Terry Davidian."

"What did he want?"

She mimicked in a deep voice, "Be a real sweetheart, Pricy-girl, and tell Tone that T.D. called."

"Pricy-girl? . . . Tone? . . . T.D.? He actually had the nerve to call me Tone?"

"Hey, he's your buddy. But frankly, if he ever calls me Pricy-girl to my face, I'll kick him in the shins."

The telephone rang. "He said he'd call back. You get it."

"Yeah . . . thanks . . . but remember it's your week to talk to Bryce Lloyd, III."

"Tony? Hey, amigo . . . it's good to hear your voice."

"Terry? I didn't think you'd want to talk to me anymore."

"Tony . . . Tony . . . sure we have our creative differences. But we're very reasonable people . . . right, partner? Actually, I called to apologize. This is big. You were completely right about the DiNetero deal. And I want to be the first to say so."

"Oh? What do you mean, I was right?"

"Scumbag. He turns out to be a real scumbag."

"I don't remember saying anything like that. He treated me nicely enough. It just didn't quite jell for us, that's all."

"Hey, enough said, Tony. You and Pricey could see what the rest of us missed."

"I don't quite follow."

"You haven't read the rags this weekend?"

"I don't read the rags . . . ever."

"Well, Tony, my main man, here's the menu. There was a big party out at a beach house in Malibu last Friday night. The police were tipped off and made a raid. They found crank, crack . . . pills . . . the whole works."

"And?"

"They also found a seventeen-year-old girl overdosed in the bedroom. She's in critical condition down at Cedars of Lebanon Hospital."

"DiNetero had something to do with this?"

"It was his house, and witnesses say he provided the girl with the drugs. He claims he's innocent. He's out on fifty thousand dollars bail . . . but it puts a damper on things, know what I mean?"

"You're saying it's a good thing I didn't sign an agreement with him?"

"Good? It's a stroke of genius. If he had the option . . . we couldn't get out on the moral turpitude clause until he's actually convicted. In Hollywood, who knows how long that and all the appeals will last? And yet, he can't do anything with it either, so we would have been in no man's land."

"You called just to tell me about DiNetero?"

"Nope . . . nope . . . nope . . . noooo. Got another reason. If you haven't got new representation yet, I'd like to sign back on . . . the same deal as before."

"Terry, I'm going to keep on turning down some things you think I should sign. I don't do that to aggravate you, but that's the way it's going to be."

"Tony, I know that. We might not see eye to eye all the time, but we know where the other one's coming from, right?"

"I suppose so."

"I do know your material. And what's more, I believe it's great stuff. I want to be a part of getting it the best exposure possible."

"I appreciate that, Terry."

"Now . . . I just happen to have another deal in the works if you give me the go-ahead."

"Do they want to change my text?"

"No sir. They like it just as it is. Promised to stick to the book, word by word."

"Are you serious?"

"Tony . . . this is a little sweetheart of a deal. As soon as you say I'm back on . . . I'll send you the contracts to review."

Tony stared out the window at the haze that hung over the Verde Valley below.

"Tony . . . are you still there?"

"OK . . . Davidian. Send me the movie contract, I'll look at it."

"All right! Tony, baby . . . great. But, just one thing. It's not a movie deal."

"What are we talking about?"

"Audio. You know . . . full-length books on cassette tapes? It's the same outfit that does L'Amour's."

Tony's heart sank. "Oh. . . ." he mumbled.

"Listen, Tony . . . amigo. This is just step one. These tapes hit the market and start circulating. . . . There'll be a lot of interest in movies. Trust me on this one. What do you say? Are we back in business?"

"Go for it, Terry."

"Hey, compadre . . . hang in with me. I'm going to get you that big deal one of these days. Then we'll sit around Bel Aire or Beverly Hills celebrating."

"Or maybe in Billings, Bozeman, or Butte. . . ." Tony laughed as he hung up the phone.

Tony sat across from Vic Lucero in the visitors' room of the Yavapai County Jail. The old man chewed on a fingernail with yellowing teeth.

He spit on the floor and choked out each word. "They . . . took . . . everthing?"

"Like I said, Vic, the machine, papers, money and torn contracts are all missing. I think someone went straight up the air vent."

"Did you check where it comes out behind the United Verde Apartments?"

"I couldn't find the vent, Vic. Where is it?"

"I told you, about a hundred paces behind the apartments."

"All I could find back there is a pile of old tires and that concrete trash bin. Is it further up the hill?"

"Trash bin? That's the vent, Shadowbrook! Didn't you look down it?"

"Eh . . . no . . . I'll go back," Tony offered. "Can you think of anyone besides you, me, and Gilette that knew what you were building?"

"None that are alive."

"You mean others have died?"

"Of old age, mainly. I've been working on this a long time."

"OK . . . just the three of us, then?"

"I don't talk about it, lest I get drunk, and I don't get drunk. Other than that spell in the spring, I ain't touched liquor in fifteen years . . . not countin' last weekend."

"What spell in the spring?"

"Up in Las Vegas . . . but it was a bust."

"What were you doing there?"

"I ran down this bunch of grad school engineers that was supposed to be mining experts. I don't think a one of them ever spent a day with his hands. I got in the front office and asked to talk to the boss. They wouldn't give me the time of day unless I left my note and schematics with them for four to six weeks. Ain't no way on earth I'm going to let them steal my machine."

"I imagine you pitched a fit?"

Lucero cocked his head. "Yep. I reckon I did."

"What does this have to do with going out and getting drunk?"

"In order to calm me down, one of them three-piece-suit boys offered to buy me a drink and some lunch. Well, I figure they owed me that much. But I reckon I overdid it a mite."

"You think when your brain got soused, your tongue got loose?"

"More than likely. But I didn't worry much about the man in the shiny patent leather slip-ons. He was just some bean counter meant to get me out of the lobby. Well, he did that. I didn't wake up for two days."

"What was the guy's name, Vic?"

"I can't even remember where we went, let alone his name!"

"Was his name Layton?"

Vic rubbed his clean-shaven chin as though he were looking for something. "Maybe."

"Did he work for M.E.T.A.L., Mineral Engineering Testing and Lab?"

"How'd you know that?" the old man sputtered.

10

From the desk of Priscilla Carey Shadowbrook:

1. Go with Tony to Prescott to visit Vic
   (Take some of Pete's sugar donuts.)
2. ASU . . . all day Wednesday
   (How many in my 7:00 A.M. Monday class?)
3. Sunday, 4:00 P.M., women's retreat planning
   (Suggest we study the book, "Awakening Your Sense of Wonder.")
4. Finish final edit on Chapter Nine
   (The "Ghost Town – 1954" scene is terrific!)
5. Have Tony wash deck & carport
   (Should we replace webbing in green chaise?)
6. Call Amanda

(Are they coming to the Labor Day
bar-be-que?)

7. Thursday, make the goodbye
   rounds
   (Honey, Celia, Pete, Randy, the
   Gillams . . . ?)

8. Pack up everything
   (Wash linens, dust, mop, vacuum,
   et. al.)

9. Title . . . title . . . title
   (The day of decision is NOW!)

10. Friday night – Pinnacle Peak
    (Me & Tony, alone!)

"You think Gilette faked the whole thing?"

Tony leaned back against the couch and stared straight up at the ceiling. "Yep."

"But who got shot down by the sliding jail?"

"No one. Here's my theory. Vic got bombed last spring and blabbed all about his blasting box to Gilette. Trying to distance himself from the fracas in Goldfield, Gilette had moved to Las Vegas . . . and went by the name Layton. He's been in and out of mining for years. He knew what he was looking at when he saw Vic's schematics. So he hatched this crazy scheme."

Price held a *Ladies' Home Journal* in each

hand and fanned herself. "Why not just come down, shoot Vic, and steal it?"

"This is better. He gets the device legally . . . does away with Clayton, so past bill collectors can't find him . . . besides, he doesn't have to kill anyone this way."

"Meanwhile Vic's in jail."

"An old man who won't live long anyway. . . . Then no one can ever challenge Gilette's right to the device."

Price brought Tony a cup of Rattlesnake Blend cowboy coffee. "Did you ever think about writing mysteries, Mr. Shadowbrook? You've got a perfect name for it," she teased. "Only . . . Shadowbrook . . . knows . . . !"

"Yeah . . . right. Mysteries are too restrictive. I mean, there are only seven decent plots. What do you do after that?"

"Well, Mr. Holier-genre-than-thou . . . when are you going to talk to the police about your Gilette theory?"

"I already did. Called the sheriff early this morning."

"What did he say?"

"Said they'd recheck the tunnel and see if they could find the handprint I told them about."

"And if they do?"

"They'll try to determine if it has any bearing on the murder."

"Has Gilette's brother showed up yet?"

Tony gulped down the coffee and felt it burn the tip of his tongue. "He called the sheriff and said he wanted to come to Jerome and collect Clayton's possessions."

"You mean the old truck and the tombstone?"

"At least the truck. He's insisting the city erect the marker on the sidewalk in front of the Nevada Hotel as a memorial to his brother."

"Whoa . . . that's rather flamboyant."

"Yeah, a permanent display of how he hornswoggled the town, I suppose. It reminds me of when Butch Cassidy and the Wild Bunch sent a photo of themselves back to that Winnemucca, Nevada, bank they had just robbed. This whole scheme is a way for Gilette to get rich and famous . . . yet have an iron-clad alibi. Someday, after the statute of limitations runs out, he'll write a book about the whole conspiracy."

"And sell a million copies?"

"Maybe I should have agreed to write his book."

Price retreated into the kitchen to answer the telephone.

Now carefully sipping his coffee and staring at the opening paragraph of Chapter

Ten, Tony glanced up as she returned to the room.

"Who was that?"

"Eh . . . maybe you shouldn't write mysteries."

"What is it?"

"That was the sheriff. He and his men are down at the Nevada Hotel. Thought you might want to come down."

"Did 'Layton' Gilette show up? I want to be there when they talk to him."

"Oh, he's there all right. But that's not the Gilette the sheriff wanted you to see."

Tony leaped to his feet. "Oh?"

"They recovered the body of Clayton V. Gilette from a ledge twenty-five feet below Vic's diggings!"

"I should have Chapter Ten finished by noon," Tony reported as Price joined him on the deck.

She kicked off her sandals, fanned her face with her hand, and found an umbrella-shaded spot on the table to set her laptop. "How are we going to end the Lucero and Gilette stories?"

"Well, for now . . . it will have to be with Victor Lucero awaiting trial for murder. Maybe by the time the author's proofs get to us we'll know more."

"How was it Lawington thought Gilette was an only child?"

"I guess their mom and dad split up when the boys were quite young. Layton was raised by his mother . . . Clayton by the father. We shouldn't have been so quick to assume things, I guess."

"You said they look alike?"

"Quite a bit. I only saw him briefly, but Layton's younger, taller, clean-shaven. Looks more like an attorney than a surveyor."

"Tony, isn't it possible that a drunk Victor Lucero did something totally out of character?"

"Like murder Gilette?"

"Yes. Everyone says that gold fever makes men do strange things."

"I just can't believe he would do that!"

"Is that because of Vic's sterling character . . . or because Tony Shadowbrook doesn't want to admit he made a mistake?"

"Well, the case isn't solved yet. The schematics and the machine are missing. Someone took them."

"What about the sheriff's theory that Vic hid them himself, figuring he'd beat the murder charge, and then go about selling them? The DA thinks Vic might have panicked when he realized how restrictive the contract was and decided the only way to break it was to murder Gilette."

"They still have some explaining to do. There wasn't any bullet hole in his head. There didn't seem to be any bullet holes at all."

"He was crushed rather badly, I presume?"

"It looked pretty gruesome for only a twenty-five-foot fall."

Price leaned over and put her head between her knees and breathed deeply.

"Eh . . . are you all right?" Tony asked.

"Let's don't talk about mangled bodies."

"The sheriff said it was lucky he hit that ledge or else he would have dropped another four thousand feet down."

"Lucky for whom?"

"Eh . . . the sheriff's search team, I reckon. Anyway, they won't know for certain about the death until they get an autopsy."

"How's Vic taking this news?"

Tony walked to the railing of the deck. "I don't know. Thought we'd drive over and check on him this afternoon, but I'm not sure what to say."

"Tony, there's nothing left for you to do."

"I suppose . . . but it's going to be tough on Friday for me to just drive away from it all. Sort of like deserting a friend in need."

Price slipped her arm into Tony's. Both of them stared out over the hazy Verde Valley below. " 'Lord, you establish peace for us; all that we have accomplished you have done for us.' "

"Your summer verse?"

"Yes. Isaiah 26:12. I'm trusting the Lord to give you some peace in this thing with Vic."

Tony turned around to face her, and leaned against the railing of the deck. "Well . . . the Lord's got just three more days to do it in."

A mufflerless sports car roared into the carport. Isabelle Broussard climbed out of a 1953 dark green MG convertible. She wore jeans and a faded red short-sleeved blouse, her long wavy black hair pulled behind her in an extremely full ponytail.

"Isabelle! Where have you been? We haven't seen you in weeks," Tony called from the deck as she hiked up the stairs.

"I've been hiding out," she admitted.

"Hiding? Where?" Price added. "I've looked all over town for you."

She plopped down in a green webbed deck chair and gazed off across the valley below. "Can I bum a cup of coffee?"

"I'll get it," Tony offered.

"You've got him trained."

"Actually, I needed a refill myself. Price usually drinks tea."

"I'm moving," Isabelle blurted out.

"You are? When?"

"Right now. I'm leaving town."

Tony returned with a cup of coffee in each hand. "Where are you going?"

"Las Cruces . . . to stay with my sister a while. Her kids are grown and she has some extra room."

"Well . . . this is our last week in town, too. We're off to Scottsdale."

"Yeah, I know."

"How have the past two weeks been?" Price asked.

"Lousy. I've been depressed most of the time."

"What's been getting you down?"

"My whole life. I've spent almost fifty years chasing after causes . . . dreams . . . visions . . . feelings. . . . Where has it got me? Living in a shack on top of a washed out copper hill, thinking of suicide. Talk about a dead end."

"Have any of the things we talked about made sense to you?"

"You mean, the Jesus stuff?"

"Yes."

"For a week or so the dreams stopped, and I felt better. But there's something that holds me back from really committing myself."

"What do you think it is?" Tony quizzed.

"I can't turn loose. I've been so caught up in the séance thing . . . the ghosts . . . the spirits. I've gotten so hooked, they won't let me go."

"You've had some trouble since we prayed with you?"

"I had a bad bout the other night . . . a week ago Thursday. The night of the murder? It shook me up . . . I've hardly been out of my room since. Maybe a new location will help."

Price turned her chair to face Broussard squarely. "What happened?"

"Well, my place doesn't have any air conditioning . . . so I was sleeping out on the front porch. It's one of those little cabins up behind the UV Apartments. I heard the gunshot down at the old jail. So I walked down the hill just a bit, but I couldn't see much from way up there. Finally, I just sat down on those old tires behind the apartments and must have dozed off. Sometime after that, I heard a second shot."

"A second shot? I thought witnesses said there was only one." Price retorted.

"But that goes along with my earlier theory. They had to shoot a hole in Gilette's hat . . . without him being in it," Tony explained.

"Of course . . . that was back before I knew Clayton was really dead."

"Well, it could have been something I dreamed or just some apparition. That's one of the problems. Sometimes I have a difficult time in telling what's real. Anyway, this time the shot sounded like it came from the bowels of the earth. In my mind I was thinking it was some sort of spirit trying to break free. Then I heard shouts . . . talking . . . I waited a long time, too scared to move and let anyone know where I was.

"All of a sudden a spirit lifted itself right out of the ground. It was dark and he was muddy . . . but it was Gilette's spirit."

"Gilette . . . you recognized him?" Tony quizzed.

"It was his spirit . . . like I say . . . this was after he was killed down by the jail."

"Where did it come out of the ground?" Tony pressed. "Was it near the concrete, eh . . . trash can behind the apartments?"

"Yes! How did you know? Then the other one came out."

"Another man?" Price asked.

"Another spirit. It was like Gilette's good and evil spirit were fighting for his soul, or something. Anyway they were carrying something grotesque . . . I presume it was his soul." Broussard stopped and looked at

Tony. "This is sounding really weird, isn't it?"

"No, go on . . . what happened next?"

"Well . . . they got in a fight. Like I said, over the thing they carried. The taller one . . . shoved the bearded one back . . . and he stumbled and fell back into the earth."

"You mean, he fell down upon the ground?"

"No, back into the bowels of the earth . . . I heard him scream . . . I can still hear his scream . . . like someone falling for a long time. I often have dreams where I'm falling. Anyway, the one that was still above ground picked up the soul and scurried around to the front of the apartments."

Price glanced over at Tony and then back to Broussard. "What did you do then, Isabelle?"

"I snuck back to my cabin and have mainly tried to hide out."

"Did you contact the police?"

"Oh, sure . . . I'm going to tell them I saw two spirits rise out of the bowels of the mountain to fight? I feel weird enough telling you two."

Tony jumped to his feet. "Come on, ladies, we're going for a ride."

Isabelle shrunk back. "Where?"

"I believe I know what you saw . . . and it

just might not have been two spirits!"

A hundred yards above the United Verde Apartments there was a barren stretch of hillside, with only a few scattered bushes, a pile of discarded car tires and a square cement riser not much larger than a trash can. The trio hiked to the tires.

"This where you saw them?" Tony asked.

"I don't want to be here. What if that tall spirit is still lurking around?" Broussard warned.

Tony grabbed her hand and led her to the concrete box. Price trailed along behind. All three stared down at the air vent.

"This isn't right . . . it's a channel for spirits!" Broussard cautioned.

"Nope. It's an air intake for a mine shaft and runs straight down to Vic Lucero's diggings. Look . . . the heavy wire grate at the bottom lifts up, and under that you'll find a wooden ladder, and a four-inch clothes dryer exhaust hose."

Price scooted closer to Tony and Isabelle. "You mean what she saw might have been Clayton and his brother?"

"It wasn't a twenty-five foot fall . . . but a fall from right here!" Tony declared.

"Is there any way to prove that?"

"Isabelle . . . do you think you could identify the taller man if you saw him?"

"Yes, I believe so."

"But wasn't it dark?" Price challenged.

"I've spent most of my life slinking around in the dark. Whether he's a man or a spirit, either way . . . I'm sure I could recognize him."

"Well, ladies . . . I think we'd better drive to Prescott."

"They nabbed Gilette on the border," the sergeant reported as he held the sheriff's office door open for Price, Isabelle, and Tony.

"Layton? You found him already?" Tony asked as they scooted past the uniformed lawman.

"The sheriff notified Mojave County to stop him for questioning. They spotted him near Hoover Dam, just about to cross into Nevada."

"Heading back to Vegas, I presume?"

"Don't know. But they're flying him back right now. The sheriff and district attorney are waiting for you in here." The sergeant led them through the light green door.

Inside were two eight-foot folding tables and a dozen metal chairs scattered around. Only two were occupied.

Sheriff Bob Hodgson tossed his hat on the table and stood as they entered. "Shadowbrook . . . ladies . . . have a chair. This is Mr. Crispe, the DA." Hodgson sat back down and opened a leather portfolio, revealing a yellow legal notepad. "You told me you had a witness who could place both Gilettes in Jerome after the crime took place. Is that right?"

"Yes, sir. This is Ms. Isabelle Broussard. . . ."

The sheriff nodded at her. "Yes, we've met before . . . under less than favorable circumstances. I believe it was suspicion of growing a controlled substance, wasn't it?"

Isabelle peered at Tony and Price. "There was no conviction. I was plant-sitting for a friend. They weren't big enough to harvest yet."

The DA tapped a black ballpoint pen on the table. "Are you telling me you believe Broussard is a credible witness?"

"Yes, sir, we are," Price said firmly. "She's been putting her life together. She was neither stoned nor drunk on that evening."

The sheriff rubbed his nose with a clenched fist. "Well, I hope so. I went out on a limb on this one. To tell you the truth, I was hesitant about apprehending Layton Gilette until I questioned the witness myself. But the sergeant insisted if Anthony Shadowbrook was as much a straight shooter as his heroes are . . . your word would be as good as all the copper in Jerome."

"I can tell you that I, for one, sincerely believe Ms. Broussard's report," Tony declared.

"Well, ma'am. . . ." The sheriff shifted forward, hands clutched on top of the notebook. "Before Gilette arrives, how about you starting from the top and telling us what you saw that night?"

Price whispered to Tony, "If she starts talking 'spirits of the dead'. . . ."

Tony looked straight at Broussard. "Isabelle, tell them exactly what you told us about those two men who climbed out of the concrete air vent, above the apartments."

There was a sharpness of focus, a clarity . . . almost a twinkle in her brown eyes. Price nudged Tony in the arm with her elbow just as Broussard began her testimony.

The report and questioning took over an hour. Tony and Price were dismissed to a waiting room. Within a few minutes, a well-dressed man was led in for interrogation.

"Was that Layton?" Price asked.

"Yep. That's Layton Gilette."

"He dresses well. That wasn't an off-the-rack suit. First-class accessories. He doesn't look like the type that would crawl through a muddy mineshaft."

"I wish we knew what was going on in there." Tony pointed toward the closed door.

"Isabelle did a good job, didn't she?"

"Do you get the idea there's some spiritual progress going on in her?"

"That's what I was thinking. I wonder if she'd be willing to stop by and visit with Pastor Wayne on her way to Las Cruces?"

"It wouldn't hurt to ask."

"Kind of exciting to think about it, isn't it?"

"Broussard coming to the Lord?"

"Yeah. It's like snatching one right out of Satan's hands."

Tony read the July issue of the *Arizona Police Officers Gazette* twice before anyone came out of the interrogation room. The sergeant finally appeared and refilled coffee cups.

"How's it going?" Tony asked.

"Gilette claims he wasn't there and refuses to say anything else."

"So, what now?"

"Well, Broussard's past reputation makes her a weak witness. The DA figures any good defense lawyer will try to make a case that you brought her in for a ringer."

"Ringer?" Tony looked at Price. "What kind of jewelry was Layton wearing when they brought him in?"

"Let's see . . . a gold and silver chain around his neck . . . a matching bracelet on his right hand, a Swiss knockoff watch on his left wrist and . . ."

"A ring?" Tony pressed.

"A large silver ring on the little finger of his left hand," she added.

Tony turned back to the sergeant. "Could I talk to the sheriff? I think I might have something to add to the discussion."

Dynamite Victor Lucero's face reflected worry. Dark-haired Isabelle Broussard's just looked tired. Layton Gilette sat with elbows on the table and hands clasped in front of him. A relaxed, perfect poker face revealed nothing.

"What have you got, Shadowbrook?" Sheriff Hodgson pressed.

"Did you happen to take any photos or castings of that handprint in the air shaft?" Tony watched Gilette slowly drop his hands to the table, then glance with disinterest toward the ceiling.

"Yep, but we couldn't pull any fingerprints off the mud."

"Did Clayton Gilette have a ring on his left hand when you found the body?"

The sergeant stepped forward and blurted

out, "Nope. No rings at all."

Layton Gilette shoved his hands under the table, glancing away from the others.

"Well," Tony continued, "someone in that tunnel was wearing a ring. As you know, Sheriff, that mud print revealed a wide-banded ring on the little finger of the left hand . . . I would guess it's a lot like the one Layton Gilette has on."

"Put your hands on the table, Gilette!" the sheriff demanded.

Layton slowly complied, revealing the silver ring. "It's circumstantial evidence. Lots of people wear rings!" he whined.

"That might be, but I'll tell you one thing. We got a good print of that ring," the sheriff reported. "It looks like murder one to me . . . 'course, if you have something to say that could convince us otherwise, this would be a mighty good time to talk."

"It was an accident!" he blurted out. "He was a jerk! The whole plan was mine and he thought he could walk away with Lucero's machine!"

Sheriff Hodgson immediately stood up. "Sergeant, would you please inform Mr. Gilette of his rights? Take Lucero back to his cell, and the rest of you wait outside. Bring in the tape recorder and the stenographer. For your sake and ours, Mr. Gilette, we want to get this down exactly as you state it."

The sheriff ushered Tony and Price to the door. "Shadowbrook," he whispered, "was there really a ring on the left pinkie on that print in the mud?"

"Yes, sir, there was."

"Good! I was hoping you didn't make that up."

"You mean, you don't really have a good photo or casting of it?"

"Shoot . . . I don't have any idea whether we do or not. It just seemed like he was about to crack, so I bluffed it." He held the door open for them. "You ever think about writing crime stories?"

Tony noticed Price's laughing green eyes. "Never," he insisted.

It was almost an hour later before the sergeant came out to tell Tony, Price and Isabelle Broussard that their testimonies were no longer needed.

"Did he really confess?" Tony quizzed.

"Yep. You mentioned that ring and it broke him. I've seen that happen over and over. A guy refuses to say anything . . . then one more fact seems to break the resistance."

"What's the charge going to be?"

"The DA is still drawing up a list. Second-degree murder seems to be the primary charge."

"What were they arguing about?"

"The story we got in there was that the whole scheme was Layton's. He went up to Nevada and found his brother in prospectin' at some near-worthless claim outside of Austin for the past couple of years. It was Clayton's idea about the tombstone. He was a little wacky about getting his name in history books."

Price tried to cool herself by shaking the collar of her blouse. "What were they arguing about that night?"

"I guess when they finally tugged that box out of the airshaft they had different ideas on what should happen next. Layton wanted to take it to Canada and sell it to some Australian mining consortium. Clayton planned to use it at his Nevada claim first, then sell it."

"So he just up and killed his brother?" Price asked.

"He claims he was just trying to take possession of the machine, and his brother fell."

"He didn't fall. He was pushed!" Broussard insisted.

"How about the tombstone thing? Was that just a diversion?" Tony questioned.

"Oh, Layton claims it was just meant to set everyone up to believe that Clayton really got killed. With Lucero in jail, they figured no one knew about the invention and the case would be solved."

Tony jammed his thumbs in the front pockets of his Wranglers. "Clayton sincerely seemed paranoid about that tombstone. I wonder if he had any idea his brother might try something like this?"

"The tombstone turned out to be prophetic," Price added.

"The sergeant pulled off his hat and wiped the sweat off his forehead. "Sort of spooky, ain't it? There are times in this business that it seems as if evil has a plan."

Just before dark, Tony, Price and Isabelle Broussard waited at the curbside for Dynamite Victor Lucero to emerge from the sheriff's office. He finally stepped out, wearing his old khakis, freshly washed and neatly pressed.

"Shadowbrook, you sprung me, and I owe you!"

"Vic, you gave us a great ending for our book. . . . You don't owe me anything."

"Well . . . I owe you and I'll make it up. That's the way things is done out here, and you know it."

"Just as long as I don't have to start eating powdered sugar doughnuts," Tony laughed.

"Now, can we give you a ride back to Jerome? Lots of folks down at the Ireland Cafe are going to want to celebrate your release."

"Well, sir . . . they'll jist have to wait until later in the week. I want to go up there to Kingman and claim my machine and schematics before some yahoo steals it out from under my nose. Besides . . . I know a fella or two in Las Vegas who might put a bid on it now that I have it finished. Think I'll go up there while I'm at it. Can I borrow your demonstration video?"

"Sure . . . it's yours. How are you going to get to Vegas?"

Lucero squinted his leathery eyes and cracked a wry smile. "I hitched myself a ride."

"Oh?"

"My attorney's going to give me a lift. I figure I better have a lawyer read my contracts from now on."

"She wouldn't happen to be an assistant public defender for Yavapai County, would she?" Tony teased.

"She's a purdy young thing, ain't she? And smart as a whip. They gave her a couple days off and she offered to drive me up."

Tony threw his arm around the old man's bony shoulder. "Dynamite Vic . . . it's been a pleasure to know you!" The two men had a hearty handshake.

"When are you and your 'daughter' leavin' town?" Vic asked.

"Friday."

"Tell Pete and the boys, I'll be back before then."

By Wednesday Tony finished the first draft of Chapter Ten. He sprawled across the living room couch scanning the finals of the other nine chapters.

"I'll punch in the corrections next week," he offered, "then you can give it a once-over. You'll be swamped at school, no doubt."

"Just like always. It'll be nice to be back to our own home . . . our own routine. This summer has been stranger than others."

"The people . . . or the environment?"

"Both, I guess. . . . I was thinking mainly of how we went home every weekend. We don't usually do that."

"Yeah, we went home every weekend to plan a wedding that never took place." He stepped toward the telephone.

"If that's Bryce Lloyd, III . . . tell him this is our last week, and don't give him our home phone number," Price called out.

"It's for you, darlin'. . . . It's your mother."

"Are they home finally?"

"No . . . they're at the Baptist Hospital . . . in Dallas."

"Dad?"

He nodded.

The phone call was long.

And teary.

Tony had iced tea and a box of Kleenex waiting on the deck for Price.

"They say the next forty-eight hours are crucial. Quadruple bypass."

"And how's your mom?"

"She's a rock, of course. But Aunt Vera broke down. Thinking about Uncle Harold, I suppose. I wish Mom didn't have to look after her, too."

"Do you need to go to Dallas?" Tony asked.

"There's no way. . . . I've got to finish this book. . . ."

"I can finish it."

"And get the girls ready for college. . . ."

"They're sophomores . . . they can get themselves ready."

"But my University classes begin on Wednesday. . . ."

"Fly home on Tuesday."

"We invited Mark, Amanda, and Cooper up for a bar-be-que."

"I'll cook steaks and we'll get the rest at the deli."

"I can't just take off . . ." Price protested.

"You have to. Darlin', you don't want to live the rest of your life thinking, 'I should have gone to see Dad.' I should know."

"But he'll probably be all right."

"And what if he isn't?"

"Are you sure?"

"Book a flight to Dallas. I'll see if Bryan can get you to Phoenix in the helicopter. Have the girls meet you at Sky Harbor with a suitcase packed."

"It will be expensive, won't it? . . . to get a flight over the holiday like this?"

"It will be the best investment all summer."

She wiped away a tear. "I'll do it."

Price glanced around at the Winslows' house. The ultra-modern, one-story home blended into the ancient copper hillside in both style and color. "Tony . . . I feel really strange about leaving you with all of this to finish up."

"Honey said she'd send her housekeeper on Thursday," Tony assured her.

"But . . . we're not quite done. . . . It's like I'm abandoning the whole project."

"Dr. Shadowbrook, you know that was a miracle to snag you an airplane ticket . . . and if I don't get you to Sedona in an hour, Bryan can't fly you to Phoenix. Grab your purse. Let's go."

The telephone rang as they headed out the door.

"Let it ring, darlin'. . . . We've got to go."

"What if it's Mother? What if something's happened to Dad?"

"Well, hurry, then. . . . I'll back the rig out of the carport."

Price ran to the Jeep Cherokee minutes later.

"Well?"

Price opened her brown leather purse and pulled out a Kleenex. She wiped the tears out of the corners of her eyes.

"Your dad?"

"Oh, no . . . it was Kit."

"What's up?"

"She wants to go to Dallas with me."

"Kit?"

"She said she's been praying for Grandpa Carey this morning and she feels like she should go to Dallas, to take care of Grandma and Aunt Vera . . . and help them fly home later in the month when Dad can travel again."

"You said Kit . . . not Kath?"

"Yes . . . the dark-haired one who takes after her father."

"But, but what about the University?"

"She said she'd just sit out this semester and try to make up some classes next summer."

"Whoa . . ." Tony moaned, ". . . I don't know. It's a tough call on the spur of the moment. Do you really think she was serious?"

"Yes."

"Well, darlin' . . . what do you think?"

"I think she ought to go."

"You do?"

"Yes. And I think she needs to stay home and go to college."

"But she can't do both."

"I know."

"Well, she probably couldn't get a flight, anyway."

"Kit said they have her on stand-by. She said she'd just camp out at Sky Harbor until a seat opens up. She figures she'd get there sometime in the next twenty-four hours. What do you think, Tony?"

"Why don't we pray about it on the way to Sedona? Then whatever you and Kit decide at the airport . . . that's what you should do."

Price pulled another Kleenex out of her purse.

"Thinking about your dad?"

"Actually . . . I was thanking the Lord for sensitive daughters. It just hit me this minute. They're all grown-up, Tony. They are young women, with their own agendas, their own dreams, their own lives, their own commitment to the Lord and their own commitment to family. And you know what part makes me shed a tear?"

"What's that, babe?"

"I like the way they're turning out. In spite of all our failures and mistakes . . . they turned out to be wonderful young women that I'm so proud to call my daughters."

"OK, Mamma. Pass the Kleenex."

Anthony Shadowbrook sat on the deck by himself.

By staying in Jerome until Friday night, he was able to punch in the final corrections to the entire manuscript. There was nothing left to do but print it up for one last grammatical edit by Priscilla Carey Shadowbrook, Ph.D. in English.

The Jeep Cherokee was crammed with everything that had found its way from Scottsdale to Jerome over the summer.

The Winslows' house had been immaculately cleaned by a woman named Maria Marias. A turquoise wooded coyote, standing four feet tall and wearing a peach-colored bandanna, was propped in the living room with a thank you note to Dick and Natalie Winslow.

Below Tony stretched Clarkdale, Cotton-wood, and to the distant east, Sedona. Above him on the mountain the lights of Jerome flickered on from one-, two-, and three-story buildings with stilts and braces to keep them from sliding into the Verde Valley.

In the cool evening breeze Tony leaned at the railing wearing jeans, green western shirt with the sleeves rolled up slightly, and old roughout boots. The big silver buckle on his belt read "Prescott Frontier Days - 1963."

Price reported from Dallas that her dad was doing pretty well, so far. Mom Carey seemed extremely relieved to have Price there.

Kit was at her mother's side. Wearing a dress. And lipstick. Emptying bedpans. Giving Grandpa a drink. And making sure the night-shift nurses gave him his medicine on time.

Kathy held down the fort at Scottsdale. There was a house to clean, a college-and-career Bible study bar-be-que to host, ward-robe decisions to make . . . and three songs to practice. She hadn't decided which to sing in the Miss Arizona Contest.

Mark, Amanda, and the cutest baby on the North American continent had changed plans and gone to San Diego to visit the child's other grandparents.

For the first time in ten weeks Tony felt he could catch his breath. He wandered back into the house and looked around for any remaining items that should go in the Jeep.

Lord . . . it's been hectic . . . crazy . . . and it zipped by at the speed of light . . . but it was a good summer. New friends . . . a new family member . . . new things learned about each other . . . and ourselves . . . some spiritual victories.

What more could we ask?

Thanks.

You've been good to us.

Again.

The telephone had what he called a Shadowbrook ring. Sometimes Tony just knew it was family.

"Hi, Dad!"

"Josh! Hey . . . how's Hawaii?"

"It's cool, Dad. Stunts are going good."

"How's your bride?"

There was a pause on the other end of the line.

"Josh? What's wrong?"

"Oh . . . listen . . . I'm crazy about Melody . . . you know that. It's like the sun rises and sets with her smile."

"And?"

"But . . . this husband thing . . . I'm not very good at it."

"What happened?"

341

"Well, today, Melody wanted to cook lunch for me. She worked all morning and made some potato salad."

"And it didn't taste like your mother's?"

"How did you know? Has Melody called you?"

"Nope. Just a guess. Don't tell me you told her it wasn't as good as your mother's."

"Yeah . . . I sort of blurted that out . . . and she ran off to the bedroom in tears and won't open the door," Josh reported.

"There you have it. Lesson number twenty-three, I think. Never . . . ever . . . compare your wife to your mother in any way. You didn't marry your mom, kid. That Melody is the sweetest girl you ever met in your life, and maybe the only one on earth, including your mother, who will let Joshua Shadowbrook be himself. Now, swallow hard, and march in there and tell her you acted like a jerk and that she never has to cook anything like your mother does. Tell her you're in love with Melody Mason Shadowbrook, and that she doesn't have to be anyone else."

"Yeah, you're right, Dad. Thanks. You always know the right thing to do."

"Not always. That's the exact same lecture your Grandpa Shadowbrook gave me about thirty-two years ago."

"No foolin'?"

"We all have to learn, Josh. Slow to speak . . . quick to forgive, is what Grandpa told me. You'll be surprised how many jams that keeps you out of."

"Thanks, Dad."

"Yeah . . . thanks, Mr. S.," a soft, feminine voice echoed on another extension.

"Melody?" Josh asked.

"Yeah . . . sorry, Josh . . . I shouldn't have picked up the phone."

"Oh, man . . . that's all right, darlin'." Josh added, "It's all my fault."

"I'm too sensitive. Insecure, I guess," Melody added.

"Well, if you two. . . ." Tony started to say, but Josh cut him short.

"Forgive me, baby, for being such a jerk!"

"Of course, I forgive you," she said. "I couldn't be upset with you more than three seconds and you know it."

"But the bedroom door?"

"It's not locked anymore."

Both extensions hung up at the same time.

He double-checked all the doors, windows, and the thermostat. Turning out the last remaining lights, he closed the front door, but hadn't put the key in the lock when a small car roared up the gravel road, lights

343

blaring in from the carport.

"Mr. Winslow? . . . . Mr. Winslow? . . . . Boy, I'm glad to catch you at home," a man's voice rolled in as the headlights on the Mercedes convertible were turned off. Tony reached inside the house and flipped on the porch lights. The voice had a familiar ring.

"Sorry, I'm not Mr. Winslow."

"Oh, I thought this was his house." The man, who looked about thirty, wore a black turtleneck sweater, black slacks, black Italian loafers.

"I'm just a houseguest."

"Tony?"

Anthony Shadowbrook stared at the young man.

"Bryce? Bryce Lloyd, III?"

"Yeah. Isn't this something? We've been talking all summer, and now we meet. Is Price here?"

"She had to fly to Dallas, Bryce."

"Whoa . . . her father? How's he doing?"

"Coming out of surgery pretty well. Thanks for asking."

"So the Winslows still aren't here?"

"No, I'm afraid not. They're in Scottsdale."

"Well, I'll catch them later. I just got up this morning saying . . . why don't I just drive over and visit the Winslows?"

"Where do you live, Bryce?"

"Palm Springs."

"California?"

"Yeah. I've got a nice place on The Pointe at Desert Mountain. If you and Price are ever in town, I insist you stop by."

"Thanks, Bryce . . . I appreciate that."

"Well, Tony . . . if they aren't here . . . they aren't here. Think I'll drive over and have some dinner in Sedona before I head home."

"You going back tonight?" Tony asked.

"Yeah."

"Take care of yourself, Bryce. That's a long drive home."

Bryce Lloyd, III turned and started down the steps. "Be sure and give Price my regards. Good night, Tony."

"Good night, Bryce."

Tony stood on the steps until the Mercedes taillights were out of view.

Lord, I still don't have a clue who Bryce Lloyd, III is!

Tony locked the front door and listened to the ringing telephone.

"It can wait. . . ." he murmured. "Everything's locked."

The phone persisted.

Tony walked through the dark to the kitchen, fumbling for the telephone.

"Shadowbrook?" the crusty voice challenged.

"Vic, is that you?"

"You expectin' Wyatt Earp?"

"No, no . . . where have you been? I've expected you all week."

"I've been wheelin' and dealin'."

"Did you sell your machine?"

"Yep. And I made myself a pretty penny. That lawyer of mine turned out to be a crackerjack when it comes to contracts."

"That's great, Vic. Where are you?"

"Down at the cafe."

"The Ireland?"

"Yep. I've got something to give you."

"I'm headed home to Scottsdale. I'll swing on by."

Evenings at the Ireland Cafe were normally a slow time.

No tourists left in town, the regulars at home in front of the television.

But not this time.

When Tony walked in, it was like the coffee-break crowd had gathered for a meeting. Sitting at the worn green Naugahyde booth near the center of the room was clean-shaven, khaki-clad Dynamite Vic Lucero. He wore a brand new khaki hat.

"Shadowbrook . . . over here!" Vic's hand leaned on a large cardboard box in the middle of the table.

"Boys," he shouted. "Calm down . . . it's time for me to speak my mind. You all know that Shadowbrook, here, wouldn't give up on me. Sort of like the Almighty appointed him to look after old Vic Lucero. Well, I offered him a partnership in my invention, but he turned it down. Like me, he still follows the code. A man's supposed to help others without reward.

"But he's got to accept this, because it's a gift. And it's against the code to refuse a gift horse."

Lucero pulled the cardboard box up. Underneath was a beautiful two-and-a-half-foot-high bronze statue of a calf roper. "Partner, this is for you. Ol' Vic don't ever forget his friends."

Tony couldn't think of what to say.

"Enough said. Now, I got a little announcement for the rest of you. I struck it rich, boys. I surely did. Not with my diggin's, but with my invention. Now, I told Pete to bring in the biggest steaks he could find. Supper's on Vic Lucero. Yes, sir, boys. I struck her rich."

The crowd roared and gathered to slap Lucero on the back and celebrate. Tony stood to stare more closely at the bronze.

"You kin' stay for supper, cain't you?" Vic

asked as he broke free of the others.

"Actually, Vic . . . I've got a daughter at home waiting for me. I better head on down the road."

"Is she purdy?"

"She makes a sunset in the Grand Canyon look like a blank slate."

Vic grinned from ear to ear. "You take your statue. And remember ol' Vic ever' time you look at it."

"That I will, partner."

"I'm movin' on too, you know."

"Where you headed?"

"I've got enough money to buy me a white frame house across from the courthouse in Prescott. I've been diggin' on this copper hill since 1927. And now . . . now it's time for me to move on."

Tony studied the wrinkled face of the old man.

"Where did you say you been diggin' all these years?"

"Eh . . . on this old copper hill," Vic repeated. "Say, Shadowbrook . . . did you ever think of a name for that book you're writin'?"

"Yep. I just did."